AND THE CORPSE IN THE QUADRANGLE

KRISHNA SUDHIR

INDIA • SINGAPORE • MALAYSIA

No.8, 3rd Cross Street
CIT Colony, Mylapore
Chennai – 600 004

First Published by Notion Press 2020

ISBN 978-1-64850-878-3

CONTENTS

DEDICATION

Dedicated to the memory of my grandmother, who told me wonderful stories when I was young.

ACKNOWLEDGMENTS

To my sons K and R in Los Angeles, you are the inspiration for this novel as well, and the ones that will hopefully follow.

To my mother in Chennai, thank you for instilling in me a passion for writing.

Thanks to the team at Notion Press for taking on this project and seeing it through to completion.

GLOSSARY OF CHARACTERS (IN ALPHABETICAL ORDER)

Amsibh: A wise and respected teacher, a mentor to Nujran

Andron: An elderly blind monk, leader of the Monks of Meirar

Arondello: A rebel leader on Hoanan's side, originally from Aaltin

Baa'chirav: A monk working as the gourmet chef on Flomo

Brenlo: A tall athletic monk from Krifaca

Dannigan: Special Agent and head of Typgar's elite forces

Danubius: A minister in Typgar's cabinet, originally from Lustraa

Donita: Tryna's friend, a student at the university

Eramsen: Head chef at the university cafeteria

Gin'kwah: A brilliant wheelchair-bound student with a progressive muscle disease

Glyoptula: A monk who has mastered most of the languages on Syzegis

Hoanan: Rababi's opponent who plotted a coup d'état, now a fugitive from justice

Iolena: Queen of Typgar, Rababi's successor as Typgar's head of state

Izvan: Head of Nadii's Internal Security

Jozak: A young monk who runs the sick bay on Flomo

Kalimo: A monk from Aaltin who can blend into the environment

Klabe: A student at the university, wears a single earring

Leongatti: Dean of the University of Western Foalinaarc

Linaea: Nujran's bodyguard and Manolos' partner

Lincus: A student at the university

Lintworth (Mr.): A teacher at the university

Lumisio and Alamira: Hoanan's parents

Maaya: A young female novitiate, a friend of Nujran

Manolos: Previously Nujran's bodyguard, turns traitor

Mbiko (Ms.): A teacher at the university

Miko: Daughter of Tyora and Zhinso

Miriana: Nujran's love interest, a student at the university

Nujran: Prince of Typgar, son of Rababi and Roone, the principal character

Nyawandus: A member of Typgar's Royal Guard

Pelorius: Amsibh's neighbor in Narcaya, an expert in martial arts

Pholtorimes: A famous detective from Aaltin, based in Zilbaros

Rababi: King of Typgar, Nujran's father who was assassinated

Rihana: An intelligence officer with Nadii's Internal Security

Rocmerin (Mr.): A teacher at the university

Ronanya: An older monk who can communicate with dead people

Roone: Formerly Queen of Typgar, Rababi's wife and Nujran's mother

Sarjenkel: A surgeon who operates on Nujran, a student of Setrosko

Sarnoff: A detective from the crime squad, a cousin of Pholtorimes

Setrosko: Physician-in-chief at the Royal Trauma Center in Loh'dis

Shamirah: A student whose body is found on campus

Sheena: Head nurse at the university infirmary

Tazloe: Nujran's roommate, a student at the university

Trimiod: A student at the university, an acquaintance of Tazloe

Tromzen: Also Amsibh's neighbor, a talented chef and skilled artisan

Tryna: A student at the university, blonde with tattoos

Tyora: Another monk, Zhinso's partner, who also befriends Nujran

Vilania: A rebel leader working for Hoanan and Yarozin

Yarozin: A former minister in Typgar, now a fugitive from justice

Yin'hua: A monk from Inchea who is a geographical seer

Zaarica: Daughter of Zenabi, Nujran's previous love interest

Zhinso: A monk, Tyora's partner, dies from a poisoned bullet

Zoltar: Captain of the Floating Monastery (Flomo)

PREFACE

The COVID-19 pandemic has transformed the world. This novel, like its predecessor, was largely written in an aircraft cabin. However, this time around, the edits and revisions were conducted on *terra firma*, in accordance with new travel restrictions.

As a first-time author, I watched the release of *Nujran and the Monks of Meirar* with both interest and trepidation. When writers publish their work, for the whole world to see, they have to be ready for any and all reactions from their readers. I was pleasantly surprised by largely positive reviews...thrilled (and somewhat flattered) that it has been embraced by its intended audience and beyond.

The writing went by faster this time. The words came at a more free-flowing pace, in part because of the novel's backdrop—this story channels the collegiate experience of our young prince. I love the grounds of American universities; they are interesting and picturesque temples of learning. I've had the honor of teaching at Bay Area campuses for over two decades, and more recently, with both my sons going through college, I've visited several university precincts. The setting for this book is a fictionalized aggregation of my memories of these locations.

The series was always planned as a trilogy; *Corpse in the Quadrangle* is the middle narrative. Nujran is a college student, going through what many undergraduates experience. But then, the discovery of a body on campus and the escape of two prisoners from a nearby jail throw the prince into a world of intrigue. Reconnecting with Amsibh and the Monks of Meirar, he undertakes new adventures replete with romance, infused with intrigue, and packed with peril. He makes fresh alliances, assumes more responsibility, and stares down danger with the courage of a prince.

I hope you enjoy reading this sequel as much as I have enjoyed writing it. As I have urged my sons and students, I will encourage you, the reader, to remember this: college is a time to forge lasting friendships and etch fond memories into our totems of time. And like Nujran, one learns that despite all the challenges encountered along the winding street of adolescence, love and hope await just around the corner.

Be well and stay safe!

Chapter One

A DEATH ON CAMPUS

It was twilight, and all was quiet, the air warm and still. Handac and landic had just started their celestial dance in the sky. Jovic, the third moon, was nowhere to be seen, allowing his companions some breathing space early in the evening. Suddenly, the stillness of the air was rent with a scream.

"What the heck was that?"

Nujran approached the window and looked out. The sound had come from the quadrangle below. Splashes of cyan and fuchsia infused the evening sky as Yarus approached the horizon in its rapid descent. His eyes took a few moments to adapt to the fading light. A small crowd was gathering near the edge of the grass.

"What do you think, Taz?" Nujran called out, turning to look over his shoulder. "Should we go down and check it out?"

His roommate, Tazloe, comfortably seated on a sofa, was staring at his hand-held device. He did not appear to react.

"Taz!" Nujran repeated, his voice louder this time. "Can you put your Zogo down for a second? There's something going on in the quad. Should we go check it out?"

Tazloe looked up and, on seeing the prince's animated gestures, slowly pulled out his earphones. "Uh…check what out, Nujran?"

"You didn't hear the scream?"

Tazloe shrugged his shoulders, said nothing, and deliberately took a long puff from his vaporizer. He then re-inserted his earphones and went back to his Zogo. Nujran shook his head, a little exasperated at his friend's overwhelming lack of interest in the situation.

"Alright, I'll go down and see what's happening. I'll be back shortly."

Nujran emerged from his room and wandered down a dimly lit corridor. The maroon bricks of the walls and ceilings formed an arch, propped up at regular intervals on the outside by tall cream pillars. A chill breeze greeted him as he turned the corner. There were several other students heading for the stairs.

They must have heard the scream as well, he thought. The stairwell was dark and smelled a little musty. *I'm sure there's mold growing on these walls. Where are those lights when you need them?*

Nujran hurried down, a couple of steps at a time. Descending three flights, he emerged through a portal leading directly into the quadrangle. The crowd had now swelled in size, and he noticed a couple of teachers rushing over to the scene.

"What happened?" he asked when he reached the group of students. He directed his question at a short red-haired youth standing next to him. He did not know the boy's name but vaguely recognized him as someone in his class.

"Oh, hello Nujran," the youth responded. Nujran felt mildly embarrassed he didn't know his name. This was not unusual at the school. The prince was something of a celebrity; everyone recognized him instantly, but it would take him a long while to know all their names.

"Someone found a body," the youth said.

"A body…down here? Really?" Nujran's voice expressed astonishment.

"Yeah. Not sure who it is."

This was perplexing. There was no reason for a body to just show up on a carefully manicured quadrangle on the grounds of the University of Western Foalinaarc. This was a premier institution, a temple for learning, where things like that did not usually happen. As Nujran wondered if he should take a closer look, a hush descended on the gathering. The whirring sound of a motor from behind him caused the students to turn their heads. Out of the sky, a low flying vehicle was descending toward them. It resembled a scooter, with a vertical pole and handlebars, but was also equipped with short wings on either side of the base. Bubbles of blue smoke emanated from an exhaust pipe beneath it.

"It's Dean Leongatti," said a lilting voice from in front of Nujran. The prince recognized Miriana, a girl from Aaltin. She was a year ahead of him, and they had first met during orientation. She had been a volunteer on one of the committees that welcomed the new students. What's that aroma I'm sensing from Miriana's clothes? he wondered. It had been years since Nujran had seen a waibonz, but their distinctive smell of cardamom and lumdumberry seemed to suddenly waft into his nostrils. He instantly recalled a shiny badge she had worn on her lapel on the occasion of their first encounter — Captain of the Waibonz Society. Does Miriana own a pet waibonz herself? Or perhaps she just fancies the furry, rolling creatures...

The flying scooter landed, and a burly man with bushy eyebrows, a sharp nose, and square shoulders alighted. The group parted down the middle, as the man whom Miriana had identified as Dean Leongatti casually made his way through them. Two teachers, who had arrived earlier, greeted him with perfunctory nods. He approached what appeared to be the body of a girl lying face-up on the grass. From where he stood, Nujran couldn't see very much more, as the crowd had quickly closed around the dean, who was now crouched over the body. The prince tried to edge his way forward through the throng, managing to catch a few words of Leongatti's initial reaction.

"I can't feel a pulse," he was saying, his fingers on the girl's neck. "She must be one of our students. I don't recognize her." He raised himself up and looked over at the teachers. "Mr. Rocmerin, Ms. Mbiko, can either of you identify her?"

There was a brief pause as both leaned over to take a closer look at the body. Rocmerin, the older of the two, shook his head, causing even more disarray to his uncombed silvery locks of curly hair. Mbiko, the younger teacher, a dark-complexioned lady with hair cropped close to her scalp, had a frown on her brow.

"She looks really familiar," she said. "I believe she's a Senior. I'm drawing a blank on her name, but I remember her from my Introduction to Politics class a couple of years ago."

"I think it's Shamirah," someone called out from the crowd. It was Miriana again. Nujran noticed that she had maneuvered her way forward and was now standing next to Leongatti. Many in the crowd gasped on hearing the name; one girl screamed. The dean raised his hand in a plea for calm.

"Are you sure?" he asked Miriana.

"I'd have to get a closer look," Miriana replied. Nujran noticed how unflustered she seemed. She had just volunteered to identify the body of a student that had shown up on campus without warning. The enormity of the situation was beginning to dawn on him.

"Let's make sure we don't touch anything," Leongatti emphasized. "Has someone informed the authorities?"

"I just did," Rocmerin replied, shutting off his hand-held Zogo and putting it away in his pocket. "The crime squad should be arriving in a few minutes."

Leongatti directed the students to move away from the body. They dispersed slowly, gathering near the edge of the quadrangle. A somber stillness had descended over the crowd. No one spoke for a while; one could almost hear a pin drop.

"Anyone know Shamirah?" someone standing behind the prince asked a few minutes later, breaking the silence.

"We had a couple of classes together," a male voice replied. "I think she's from Ersipia."

Nujran couldn't recall another incident like this happening during his year at college. In fact, nothing out of the ordinary had occurred thus far. His first year, which had ended a couple of months earlier, had been remarkably uneventful. He had spent a quiet summer on campus, and the new academic year had just begun. A body turning up mysteriously was certainly more than a little strange. *How had she died?* he wondered. *Was she ill, and had she perhaps collapsed on the way back to her room? Could she have encountered an unfortunate accident?* And worse still, *could there have been some foul play?* He shuddered a little at the last thought.

A short while later, the members of the local crime squad appeared on the scene. They were dressed in purple uniforms, with crimson hats that seemed to bobble up and down on their heads.

"The bobbleheads have arrived," whispered a young man standing just behind Nujran.

A few students snickered, then quickly became serious again, reminded of the gravity of the situation. The leader was a large hatless man who introduced himself to Leongatti as Detective Sarnoff. Nujran noticed large beads of sweat on his forehead, some of which were slowly trickling down his temples on to his face. For some reason, the prince was reminded of Pholtorimes, the famous sleuth from Aaltin. Pholtorimes had been a great help to King Rababi when terrorists struck in Loh'dis, as part of a tortuous plot by the king's political opponent Hoanan to stage a coup. A wave of sadness suddenly descended on Nujran. He shivered, as though touched by a chill wind.

I miss Father so much, he thought. *There is a great deal I would have liked to learn from him, but he's gone. I wish we had more time together.*

"Who here can identify the girl?" Nujran's thoughts were interrupted by Sarnoff's grating voice.

"She's a Senior, her name is Shamirah." It was Miriana again, volunteering the information.

Sarnoff asked her to come forward, then called out, "Anyone else who knew her, please stay. We have some questions for you. The others should return to their rooms. We'll call you if we need to."

Nujran considered if he should stay or return to his room. Though he didn't really know her, he had heard the deceased girl's name a couple of times during his year at the university. His curiosity was aroused, and he might learn a bit more about what had happened by hanging around. On the other hand, Sarnoff would have many questions, and he realized he had precious little to contribute. In the end, he decided it was best to go back to his room.

The short red-haired youth accompanied him as he made his way back toward the building. "What do you think happened, Nujran?"

"I have no idea. I'm sure the detective will work it out."

"Has a murder ever happened on campus before?"

"Wait a minute...I don't think we should be jumping to conclusions," the prince replied. "We don't know the cause of death."

"What else could it have been?" the youth inquired.

"Well, there are multiple ways a person could die. Natural death, an accident, suicide, and of course murder. Any of these might be the underlying cause here."

"Your father was murdered, wasn't he?" the youth asked.

Nujran was starting to find him exasperating. He did not reply but instead quickened his pace.

"Were you there?" the youth continued. "Did you see it happen?"

Nujran's annoyance was increasing exponentially. "I'd rather not discuss it," he replied gruffly.

"Oh, I'm sorry." The youth just realized that he had struck a nerve with his questions. "I didn't mean to..."

"It's alright. Don't worry about it."

There was a brief uncomfortable silence. They proceeded briskly through the corridor and up a few flights of stairs, Nujran bounding ahead. As he strode toward his room, he felt a lot calmer, his irritation apparently exorcized by the exercise. He slowed down, turned around, and said, "I don't know your name."

"I'm Lincus," the youth replied. "I'm from Yarwone."

Nujran smiled. "That's where my mother is from."

"I know. She's the most celebrated person from our country. We're all very proud of her."

The prince now felt himself warming up to this lad. "Your questions brought back painful memories," he remarked. "But still, I shouldn't have snapped at you. Yes, I was there when my father was killed. He died with his arms wrapped around me. The assassin was one of my trusted bodyguards."

A barely audible gasp emerged from Lincus' lips. "I'm so sorry, I didn't know that."

There was another awkward silence. Lincus' questions had reminded the prince of his father's assassination. It had been a time of great upheaval, not just for his family, but for all of Typgar. Riots had broken out in the streets outside his home, and shopkeepers had fled the scene in the aftermath of widespread looting. The rebels under Hoanan, who had instigated the unrest, had eventually been defeated. Both Hoanan as well as Yarozin, the mastermind of the plot, had been captured and imprisoned. Iolena, his father's former Minister for

Defense, was now Typgar's head of state, the democratically elected ruler. She had won the election that Rababi's murder had triggered.

"I'd better go now," said the prince. "I've got assignments to complete. Nice seeing you again, Lincus."

Back in the room, Tazloe was reading a magazine. His vaporizer was on a small square table next to him. As Nujran walked in, he raised his head and inquired, "So, what was all the fuss about?"

"They found a body. One of our seniors apparently, a girl named Shamirah."

"Wow! Do you know what happened?"

"They're not sure. The crime squad guys are here and are investigating."

"Did you say her name was Shamirah?" Tazloe asked. There was a frown on his brow.

"Yeah, do you know her?"

"Not really, but something about the name rings a bell."

"Apparently, Miriana knew her. She was from Ersipia."

A silence descended on the room. Tazloe returned to the magazine he was reading, Nujran to his thoughts.

She's not just a corpse in the quadrangle. She's a real person. Her parents would surely be devastated when they receive the news.

Nujran was no stranger to death. In addition to his father, Rababi, there was also Zhinso, a monk who he had befriended. He had been tragically shot when rebels had boarded their ship. It turned out that the bullet was poison-tipped, and the monk perished before an antidote could be found. Zhinso's passing was the young prince's first exposure to death, and the experience had affected him profoundly.

His roommate's voice interrupted his thoughts.

"I'm hungry, Nujran. Want to go grab a bite to eat?"

"Was going to start an assignment, Taz. I guess I could work on it later. Give me a few minutes, and then let's go to the dining hall."

A short while later, they emerged from their room, walked downstairs, and turned to their right, in a direction away from the quadrangle. Shortly after, they entered a large hall with a high ceiling and long tables of dark wood. The enticing aroma of grilled meat greeted their nostrils as they walked in. Bright lamps dangled from long cords, bathing areas of the room in a yellow glow. Several students were already there, and there was an audible buzz of conversation. Nujran strolled over to the serving station and helped himself to a bowl of hot soup. As he made his way back to the tables, he looked around to see where Tazloe had gone. His roommate was now chatting animatedly with a young lady dining alone in a corner of the room.

He dragged me down here saying he was hungry, but he's busy trying to get a date, Nujran thought to himself, a smile playing on his lips. *That's classic Taz-man…I should probably give him some space.*

Just then, the door opened and Miriana walked in. Nujran watched her as she sauntered over to the machine that dispensed drinks. She was wearing a tracksuit that hugged her frame, showing off her slender curvy form. *She's really pretty,* he thought to himself. *A nice physique too.* She filled up a glass and turned around. Seeing Nujran standing by himself with a bowl of soup on his tray, she headed over in his direction.

"Are you by yourself, Nujran?" she asked. "Mind if I join you?"

Nujran seemed surprised by her direct approach. "Sure, do sneeze," he said.

She looked back at him, puzzled.

He quickly corrected himself. "I mean, do please." They both chuckled, then sat down at an empty table across from each other. "No food, just a drink?" Nujran asked.

"In a little while perhaps, not quite hungry yet. I had a late lunch."

"I thought that Sarnoff and his folks from the crime squad would still be interrogating you," Nujran remarked.

"No, it was just a brief interview," Miriana responded. "But they've taken my contact details, and I'm sure there's more to follow."

"So, you knew Shamirah?"

"Yes, I did, for about a year now."

"Was she a friend of yours?"

"Not really, she was an acquaintance. I don't think she had many friends."

"Why was that?"

"She was a bit anti-social. Oops, I shouldn't have said that…that's not very nice of me. But she wasn't easy to get to know. She kept her distance. And now she's dead; it's very sad."

"Do they suspect foul play?" Nujran inquired.

"I'm sure that's on everyone's mind. I really don't know. A lady from the crime squad asked me a few questions, but they didn't really let on what they were thinking."

"I remember accompanying my teacher, Amsibh, on a series of eyewitness interviews," the prince said. "This was immediately after the terrorist attacks on Loh'dis a couple of years ago."

"Yes, I remember that attack. Everyone does. I was still at home then."

"Where is home?"

"Zilbaros," replied Miriana.

"Ah, Pholtorimes' home country," Nujran muttered softly.

"Who?" Miriana looked puzzled.

"A detective I knew. He came to Loh'dis and helped us through the crisis that followed the attacks."

As Nujran chatted with Miriana, he found himself drawn to her pleasant persona. She seemed unselfconscious, and her voice had a musical quality. He had interacted with other students from Aaltin before and had generally found them friendly and easy to get along with. He wondered if she had a boyfriend but thought it imprudent to ask. Abruptly, his thoughts were interrupted by the vibration of his Zogo. He extracted it from his pocket and looked at the number flashing on the screen.

"Sorry, Miriana, I've got to take this call."

He got up from the table, wandered over to an empty area of the dining hall, and pushed a button.

"Hello, Nujran," a voice said as the screen lit up. It was his mother, Queen Roone.

"Hello, Mother," Nujran responded. "We've had a tragedy on campus today."

"Oh dear, what happened?"

"A student's body was found in the quadrangle. We really don't know how she died."

"That's so unusual," Roone's voice now sounded anxious. "Are the authorities there to investigate?"

"Yes, Mother, they are. I'm sure we'll find out more over the next few days, as the story unfolds."

"Keep me informed, Nujran. But I called for another reason. I didn't really want to worry you, but Iolena insisted that you should be informed."

"What's the news, Mother?" asked the prince.

"There was a prison break earlier today in Eastern Foalinaarc. It was Yarozin and Hoanan. They've both escaped and are on the run."

Chapter Two

FUGITIVES IN THE WOODS

"Can't you move faster, Hoanan?" The voice was gruff, the tone uncompromising.

"I'm trying my best, Yarozin. This is not easy…the terrain is pretty steep."

"It's not the terrain; it's you. You should have been exercising in your cell regularly, like I told you to. Instead, you've been gorging on prison food…and getting fat."

Though overtly rude, Yarozin wasn't far off the mark. Even as a politician, Hoanan hadn't really taken care of himself physically. He had gradually put on weight after he lost the election to Rababi, and following his capture and imprisonment, this had only become worse. The food in Foalinaarc's jails was always plentiful, albeit not of the finest quality; Hoanan had indulged himself without restraint. His face had become fuller, an additional chin had appeared, and his girth had enlarged significantly. By contrast, Yarozin had stayed fit during his incarceration. He had diligently worked out several hours a day in solitary confinement. Furthermore, during the one hour per week he was allowed into the prison yard, he made full use of the exercise equipment at his disposal. The other prisoners generally tended to avoid him, keeping their distance from the notorious mastermind of Rababi's assassination. Hoanan was his only friend behind bars, and they had plotted their escape together.

"Where are we headed?" Hoanan asked, breathing heavily as he posed the question.

"If I'm correct, there should be a stream on the other side of this hill," Yarozin replied. "We can rest beside it for a while, hydrate ourselves, then look for something to eat."

"But we're a long way from civilization," Hoanan pointed out. "What food are we likely to find around here?"

"Well, what little we managed to bring with us from the prison is finished. So now we have to rely on nature."

"I've never had to do that before," complained Hoanan.

"Get used to it," snapped Yarozin. "It's going to be berries and whatever else we can find over the next few days. With some luck, we might be able to guddle some fish from the running waters of the stream. In any case, your days of gourmet prison food are over."

They continued their journey, Yarozin pulling ahead of Hoanan, moving quickly up the narrow path to the top of the hill. Their prison break had taken place just prior to midnight, on the previous day. Yarus was now nearing its zenith, so they had been on the run for about half a day. It was starting to be quite warm, and while scattered trees along the path offered intermittent and welcoming shade, there were bald, unprotected areas of the hillside where the heat was oppressive. Both men were showing signs of discomfort, and Hoanan was now short of breath and visibly sweaty.

"I really need to rest soon." Hoanan's tone was plaintive. "I feel weak...can we take a break, at least for a short while?"

"Not much further now," Yarozin responded. His tone was matter of fact. "I see the stream, and the path is going to be downhill from here. And consider yourself lucky that I was able to acquire comfortable shoes for us both. We would have never made it this far in prison slippers."

"Yes, I meant to ask you: where did you get these shoes?"

"I had them stolen from the warden's office. Apparently, he has quite a supply. I think these are the QuonJon 4 versions that came out last year."

"Oh yeah, they're made with extra plugarnium silk for a sock-like feel...they sort of cuddle your ankles in a fashion that I really—"

"Shut up, Hoanan! What have I told you about economy of words? Be concise; it's really not that difficult, you dumb, stupid buffoon."

"Alright, alright...no need to get nasty."

They walked rapidly, propelled downward by gravity so that even Hoanan was able to pick up the pace. Yarus' rays were now beating down on them unrelentingly. Rivulets of perspiration flowed down from their foreheads, irrigating their cheeks and jowls. As they approached the stream, the welcome sound of rushing water greeted their ears. They tore off their clothes and dove in, bare-bodied except for their undergarments.

"That feels so good," Yarozin said when he came up for air. Hoanan agreed, nodding his head, as he paddled around clumsily with his chin just above the water level.

"Don't we need to find some other clothes?" Hoanan asked, looking over at the yellow prison overalls they had left on the bank.

"All in good time," Yarozin replied. "We'll need to get them from someone along the way."

"So where exactly are we?" Hoanan inquired, his eyes taking in a wide arc of the landscape as he spoke.

"Somewhere in the hills of Central Foalinaarc, I believe. The prison was close to the eastern border, over that way. We've traveled quite some distance westward through the Erissa mountains, but we still have a long way to go."

"How did you figure all that out?"

"I made friends with several of the guards. Most of them were quite helpful, actually. While you were busy consuming food, fattening yourself, and evolving into the corpulent tub of lard that you are, I was collecting information."

"Now there's no need to keep insulting me, Yarozin," Hoanan protested. "We're in this together; I am your ally. And I do appreciate all your help, including the shoes, of course."

Yarozin did not reply. He slowly rose out of the water, craning his neck and tilting his head. He seemed to be listening intently, focusing his attention toward the woods across the stream.

"I can hear something in the distance," he said. "I think there are people out there." He motioned to Hoanan to get out of the water and back on the bank. They grabbed their clothes and hurriedly retreated, taking cover behind a tree. Peering out from behind the trunk, they waited for several minutes. Hoanan wondered anxiously if they had been seen. A few moments later, a group of youths emerged from the woods, stripped down to their bathing suits, and entered the water from the opposite bank.

"They look like students," Hoanan muttered.

"Possibly," Yarozin responded. "Maybe they're on a camping trip in the woods."

"We should kill them. They will surely report seeing us."

"Not if we stay out of sight."

They fell silent and, from their vantage point, watched the youngsters play around in the stream. The group had a mix of boys and girls. From the obvious familiarity on display, they were likely a group of friends. One of them noticed a tree trunk that had fallen across the water further upstream and pointed to it. One by one, they climbed out of the water, made their way to the log, ambling in single file over it to the midpoint. And then, in the carefree manner typical of youthful exuberance, they re-entered the stream in quick succession.

A couple of them just jumped in feet first; two others dove in, arms stretched forward and downward. The last two, clearly the most athletic in the group, insisted on doing backflips before hitting the water, drawing applause and laughter from the others. They swam back toward the hidden fugitives, got out of the water again, and repeated the process.

"This is getting annoying," Hoanan said to Yarozin, after watching their seemingly endless routine a few dozen times. "Are we just going to sit here and wait?"

"I have an idea," Yarozin replied. "Stay here."

"What do you think you're doing?" Hoanan asked, keeping his voice down to a low whisper. "I thought you said we should remain out of sight."

Yarozin did not reply. He emerged from behind the tree, still in his undergarments, and sauntered down to the stream. The youths were making their way back toward the tree trunk, walking by the water's edge on the opposite bank.

One of them, a stout young man with black hair, suddenly turned around and noticed Yarozin. "Hey guys, there's a man over there," he called out.

The others stopped in their tracks and swiveled around to take a look.

"What the..." cursed one of the boys, with a lean and lanky build. There was a look of astonishment on his face.

Hoanan thought he heard a muffled scream emanate from one of the girls. Yarozin must have presented a most outlandish appearance. Although he had stayed slim and physically fit during his stint in prison, his grayish-white hair had grown rather long. He had used a hairband obtained from one of the guards to maintain it in a ponytail that came down to waist-length behind him. His beard had also grown and was an odd mix of black and white with startling yellow streaks. To add to this, he was now only dressed in underpants.

"Must be a homeless man, living in the hills," murmured one of the girls. There was compassion in her voice. She was a tall brunette, and she wore a multicolored bead necklace around her neck. "Poor soul, he probably has not eaten in a while."

"He looks mentally ill," one of the boys commented. A single earring he sported in his left earlobe glistened in the light of Yarus.

"We should be careful," chimed in another girl with long wavy blond hair. Her friend, another blonde, with tattoos adorning her arms, nodded in agreement.

The stout boy who had first noticed Yarozin said, "We should just ask him who he is." The others pondered this seemingly practical strategy for a moment.

"Who are you, sir?" the brunette with the compassionate voice called out.

They received no response. Yarozin appeared not to have heard them. There was a pregnant silence, as he approached the water's edge. Suddenly, something strange happened that took all the onlookers by surprise. Yarozin's body appeared to rise a little, a small gap now visible between his feet and the ground. He then continued his advance over the water's surface.

"What the..." said the lean and lanky lad, prone to cursing, once again. "Holy Nubzoly! The guy's actually levitating! I thought it was only possible with a jetpack."

Hoanan, still well concealed behind the tree, let loose a loud gasp. Obviously, this was a complete surprise to him as well. Yarozin advanced slowly over the water, his feet a few inches over it, and came to a halt just short of the opposite bank. He looked up at the youngsters, appearing to take a great deal of satisfaction from their incredulous looks.

"No need to be alarmed," he called out, a reassuring tone in his voice. "I'm a wandering monk, in search of food. I have not eaten in days." He waited a few moments for what he had just said to sink in. "Can you help me?" he continued. "I'm in desperate need of some food."

There was a long silence, as the young men and women pondered what they had heard. The tall brunette broke the silence. "I'm sure we can assist," she responded kindly. "Are you alone?"

Yarozin gestured over his shoulder toward the tree behind which Hoanan was hiding. "There's another monk over there, behind that tree. He's quite unwell and too weak to walk."

She turned to the others. "We can give them some of our food, can't we, guys?"

A quick discussion ensued among the group. There appeared to be some differences of opinion, as some were shaking their heads and others were nodding. But after a short while, a consensus appeared to have been reached, and the brunette spoke again.

"If you wait here, sir, we will go and fetch you some food."

The group walked briskly back toward the woods. Yarozin stayed where he was for a few moments, his feet immobile above the water's surface. But sensing Hoanan's eyes boring into his back, he turned around. His torso twisting backward, he looked directly at his partner-in-crime, winked deliberately, and gave him a wave. He then turned and faced the woods expectantly. For a while, all was quiet, and Hoanan wondered if the students had turned their backs on them and fled the scene. But his concerns were for naught, and Yarozin's patience was soon rewarded. The group returned, a couple of the youths carrying several large paper bags. They beckoned to Yarozin, and he levitated toward them, then slowly landed on the opposite bank. They handed him the bags, which he gathered up in his arms, each of his hands grasping a couple in addition.

"Thank you, young people," he said. "I truly appreciate your kindness."

As they turned to leave, Yarozin remarked, "You look like students. Where are you from?"

"The University of Western Foalinaarc," the stout boy answered.

"Have you heard of it?" asked the lean and lanky lad.

"Only by reputation," Yarozin replied. "I don't believe I've visited, though."

"Yes, it's fairly well known," added the brunette. "The most sought-after university in Foalinaarc, and probably in all of Syzegis. Famous people send their children there."

"You're all children of famous people, I take it then?" Yarozin inquired with a smile.

"Not really," the brunette replied. "But we may be the only ones at the school who're not."

The other two blonde girls giggled. The one sporting tattoos on her arms chimed in, "There's a student called Nujran in my year. Do you know that name? He's the Prince of Typgar, son of Rababi and Roone."

Yarozin abruptly fell silent. But if the youngsters had been particularly discerning, they would have observed a curious expression on the face of this scantily clothed man, who had just levitated over water. It was like he had just received some intriguing news. He remained frozen for a few moments, arms clasped around the paper bags, evidently lost in his thoughts.

After what seemed like an interminable silence, the boy with the single earring spoke. "Alright, guys, it's time for us to leave." He turned to Yarozin. "Enjoy the food, glad we were able to help. Hope your companion gains back his energy and recovers soon."

They marched off toward the trees, conversing animatedly. At the edge of the woods, the brunette looked back and waved, but Yarozin remained motionless. Several minutes later, he turned around, walked down to the water, then levitated back toward his comrade. Having traversed the stream, his feet slowly descended and hit the ground. He strode purposefully toward the tree and put the paper bags down in front of Hoanan.

"That should be enough food to last a while," he commented. "I did consider killing those kids. I would have done so if they had not given up any of their food. But in the end, they turned out to be pretty generous, so I spared their lives."

Hoanan was staring at his friend, mouth open, a quizzical look on his face.

"What's the matter, Hoanan? You look like you've been struck by lightning." Yarozin's tone was mischievous.

Hoanan remained speechless momentarily, then asked, "What was all that about?"

"What do you mean?"

"I mean…when did you learn to levitate? And how come I've never seen you do it before?"

"A long time ago. But, I'd lost the skill for a while. Being focused in prison, and returning to peak physical shape, restored it."

"Wow…I didn't know."

"The prison experience wasn't all bad, really. I found myself embracing the silence of solitude more than anything. But once I had repaired my mind, I was able to repair my body. You know… in order to levitate…your body has to be in sync with your mind."

"And where did you learn it? Levitation, I mean…I thought only monks could do it."

"You're not as stupid as you look." There was a hint of derision in Yarozin's tone. Staring into space, he continued, "I did, in fact, learn it as a monk. In my youth, I was part of an ancient order. They called themselves the Monks of Meirar."

Chapter Three

THE INVESTIGATION BEGINS

"So, what did Sarnoff want to know?" Nujran asked Miriana. Observing that she was seated by herself on a bench outside the campus library, he had approached her and planted himself beside her.

Miriana looked up from the book she was reading. Large and heavy, it was vaguely reminiscent of the massive volumes on statecraft Nujran had seen in his father's library, back at the palace in Loh'dis. Miriana's text was opened to a page showing a detailed cross-sectional image of a person's chest.

"It was a fairly lengthy interview," Miriana replied. "We spoke for at least a couple of hours. He asked a lot of probing questions. Fortunately, I had done some background research, in anticipation of the inquiries I knew he was going to make."

"And how did you do that?" Nujran's face showed surprise, his voice barely hiding his admiration.

"Well, over the last couple of days, I talked to a number of different people on campus, who may have known Shamirah. She was from Ersipia, you see, and they have their own social club."

"Just for students from Ersipia?"

"That's how it started. But now, it's also for those from Baariya and Dranjon. Those nations share a similar culture. They speak different languages, as you know, but their food, music, dances, and so on are remarkably similar."

"Perhaps they were actually one people sometime in the past?"

"Yes, it's possible; I'm not really sure. Sometimes these national boundaries are pretty artificial, anyway."

"Agreed. I remember Danubius telling me as a child that you see no borders when you look at Syzegis from space."

"Danubius? Who's that?"

"He was a minister in my father's cabinet. He's retired now. He was originally from Lustraa. Turqtooth, we'd call him as kids; teeth so turquoise, you'd think you were looking at the cool waters of Lake Wahidubi. He was an intrepid explorer in his youth…the guy had actually traveled to other planets with nothing more than a knife and some guckmint."

"Wow, that's so interesting. I've never seen teeth even remotely turquoise…in fact, I can't remember seeing teeth any shade of blue! Maybe he ingested something on another planet that caused the color change?"

"No idea," Nujran responded. There was a silence as both students contemplated Danubius' teeth and his inter-planetary travels. A few moments later, the prince spoke again.

"So, was Shamirah a regular at the club for Ersipian students?"

Miriana was just about to reply, when her book started to wobble vigorously on her lap. Soft rhythmic music emerged, slowly growing louder and more melodious, and then there was a brief flash of light. A hologram appeared just over the open pages, displaying a beating heart that seemed to be dancing to the tempo of the music. As Nujran looked on, the image began to rotate and the heart split open, revealing chambers filled with blood.

"That's really impressive!" exclaimed the prince. "It's amazing how the images just pop out of the pages."

"Yes, they literally bring the textbook to life. It's so much easier to study anatomy when you can visualize it so clearly. One just grasps things much faster. And beats reading all the lessons in detail…so time-consuming!"

"Are you planning to be a scientist, Miriana?" Nujran asked.

"I'm not sure yet," Miriana replied. "I often imagined myself as a veterinarian. I love animals. I have a pet waibonz at home. I miss him terribly."

"Yes, I remember…you were wearing a badge—Captain of the Waibonz Society—when I saw you first."

"When was that?"

"Shortly after I arrived…during new students' orientation."

"Ah, yes…that was a phase. I've passed the baton on to someone else."

"Have you thought about a career in medicine, Miriana? I think you'd make a really good doctor."

"I've been considering that quite seriously, Nujran. I've been told I have an inquisitive mind, and I do enjoy helping people. The body is an incredibly fascinating machine...so complex. I have a lot to learn." She slowly shut the book, causing the hologram to melt into its pages and eventually disappear from view. When it was fully closed, the music stopped.

"Does Sarnoff believe that Shamirah was murdered?" asked Nujran, deftly directing the conversation back to the investigation.

"I did ask him that a couple of times. Initially, he was quite evasive, but the second time, he just replied that they hadn't confirmed anything yet."

"And what do you think, Miriana? Surely you must have an opinion by now."

Miriana was silent. She didn't respond for a few moments. The book on her lap was starting to shudder again, threatening to fly open and reveal some other interesting anatomical structure.

"Well, there was something different about her," she finally said. "I can't describe it precisely, but she gave me the impression she was struggling to fit in. Like, you know...a dillydroob in a sycamund bush. And it couldn't have just been because of where she was from."

"A dillydroob? What's that, Miriana?"

"It's a giant yellow blossom...sycamund bushes only have tiny purple flowers."

"This is starting to sound like a real mystery, Miriana...Shamirah's death, I mean."

"Indeed, Nujran. Sarnoff seems determined to solve the case, and I hear that his team of bobbleheads is pretty competent. They're interrogating a lot of folks on campus, asking tons of questions. I'm sure that over time..."

She was interrupted by a voice from behind them. They turned around to see Tazloe running in their direction.

"Have you heard, guys?" He sounded breathless and a little anxious. "They've escaped from prison."

"Slow down," Miriana said. "Who escaped?"

"Yarozin and Hoanan...they've broken out of jail. They were being held somewhere in Eastern Foalinaarc, but apparently, they're now fugitives on the run."

"Eastern Foalinaarc?" inquired Miriana, a quizzical look on her face. "I thought they were in the Central Prison in Loh'dis."

"You're right, Miriana," Nujran observed. "That's where they were incarcerated immediately after their trial. However, Queen Iolena was concerned that their presence in Typgar was a rallying point for a renewed insurgency. So, she spoke with Foalinaarc's rulers and negotiated a transfer to an isolated prison there, near the border with…"

"You don't seem surprised, Nujran," Tazloe interrupted. He then took a long whiff from a vaporizer that he was holding in one of his hands.

"That's because I already knew, Taz. My mother had informed me of this a couple of days back. She asked me not to share the news, though. But I was pretty sure that it was only a matter of time before it would get out. How did you hear?"

"I was watching the news on the cafeteria screen, and they just announced it. I thought it was important that you know. There was a time when they came after you, right?"

Nujran did not respond immediately. His mind flashed back to the tribulations his country had experienced. Hoanan had briefly staged a coup d'état in Loh'dis, and the entire planet had believed he was the villain of the peace. But in the end, Yarozin, then a minister in Rababi's cabinet, had turned out to be the unexpected mastermind behind the scenes. Early in the conflict, Hoanan had indeed directly threatened Nujran, causing his parents to fear for his safety and send him away from the palace with his teacher, Amsibh.

"You should probably put that vaporizer away, Taz," Miriana suggested, a smile on her face. "Some of our professors are on the prowl. They might confiscate it if they see you. And I don't mean to lecture you, but that stuff you're inhaling is bad for your lungs."

Tazloe shrugged his shoulders but said nothing.

Miriana then addressed the prince, cutting into his thoughts. "Are you alright, Nujran?"

"Huh...yes, I am. Sorry, my mind was wandering there. You're correct, Taz...when Hoanan issued his threats, he mentioned me directly. That really spooked my parents. And that's why I was asked to leave Typgar with my teacher. I actually fell captive to his men at one point, but Amsibh managed to turn the tables on our captors. Those were scary times, but I guess I learned a lot too."

"Wow, you've certainly seen a great deal, Nujran." Miriana sounded genuinely appreciative.

Tazloe nodded in agreement. "Yeah, my life has been quite boring so far, compared to yours."

"It would be nice to hear more about your adventures," Miriana remarked. "I have read some accounts in newspapers and magazines, but nothing like hearing it directly from the source."

"I'm his roommate, and I know very little about him," Tazloe noted, turning to Miriana. "He doesn't speak very much about the rebellion."

"I guess I've suppressed some of those memories, Taz. But there were some good times too, not just with Amsibh, but also his friends Pelorius and Tromzen. Some of the finest men I will ever know. I learned so much from them." Nujran fell silent for a few moments. "And then, of course, there were the Monks of Meirar, an amazing group of people!" Nujran's face now brightened, and his eyes seemed to sparkle as he reflected on his friends.

"You'll have to tell us about them sometime," said Miriana. "I would love to hear those stories, I really would. But right now, I have to study for an anatomy test tomorrow. See you later, guys."

Miriana picked herself up, tucked her massive textbook under her arm, and left. Nujran and Tazloe wandered back toward their room. As they approached the quadrangle, the prince spotted Sarnoff from a distance. The area in the quadrangle where the body was found had been cordoned off with thin poles and multicolored tape. Sarnoff was crouching within the enclosed area, almost down to his hands and knees. Drawing closer, Nujran suddenly spotted something he hadn't observed before. Sarnoff was facing away from them, and on the back of his head were a pair of rear-facing eyes, exactly like Pholtorimes had! Even earlier, Nujran had felt that there was something about Sarnoff that reminded him of the great detective from Aaltin. Now, the additional pair of eyes affirmed the resemblance even more. *Were they perhaps related? Or maybe they were just from the same part of the planet?* As these thoughts played around in the prince's mind, Sarnoff turned around. He had spotted them approaching despite apparently facing the opposite direction, a trick Nujran had seen Pholtorimes perform repeatedly.

"Best to keep your distance, boys," Sarnoff called out. "This part of the quad is still off-limits."

"No problem," Tazloe responded. "We were just on our way back to our rooms."

The boys walked past the restricted area, but Nujran's curiosity got the better of him. He trotted back and addressed Sarnoff. "Detective, can I ask you a quick question?"

The detective turned around, a frown on his brow. "I'm a little busy, as you can see…what's on your mind?"

"Are you related to Pholtorimes of Aaltin?"

There was a brief silence. Sarnoff stared at Nujran, his frown relaxing and replaced now by an expression of surprise on his face. "As a matter of fact, I am," he replied, a moment later. "How do you know Pholtorimes? And how did you guess I am his relative?"

"Well, you resemble him a lot," the prince replied, deciding it was probably unnecessary to mention the additional pair of rear-facing eyes. "He helped us during a difficult time in Typgar. I actually had the privilege of interacting closely with him."

"That's remarkable," said Sarnoff, as he emerged from behind the security tapes, clearly interested in conversing now. "And who might you be?"

"He's Nujran, Prince of Typgar," Tazloe declared. "And I'm his roommate, Tazloe."

There was silence again, as Sarnoff digested this information. And then, his face broke into a warm smile, as he extended a hand to the prince. "It's good to meet you, Nujran. I've always had the greatest respect for your parents. So tragic, what happened to the king…he was truly a great man." He paused for a moment and then continued, "Pholtorimes is my cousin, and I owe a great deal to him. He's the one who encouraged me to be a detective."

"Sorry if this sounds rude, but does everyone in your family have two pairs of eyes?" Nujran inquired, his curiosity getting the better of discretion.

Sarnoff threw his head back and guffawed. "We do, indeed, Nujran…we do, indeed! And it certainly helps us in the detective trade. That's probably why many in my family are in this profession."

"You have…two pairs of eyes?" Tazloe seemed dumbstruck as he posed the question.

"Nice to meet you, Tazloe," said Sarnoff, suddenly realizing he had only greeted the prince and not his friend. "And yes, I have an additional pair of eyes on the back of my head." He spun around and pointed to them, causing Tazloe to let out a gasp. Encouraged by the obvious interest Tazloe was displaying, Sarnoff continued, "In essence, my visual input is doubled, and I don't need to turn around. Very handy indeed in my line of work, as you can imagine."

"I'm sure you're busy, detective," Nujran chimed in. "Our apologies if we disturbed you. We'll be heading back to our rooms now."

"Wait a minute, guys…did you know Shamirah, the dead girl?"

"Not really," Nujran replied. Tazloe shook his head, indicating he did not, either.

"Hmmm…looks like she didn't have many friends," said the detective. "That's made our investigation more difficult; there's not a whole lot of information on her. She seemed to be a bit of a recluse… it's been hard to find students who actually interacted with her."

"I understand that Miriana knew her," Nujran noted. "And I believe you have spoken with her, at some length."

Sarnoff nodded. "Ah yes, Miriana…a very helpful person. I've given her a few tasks; she's acting as our eyes and ears on campus. She could make a good detective, one day."

"She actually wants to be a doctor," said Nujran.

The detective scratched his chin. "That's interesting. You know, there are similarities between the two professions. Both require keen powers of observation and good listening skills. Deductive reasoning is essential in both fields. And above all, both need a good understanding of people…how they think, behave, and respond in stressful situations. I can go on and on…"

"That's fascinating, detective," said Nujran. "Thanks for your time, we'd better leave you to your work."

"If you hear anything of relevance to the case, don't hesitate to contact me," the detective called out after them as a parting shot.

They made their way across the quadrangle to their rooms. Settling in, they reached for their books, in preparation for class later that afternoon. It was a warm day, and Tazloe had an oscillating fan set up that produced a strong breeze. He sluggishly picked up his "One Thousand and One Humane Ways to Train a Waibonz" for his Animal Science class. Nujran decided to postpone serious study and instead selected "Zogo Tips and Tricks" from his bookshelf. He had recently acquired a new device and was struggling with its novel features, so he thought that maybe a book might help. Tazloe certainly did not agree and had mocked him gently for it. "Just play with it, Nujran; you don't need a book to work these things out." The prince settled down into a large brown armchair, a classic piece of furniture designed in Lustraa. "This dundoo leather is magnificent; it just couldn't be any softer!" he exclaimed. It was a gift to him from Minister Danubius when he departed for college. A couple of pages into the book, his eyelids were starting to feel heavy. Not surprisingly, he dozed off but was awakened a short while later by a loud knock on their door.

"Taz, someone's at the door," said the prince. Tazloe, who was listening to music through his earbuds and likely under the influence of chemicals he had inhaled during the day through his vaporizer, was completely oblivious to the knocking. Exasperated, Nujran lifted himself off his reclining chair and made his way to the door. When he opened it, he found Miriana outside. She looked distracted and was pacing up and down in the corridor outside. On seeing Nujran, she stopped and spoke tersely, a sense of urgency in her voice.

"I've just found out something, Nujran. I need to talk to you. It's urgent, do you have a minute?" She seemed a tad short of breath.

"Sure, Miriana."

She dropped her voice to a whisper. "It's just for your ears, not Tazloe's...where can we speak?"

"Taz has his earbuds on; he's not going to hear anything. He's probably got his music playing at full volume. Why don't we go over to the dining table and chat?"

They walked back into the room, behind the sofa where Tazloe was sprawled out, his eyes closed, head bobbing from side to side in obvious enjoyment of the music he was listening to. Just past a parapet adorned with cups and mugs of various sizes was a rectangular dining table with four chairs. Miriana took a seat on one of them.

"Would you like something to drink?" the prince asked.

"No thanks," answered Miriana, as Nujran sat down across from her. She leaned forward over the table and spoke softly, her words barely audible. "I've been chatting with everyone on campus who knew Shamirah. I've uncovered a secret, something about her that only one other person on campus knew. He's a student from Ersipia and knew her before she came here. Apparently, their families were close. But her folks made him promise that he would tell no one, so he kept his word and didn't disclose it to anybody. I'm not sure if he meant to tell me, but we were just having a conversation about her, and it sort of slipped out." Miriana's speech was rapid, the words pouring out in a torrent.

Nujran's curiosity was aroused, but his voice remained calm. "So, what's this secret, Miriana?"

"You can't repeat this to anyone, Nujran. Do you promise?"

"Yes, I promise."

"I'll be sharing it with Sarnoff shortly, of course. It's relevant to his investigation."

"Well, what is it?" Nujran now sounded impatient. This had been a long preamble, and the secret had still not been revealed.

"Alright, here goes. Shamirah used to be Shamir. She was once a boy. She underwent gender reassignment before she came here."

Chapter Four

JET HOCKEY IN THE GYM

There was a long silence as Nujran digested the significance of what Miriana had just revealed. It was, without doubt, the last thing he had expected to hear. Granted, he had not known Shamirah well, but the revelation was still astounding. He searched his memory for someone else he might have come across who had changed their gender. That such individuals existed had occasionally been discussed in hushed whispers at the palace when he was growing up, although he could not recall having met any such person. Perhaps one of the many visitors to his father's court or the palace had also harbored such a complex secret, but if that was the case, he had not known anything about it. A thought then crossed his mind.

"Miriana, you said it was relevant to Sarnoff's investigation. Why do you think so?"

"Well, isn't it obvious, Nujran? She might have been killed *because* she's transgender."

"Hmmm, but aren't we a broad-minded student community, here in Western Foalinaarc? We accept each other for who we are. It shouldn't really matter where someone comes from, or what their orientation is. I would have thought this is one of the reasons our university is so popular… a magnet for students around the world."

"In theory, yes...we have a reputation for being a welcoming campus. But bigotry and hate can run deep. Perhaps someone uncovered her secret and resented her or, worse still, hated her for it."

Nujran frowned. "Enough to kill her? That seems a bit extreme."

"Bigots don't behave rationally, as you well know. There's plenty of examples of that in history. It's not so long ago that they burned women alive as witches, just for independent thought."

"I guess it's possible someone knew her secret, and she paid a price for it. In any case, it does make sense to bring it to Sarnoff's attention."

Miriana nodded. "I was actually on my way to see him before afternoon classes start. Would you like to come along?"

"Sure," replied Nujran. "Just give me a second to grab my backpack."

A short while later, they descended the stairs and crossed the quadrangle in silence. Sarnoff was nowhere to be seen, so they approached a woman in a purple uniform, wearing a crimson hat that bobbled vertically on her head. She was guarding the restricted area, leaning over the security tape, prodding the ground with a staff.

"Is Detective Sarnoff around?" Miriana asked the guard.

The woman turned to them but didn't answer immediately. She appeared to be gauging their intent, carefully studying Nujran first and then Miriana.

"Is Detective Sarnoff still here?" Miriana asked again.

"I heard you the first time," came the reply. "Why do you need to see him?"

"We have some information that might be pertinent to his investigation," Nujran volunteered. "He told us to contact him if we heard anything of relevance."

"Well, you can tell me what you heard. I'll pass it on to him."

Miriana and Nujran looked at each other. Miriana then spoke, "Actually, the information is of a sensitive nature. We'd prefer to deliver it to him directly."

"I see," the guard responded. She did not appear to be in any hurry to connect them with Sarnoff. "He's left campus and headed back to the office. He may return later this evening, but I'm not sure."

"Could you let him know that Miriana and Nujran would like to speak with him?" Miriana sounded a bit testy now.

The guard seemed unperturbed by Miriana's tone. She took out a small device that resembled Tazloe's Zogo from her pocket and began to send a message on it to someone. She looked up briefly as she was typing. "How do you spell them?" she inquired.

"Spell what?" asked Nujran.

"Your names," the guard replied.

"M-I-R-I-A-N-A and N-U-J-R-A-N." Miriana's voice was raised, exasperation apparent in her voice, as she spelled out their names.

Again, the guard appeared not to notice Miriana's frustration. They waited as she continued to type her message, her head bowed and brow furrowed in concentration. When she finished, she looked up. "Alright, I've sent it. I'm sure he'll get back to you when he receives the message."

They proceeded slowly across the quadrangle. Nujran observed Miriana shake her head from side to side. *She's easily annoyed*, he thought. He decided it was prudent to keep his impressions to himself. On the other hand, Sarnoff had encouraged them to get in touch if anything new came up. And the new facts that had emerged on Shamirah were certainly important. *So, perhaps she's right to be annoyed.*

"I hate incompetence. Doesn't she understand I have information pertinent to the case?" Miriana's impatience was now on full display.

"I'm sure the message will get to Sarnoff," said Nujran reassuringly. "What class are you heading to now?"

"History," Miriana replied. "We're studying the ancient cultures of Aaltin. They go back thousands of years…it's all quite fascinating. Apparently, many of them used to worship Yarus as a Sun God. They'd go outside to water their crops and look up to the sky, shouting in unison, 'Al-rye dor trea Issuh Yarus,' meaning 'Thank you, oh mighty Sun God.' I really love this stuff." The prince's deft ploy to change the subject seemed successful. Miriana sounded much calmer now.

"Interesting…does the practice still continue?"

"I believe it does, deep in the heart of Zilbaros. There are tribal communities that still live the same way, not having changed much over the millennia. In fact, there's a temple atop a mountain at a place called Ucham-Uchip, where visitors still come from far and wide, not just for the spectacular views, and a peek into history, but to actually perform rituals to Yarus, even in this day and age."

"Wow, that's amazing. Have you been there?"

"Not yet, but I intend to."

"Anyway, have fun in history class. I envy you. I have to go to a boring political science lecture now."

"Boring…really? I thought politics was in your blood, Nujran."

"Yeah, that's what everyone expects of me, right? Honestly, I like statecraft and enjoyed hanging around my father's colleagues growing up. But when it's dissected and analyzed to a mind-numbing degree, that takes all the fun out of it."

"Are you heading to the gym later this evening?"

"Yes, Miriana, see you there after class."

The gymnasium at the university, colloquially known as the Briztanga, was an impressive edifice, a circular structure capped with an enormous orange brick dome. The exterior wall was painted with colorful scenes of the school's past sporting triumphs—everything from Captain Lingbot Dinkevzian's winning puck toss to the underdog upset against Funtyrda University's dreaded Funbluzids from Lustraa. There was a cobble-stoned path around the circumference that was lined with statues of famous athletes from all across Syzegis, inspiring figures of gladiatorial prowess.

Nujran arrived there a little later than he had planned. Although his classes had finished on time, he had hung out to chat with some of the other students after the last lecture. Yarus had commenced its descent in the evening sky, lengthening the shadows on the ground. He walked up the steps at the entrance to the building, passed between a pair of tall pillars, and then through the main doors. Turning immediately to his right, he entered a spacious hall lined by levitating bleachers along the perimeter. Anyone atop them seemed weightless. A tall temporary structure, shaped like an inverted bowl, had been erected in the hall, occupying about three-quarters of its ground area. The walls were transparent, made of some sort of metallic meshwork. Two groups of students were floating in the air. One team was dressed in creamy yellow shirts and dark green shorts with an embroidered red dragon on the shirt pocket. The other sported maroon shirts and white shorts, with the shirt pocket displaying a green frog. All had small jetpacks on their backs and sticks in their hands.

"Ever watched a game of jet hockey before?" Nujran turned to see Miriana right behind him.

"No, but I've heard of it," the prince answered. "Wasn't it invented in Orepio?"

"Yes, in Yarwone, actually. The Yarwonese Hills provided the perfect altitude for optimal jet hockey practice. Their players were unrivaled for decades. But you know this, don't you? Yarwone is your mother's country, isn't it, Nujran?"

"Yes, it is. But I grew up in Typgar and only visited Yarwone during summer vacations. I know they're obsessed with sport there.

Apparently, most of the games played on our planet originated in that region."

"This one's a fairly recent invention. The technology has become quite sophisticated. The jet packs are called boostgooms...the players have to steer their boostgooms while going after the ball. And, if that's not difficult enough, there's an additional twist."

"What's that?"

"The balls have limited lifespans, of variable length actually. Just as you're chasing one, it's likely to disintegrate or explode into billions of yongarta particles, and another will appear somewhere else in the dome. So, it's a combination of maneuvering the boostgooms to stay afloat, skillful use of the hockey stick, and an element of luck. And just to complicate things even further, the climate in the dome changes at random from extremely warm to freezing over the course of a game. You'll be sweating and then shivering within seconds. Takes endurance and dexterity to keep up."

"Wow, that sounds extremely challenging! Have you tried it, Miriana?"

Miriana smiled. "Yes, I have. But I'm not very good at it. Truth be told, I'm not really adept at any sport."

They sat down on the bleachers and observed the game for a while. At first, things were slow, almost as if the players were getting accustomed to the aerodynamics of their individual jetpacks. Then, all of a sudden, the teams picked up the pace, and very soon it was a blur of colors flashing around in the dome. As he watched, a thought occurred to Nujran, bringing a faint smile to his lips. He turned to his companion.

"I've mentioned the Monks of Meirar to you, right, Miriana?"

"Yes, just once. You were going to tell me more about them."

"Well, they're a remarkable group of people. They travel around Syzegis on a ship called Flomo, a Floating Monastery. They each have individual talents, some of which are quite spectacular. But one common skill they all have is the ability to levitate."

"That's incredible!" exclaimed Miriana. "You've actually seen them do this?"

"Yes, indeed. And what's more...I've tried it myself, as a matter of fact. I never really mastered it, but I did succeed in floating over water on a couple of occasions."

"Are you serious, Nujran? Or are you just pulling my leg?"

Nujran laughed. "I'm serious, Miriana. I did levitate; I'm not making this up. Or at least I believe I did. But the reason I thought about them now was the jet hockey game we're watching."

"What's the connection?"

"Isn't it obvious, Miriana? The monks would be able to play without the need for jet packs! They could just float around on their own, using their powers of levitation. Wouldn't that be so cool?"

"What an intriguing idea!" Miriana looked at the prince, her expression melting into a smile. "You know, Nujran...you really are fun to be with. When I heard you were coming here, I thought you'd just be a spoiled prince. I guess the experiences you've had, and the things you have witnessed, have made you quite interesting."

Nujran beamed, savoring the compliment. His understanding of the opposite sex was limited to his long friendship with his childhood friend Zaarica and his brief flirtation with Maaya, one of the young novitiates on Flomo. *I know so little about women...I have much to learn. Is Miriana coming on to me, or is she just being friendly? What does she really think about me?* His thoughts were interrupted by Miriana, posing a direct question.

"Nujran, do you have a girlfriend?"

"Not exactly." The prince seemed somewhat taken aback.

"That's an odd response...not exactly. What do you mean?"

Nujran pondered for a moment. "Well, it's like this. I had a friend at the palace, Zaarica. We've been really close for a long time, since we were kids, actually. But when the time came to go to college, things changed. I got admission here, while she decided to go to a school in Typgar, not far from Loh'dis. We then parted as friends, promising to stay in touch. We didn't specifically discuss breaking up, but I think we both clearly understood we were moving on."

"Oh, I see." Miriana was looking directly at Nujran now. "So, if I asked you out on a date, you'd be alright with that?"

The prince considered the question briefly. As he did, he felt mildly embarrassed. *Perhaps I should have asked her out,* he thought. *Isn't that the usual convention?* Aloud, he replied, "Yes, I'd be fine with that, Miriana."

"Well, it's a date, then," said Miriana, smiling as she spoke. "Not an overly-enthusiastic response, but a 'yes' nonetheless."

"Oh, sorry, Miriana. I'm just being totally honest. It's only fair that you know about Zaarica." There was silence for a few moments, and then Nujran spoke again. "I'd love to go out with you."

"Dinner tomorrow night?"

"Sounds really good." Nujran's tone was distinctly more eager now. He wanted to learn more about Miriana, and several questions crossed his mind, but he decided to save them for later. Suddenly, out of the blue, there was a loud bang, followed by voices shouting, then an audible thud. They looked up to see what had triggered the commotion. It soon became apparent that two of the students, from opposing teams, had bumped into each other in mid-air, crashing down to the ground as a result of the collision.

Miriana stood up. "That didn't sound good. I hope they're not hurt."

"Let's go have a look," said Nujran.

They approached the netted dome. Miriana lifted up the bottom edge that was resting on the floor. They crawled under, making their way to the gathering near the center of the dome. They worked their way through the crowd, gently elbowing past the other students. As they reached the center of the throng, they observed a young man writhing around on the floor, grunting in obvious pain. Someone removed his helmet, and Nujran immediately noticed a large single earring glinting in his left ear. Next to him was a girl lying on her side, long blond hair streaming down from beneath her helmet and obscuring her face. What was instantly apparent, though, were her arms covered with multiple tattoos.

"We need to call for help and get them to the infirmary," a voice called out. "Don't move them; it's not clear what injuries they have. We don't want to make things worse." It was one of the physical education teachers who had walked into the gymnasium. Nujran didn't know his name, but from his distinctive accent, he appeared to be from Lustraa.

Miriana had pulled her Zogo out of her pocket and was dialing a number. The prince heard a couple of rings, and then a voice answered. Miriana spoke into the device, "We have a couple of students injured in the Briztanga. Can you send someone at once, please?"

The teacher, whom the others had addressed as Mr. Lintworth, was kneeling on the ground and speaking with the injured students. A few moments later, a man and a woman in light blue uniforms rushed in through the door, bearing leather bags in their hands. They ducked under the edge of the dome, approached the fallen students, and knelt on the floor beside them. An assessment of injuries was quickly made, following which they delved into their bags. Cervical collars were produced and expertly wrapped around the necks of the injured students. Then, extracting oblong pieces of stiff fabric, they placed them on the ground and tapped them. As the crowd watched, the fabric expanded lengthwise into stretchers, which the uniformed medics placed next to the students.

Seeking help from a couple of the onlookers, the medics gently transferred the students on to the stretchers. They tapped the stretchers again a couple of times, and the sides curled up to prevent the students from rolling off. They pushed a flashing blue button near the foot end, and each stretcher slowly raised itself, staying afloat a few feet above the ground. "That's a really good sapphiron," one of the medics noted to his associate, pointing to the blue button. "I've seen some break after a couple of uses. But hey, you get what you pay for, right?" The medics then gently guided the stretchers toward the edge of the dome, under the netting, and then out through the door.

"They're in good hands now," Mr. Lintworth called out. "Perhaps a couple of you could accompany them to the infirmary."

"We'll go," Miriana volunteered, beckoning to Nujran. They ran out of the gym after the medics.

They caught up with them and walked alongside the floating stretchers. The light of Yarus had all but faded now, all three moons were in the sky. As they approached the infirmary, the blonde girl with the tattoos on her arms spoke to the prince. "You're Nujran, aren't you? Prince of Typgar, right?"

"Yes, he is," Miriana answered on his behalf.

"We were talking about you the other day," the girl continued.

"Really?" Nujran seemed nonplussed. Although a celebrity in the campus community, it always came as a surprise to him that he was a person of interest to other students.

"Well, you're not going to believe this," remarked the youth with the single earring, lying on the other stretcher. "We were going to come and talk with you about something really important. We think we may have seen Yarozin and Hoanan."

Chapter Five

A MATTER OF SURVIVAL

It was late in the day, and an indigo hue had begun to permeate the early evening sky above the trees. Handac had just made its entrance, but the other two moons were not yet visible. On the ground below, in the hills of Central Foalinaarc, the fugitive duo was making steady progress westwards. The terrain was still extremely rough, and day by day, nourishment was becoming harder to come by. Their earlier encounter with the students had been a lucky break; the food they had generously provided had sustained the escapees for a few days. But two weeks had passed since the last of their supplies were consumed, and an air of desperation had set in. They were now reduced to aggressively foraging in the woods, seeking out and feeding on anything edible they could find.

"What are we going to do for food, Yarozin?" Hoanan inquired. "I don't want to die of starvation, out here in this remote location, far from civilization."

"Well, at least it's caused you to lose some weight," Yarozin snapped. "So, count yourself lucky; you're a lot fitter now."

Hoanan did not respond. Under constant fire from repeated salvos of Yarozin's insults, he had developed a thick skin. On occasion, he would think of an appropriate rejoinder...about Yarozin's ghastly stench of rotten fish, for instance, or his consistently unsavory personality. But usually, by the time he had conjured up a seemingly perfect riposte, the moment had passed, so he usually ended up saying nothing.

They had survived for a while on leaves and berries. But as they made their way westwards through the mountains, the terrain had progressively become more hostile. Trees were sparse, and the vegetation was largely shrubbery, with little to offer as food.

"Another few days, and we should reach Western Foalinaarc," Yarozin observed optimistically.

"That's what you said several days ago," Hoanan retorted dryly. "We might be dead long before that."

Their progress was now much slower than it had been immediately after their escape. They were fatigued and dehydrated. Their last encounter with a stream had been a few days earlier, and the water they had managed to store had run out. Their lips were dry and parched, their muscles ached, and their energy levels were extremely low. Just standing up was a significant effort, and each step they took seemed more painful than the last. Even Yarozin, who was the much fitter by far of the two, was starting to show signs of extreme stress.

"We have to stay alive, Hoanan. And we will."

"So, what's the plan, Yarozin? Why are we heading to Western Foalinaarc?"

"Well, for one thing, that's where we're going to find food and water," answered Yarozin. "And what's more, that's where Nujran currently resides."

"Nujran? Rababi's son?"

"Yes, he's studying at the University of Western Foalinaarc."

"How do you know that?

"The students who gave us their food were from there. One of them mentioned that Nujran was studying there."

"And why are we interested in finding him, Yarozin?"

"He's the key to our plans, Hoanan. Do I really have to explain everything to you? For heaven's sake, you are the single most inept nincompoop I've ever had the displeasure of communing with! But alas, you are all I have for now. Let's stay focused on finding food...I'm sure you'll at least be interested in that, you chub-lord."

Hoanan said nothing. Overwhelmed by fatigue, he had little interest in responding to Yarozin's barbs. They continued to walk one behind the other. Yarozin took slow but deliberate steps, looking straight in front of him, with the comportment of someone singularly fixated on a goal. Hoanan was now staggering noticeably, yet trying hard to follow Yarozin's lead.

"Slow down, there's something ahead." Yarozin was pointing downhill toward a large object lying across the path. The light was fading, and it was not easy to determine what it was from their vantage point. They approached cautiously, straining their eyes for any signs of movement, but the object stayed resolutely still. When they were a few feet away, Yarozin spoke, "It looks like a body."

"An animal? Could be a mountain goat. They're said to inhabit these hills. Surprising we haven't seen any so far. Let's hope it's one. Would love to sink my teeth into that meat."

"I don't think so, Hoanan. It's a dead man. Or maybe a woman."

"A corpse? Out here in the middle of nowhere? That's strange, Yarozin, don't you agree?"

"Could be a traveler who lost his way. Let's first make sure he's dead, and then we can search him for food."

It turned out to be a male, someone who had perhaps collapsed and perished in the mountains fairly recently. There was a backpack next to the body, but to their dismay, it contained no food—just a camera, a ball of string, a hunting knife, a heavily stained towel, and an empty water bottle.

"Well, looks like we're out of luck, Yarozin. No food or water in his sack. What are we going to do now?"

Yarozin did not respond immediately. He stared hard at the body and then looked up. "We could eat him, Hoanan."

Hoanan stared at Yarozin, a look of disbelief on his face. "What do you mean?"

"Well, it's a reasonably fresh cadaver, and he's a large man. There's a lot of meat there. With some luck, I think we could nourish ourselves for at least a few days."

"But what you are suggesting…that's cannibalism!" Hoanan was clearly surprised by Yarozin's suggestion.

"Yes, that's true," Yarozin admitted. "All things considered, though, do we have a choice? We're out here in the woods with no supplies. We haven't eaten for several days. There doesn't seem to be any wildlife around. If we don't eat something soon, we are both going to starve to death."

Yarozin had presented his rationale with his usual bluntness. While the idea still seemed appalling, the argument was convincing. Hoanan felt his stomach cramp up, the pangs of hunger literally gnawing at his insides. He was weak, experiencing frequent dizzy spells, and had little vigor left to counter Yarozin. Nevertheless, the thought of doing what his comrade had just suggested made him slightly nauseous. He leaned over and tried to vomit, but nothing emerged from his mouth.

"We should try and light a fire." Yarozin was gathering sticks and twigs from the ground around them. "Can you find a couple of stones we could use to ignite it?"

"What do we need a fire for?" Hoanan's voice sounded weak.

"To cook the meat, of course," came the reply. "I'm not eating any of it raw."

"You really are going to go through with this, aren't you, Yarozin?"

"Yes, I am. As I already told you, we don't have a choice."

Very soon, Yarozin had collected enough sticks and brushwood, clearly in abundant supply around them. He tied them together loosely with a piece of string, cut from the ball they had found in the man's bag. He then pulled out the knife, deliberately walked over the body, and bent down over it. He returned with something in his hands and placed it beside the pile of wood. Meanwhile, Hoanan had wandered off into the vegetation, and a short while later, emerged from a clump of bushes with a few pebbles of different sizes in his hands.

"Have you ever lit a fire before?" Hoanan inquired.

"Yes, as a young monk, we had to from time to time. During our travels, we learned to spark the flames through deep concentration," replied Yarozin. "I became more efficient with the skill during my twilight days as a monk. It's been a while, though. Let's hope I can do it."

He selected a couple of coarse, glimmering pebbles, held them close to the brushwood, and rubbed them briefly against each other. He then closed his eyes and appeared to be concentrating hard. Nothing happened, so he tried again. There was still no result.

"Are you sure you know how to do this?" asked Hoanan. "Seems like you're just mucking about to me. How does that famous adage go? Ah yes, where there's smoke, there's fire. And I don't see any smoke, as of yet."

"What a preposterous use of a saying…so intentionally metaphorical! You just have to be patient. Where did you get these pebbles from?"

"I found them under some trees."

"Did you have to dig them out, or were they fully exposed?"

"A little digging, not much."

"I see."

"So, what's the problem, Yarozin?"

"Well, they're somewhat damp. Probably moisture from the tree roots. They have to be really dry to ignite a spark."

"Perhaps we could use the towel in the bag."

"That's your first good idea, Hoanan. Toss it over."

Yarozin started drying the pebbles with the towel. He worked slowly but meticulously, concentrating on each one, giving it the same degree of attention a jeweler would while polishing a precious stone. The light from Yarus had now faded, all three moons were in the sky. The clearing by the path where they were seated was brilliantly illuminated by the lunar trio, the gray stones taking on a bluish sheen in the light of the moons. It was a still night with no breeze; the air was beginning to cool down a tad. Hoanan had perched himself against a rock and was starting to doze off, when suddenly he was awakened by a triumphant shout.

"There it is!" Yarozin exclaimed. "I've got it going."

Sure enough, the pile of wood over which Yarozin was kneeling was glowing a bright purple, and occasional tongues of red and blue flames emerged.

"We need a bit more wood," he called out.

Hoanan sauntered over, gathering a few more sticks as he approached. He handed them to his comrade, who threw them on to the fire. A few moments later, Yarozin's efforts were rewarded with a crackling bonfire, bright multicolored flames swaying in front of their eyes.

"Time to start cooking," Yarozin announced, a tone of satisfaction in his voice.

Hoanan grimaced a little. "You have the meat?"

"Of course I do," Yarozin answered. He leaned down to where he had placed the cut on a rock beside him, impaled it on a long stick, and proceeded to dangle it over the flames. It started to smoke a little, and Yarozin patiently rotated the stick, watching intently as it cooked.

"I'm not sure I want to eat it," Hoanan declared, wondering quietly from which part of the corpse Yarozin had extracted it. "Smells a bit odd. Human meat...it's not that appetizing."

"Well, it's not a prime steak…but as I said before, you don't really have much choice, Hoanan," Yarozin observed, disdain apparent in his voice.

"Well, I refuse to eat it. I would rather starve."

"It's very likely you will. I don't see any other food around."

The two men fell silent. Red, blue, and purple colors now danced on their irises, as they stared at the fire in front of them. A short while later, Yarozin proclaimed, "I think it's ready." He cut the piece of meat into two halves with the dead man's knife and skewered each half with a short stick. He offered one to Hoanan, who turned his head away. Yarozin sat down beside the fire and looked at what he was holding. And then, he hungrily bit into the meat. His companion looked on, an expression of disapproval on his face.

"Tastes salty," Yarozin remarked. "Could have done with a bit more cooking, perhaps."

Hoanan did not reply. A gentle breeze emerged from the woods. The flames continued their dance in front of them. Except for the crackling of the fire, the night was quiet.

When he finished eating, Yarozin looked up at Hoanan. "It wasn't that bad," he said. "I guess I'm officially a cannibal now."

"That's a disgusting thought," Hoanan responded quietly. "You're clearly more adventurous than I had realized."

Yarozin shrugged his shoulders. "It's a matter of survival, Hoanan. Eat what we can or die here in the woods."

Chapter Six

A VISITOR TO CAMPUS

The infirmary at the school was an enormous rectangular chamber, well illuminated by the natural light of Yarus streaming in through large square windows. There were beds lining each of the long walls, and a comfortable leather armchair with a reclining back beside each bed. On the far side were a couple of machines, draped in plastic covers, evidently to prevent them from gathering dust. A male nurse was seated near the entrance to the room, mulling over a chart spread out on a desk in front of him, intermittently entering a few hand-written notes. The room had only two occupants, the students who had recently been hurt during jet hockey practice.

Nujran and Miriana had come to visit the injured duo on the morning following the incident in the gymnasium. It turned out that the blonde girl with tattoos on her arms was named Tryna, after the Syzegian goddess of exuberance. The youth with the single earring was Klabe, a name meaning frugal in his native tongue. *How delightfully ironic, exuberance and thrift,* Nujran thought. Fortunately, their injuries were not major—multiple bruises, a scratch here and there barely visible to the uninformed, but no broken bones—and they were making a speedy recovery. Although confined to their beds, they remained in good spirits. Responding to a question from the prince, they eagerly related the details of their encounter with the vagrant monk and his seemingly desperate request for food. "He looked authentic and sincere," Klabe remarked. "None of us have seen a person levitate before, so needless to say we were all astounded when he first emerged."

"We know there were two of them," Tryna said. "The one who approached us indicated that there was another man concealed behind a tree."

"He looked emaciated, so we assumed he was homeless," said Klabe.

"Emaciated?" Nujran's brow was furrowed.

"It's a medical term," Miriana pointed out. "He means he was thin and wasted."

"Klabe often likes using big words," Tryna noted.

"My father was a linguistics expert, so I picked up a sesquipedalian way of speaking," Klabe explained. "Which means that I like using long words like sesquipedalian..."

Everyone laughed.

Not quite what one would expect from someone with a name that means 'frugal', Nujran thought. "So, when did you start suspecting that they might be the fugitives?" he asked, out loud, drawing the group's attention back to the subject at hand.

"Well, at the time, we had no reason to doubt his story," Tryna observed. "Naturally, we took pity on them and offered as much food and water as we could. We just saved enough for us to make it back to campus."

"When we got back, the news of the escaped convicts was on everyone's lips." Klabe turned to the prince. "Naturally, my first concern was about you. I remember the chaos they unleashed in your kingdom. A systematic campaign of terror, a lot of death and destruction and, in the end, a failed coup."

And I lost my father in the process. Nujran's shoulders sagged just a tad, like a burden was weighing him down. He remained silent, though, as Klabe continued, "I recall reading a news item on their incarceration in a prison in Eastern Foalinaarc. That's not too far from where we spotted these so-called monks."

"Did you actually see the second man?" Miriana inquired.

Klabe pondered for a moment. "No, I did not. But Tryna's friend Donita was positive that she did."

"She described him as a large man," said Tryna. "She got a pretty good look at him apparently, even though he was trying hard to stay concealed behind a tree."

"At any stage during the encounter, did you feel your lives were at risk?" Miriana asked.

"Not really," Tryna answered. "On the contrary, some of us felt sorry for them."

"Now, let's be clear…we can't be sure they were Hoanan and Yarozin," Klabe admitted. "But the circumstances are certainly suspicious. A couple of well-known prisoners escape at around midnight. Then half a day later, two mysterious men purporting to be monks show up in the woods not far from the scene of the break. It may be a coincidence, but I have a pretty strong feeling that the men we saw were the fugitives."

"Do we know if either Yarozin or Hoanan can levitate?" Miriana enquired, addressing her question to no one in particular.

Nujran had fallen silent during the latter part of the conversation. He looked at Miriana, pondered for a moment, then spoke. "Not sure…I'm unaware that either possesses such skills. Although Hoanan was in the news a lot in those days, I don't recall anyone mentioning levitation as one of his abilities. As for Yarozin, I met him a few times when he was Minister of Internal Security, but honestly, I didn't really know much about him. Like everyone else at the palace, I was astonished to hear that he had masterminded the rebellion. And if he has any special talents, I certainly wouldn't know about them."

"We should let Sarnoff know," Miriana commented. "This is pretty important information. He needs to pass it on to the relevant authorities."

Nujran left the infirmary a short while later with Miriana. It was mid-morning, and a typical late autumn day in Foalinaarc. The sky was a brilliant navy blue, with a few scattered clouds floating across the expanse, aided eastwards by a gentle breeze. As the prince and his companion approached the edge of the quadrangle, they saw Lincus hurrying over toward them. He stopped when he was close, catching his breath before he began to speak.

"Dean Leongatti is looking for you, Nujran. Apparently, you have a visitor."

"A visitor?" the prince asked. "I wasn't expecting anyone."

"I'm not sure who it is." Lincus' words were pouring out rapidly, his voice now a trifle shrill. "But someone from the main office came by your room and asked for you. I happened to be passing by and offered to go and find you. Taz said you might be in the infirmary, so I was heading that way."

"You'd better go and see Leongatti." Miriana looked serious. "Perhaps it's Sarnoff, responding to our earlier message. About time too, I thought he would have got in touch with us earlier."

Nujran strolled across the quadrangle, past the location where Shamirah's corpse was discovered. An ominous silence prevailed... the security tape was still in place, but the area was now unguarded. He proceeded down a couple of lengthy corridors, imparting the obligatory nod to students as they walked past. He then emerged into a lush garden, lined by arrays of tall ulolo trees and thickets of short, colorful flowering bhos bushes, both characteristic of Foalinaarc's dry vegetation. Wandering up a cobble-stoned path, he entered an older red brick building. Its exterior had a wrinkled appearance, almost like it wore time on its stucco. He stepped into a room with a high ceiling, empty except for a glass tube-like structure in the center. He observed that the tube seemed to penetrate the ceiling and assumed it was some sort of elevator. He proceeded toward it, when a female voice addressed him through a speaker embedded on a panel in the elevator door.

"Ahem...Dean Leongatti's office, please identify yourself," the voice requested.

"I'm Nujran. I was asked to come here."

There was a brief pause. "Come on up," the voice said. "The dean is expecting you."

The curved glass doors of the elevator opened invitingly, and Nujran entered. As he ascended slowly toward the ceiling, he noticed that the walls of the room were adorned with shelves bearing trophies and shields, mementos of past victories in inter-collegiate competitions and tournaments. The elevator penetrated a circular opening in the ceiling, first bringing into view a carpeted floor, then plush antique furniture that, for the most part, was made of dark wood. As he came to a halt and the elevator doors opened, Nujran realized that he was on one side of a large elliptical room. Diametrically across was an ornate rectangular table, bearing the university seal. Seated behind the table was Dean Leongatti, wearing a deep purple jacket, an orange sash draped over his square shoulders. He sported a tall black hat that matched the color of his bushy eyebrows, and a pair of horn-rimmed circular eyeglasses perched low down on his nose.

Why is he wearing a hat inside? the prince wondered. *It certainly enhances his already imposing appearance. Perhaps that's the intent.*

Aloud, he said, "Dean Leongatti, you wanted to see me?"

Leongatti's chair was half-turned, and he appeared to be facing a whiteboard near the wall. In his hand was a gold pen-shaped object, which he was waving around, and as he did, letters and words took shape on the whiteboard. The dean seemed to be the only occupant of the impressively furnished office. There were glass windows all around that afforded panoramic views of the campus. In between the windows were high wooden shelves lined with books and leather-bound volumes of various colors and sizes. There was a high-backed armchair facing the dean's desk, with maroon leather upholstery that reminded Nujran of the furniture in his father's chambers back at the palace in Loh'dis. To the prince's right, near one of the long arcs of the oval chamber, was a resplendent sofa that caught his attention. It had gold threads embroidered on to blue fabric, and Yarus' rays were bouncing off the gold, causing it to sparkle brightly. In front of the sofa was a coffee table with a large pitcher and four mugs arranged neatly on a tray. Above the sofa, between two rhomboid windows, was an unusual circular clock perched on the wall. It had the face of a man whose long slender whiskers served as its hands. The odd angle displayed by the mustache gave the face a twisted and rather comical appearance. There was a series of flashing numbers on the man's forehead. The prince stared at it, then realized they indicated the day, month, and year. As his gaze was riveted on this strange object, it suddenly started to speak to him.

"Hello, Nujran, it's really good to see you again!"

Nujran was momentarily astounded. He hadn't expected the clock to address him, yet there was something about the voice that seemed vaguely familiar.

"I'm probably the last person you expected to see," the voice continued, appearing to originate this time from the pitcher on the coffee table. A grin now appeared on Nujran's face, as his eyes searched the room for the source of the voice. He moved forward, approaching the dean's desk, and it was then that he noticed that the high-backed armchair was not empty. Seated comfortably in it was a man with an oddly-shaped hat perched on his head and long gray hair that seemed to merge with his flowing beard. He stood up and raised two of his four arms, inviting Nujran into an embrace.

"Maestro, it's so good to see you! Still your usual playful self, throwing your voice around the room." The prince ran into Amsibh's arms, clasping him in a warm embrace.

"You must be a really special young man," Leongatti noted, looking across the desk over his eyeglasses, a smile on his face. "Your teacher has traveled a long way just to see you."

Amsibh was beaming. "He is special, Leon." Nujran had never heard anyone address the dean this way.

Leongatti chuckled. "I know…he's Rababi and Roone's son, Amsibh. But on campus here, he's just another student, right, Nujran?"

The prince was about to respond, but Amsibh interjected, "No, it's much more than that, Leon. He once saved my life in the heat of battle. He's a brave, quick-thinking young man."

"Oh, really it was nothing, maestro. Linaea told me to get you out of the helicopter, so I just followed her instructions."

"That may be true, but I survived the accident, and am standing before you today, because of the speed with which you reacted."

"When was this?" Dean Leongatti asked, now quite interested in hearing more.

"It was during the late stages of the conflict with Hoanan's rebels to retake Typgar," the maestro answered. "Our helicopter crashed, and I had passed out. Had I remained in the helicopter, I would have been burned alive in the flames or suffocated to death by the smoke. Nujran rescued me…I shall always be grateful."

Nujran felt a wave of opposing emotions. He was certainly pleased with the praise from the maestro, but once again, painful memories began to invade his mind. Immediately after dragging Amsibh out of the helicopter, they had entered the palace courtyard. And it was a short while thereafter that Rababi had emerged, made his way toward Nujran, and then succumbed to the assassin's bullets as he held the prince in his arms.

"What's the matter, Nujran?" The maestro had noticed the prince's change in expression and realized he may have touched a nerve.

"Thoughts of my father just flooded back, maestro. I'm sorry…this happens every now and then…I'll be good in a second."

"It's perfectly alright, no need to apologize." Leongatti's tone was gentle as he walked over to Nujran and gave him a pat on his back. "It's just over a couple of years since you lost your father. You probably didn't have much opportunity to grieve back then. So, it's going to hit you from time to time, and rather unexpectedly."

Nujran rubbed his eyes with the balls of his hands. "I'm ok, thank you, sir." He then turned to Amsibh. "So, what brings you to our campus, maestro?"

"You know that Yarozin and Hoanan have escaped from prison, right? Iolena is very concerned. She contacted me to ask if I could visit you."

"Oh, I see. What's her concern, specifically?"

"Well, there are vague rumors of sightings in Central Foalinaarc. If these are true, then they're heading westward."

Nujran's thoughts drifted to Tryna and Klabe. He decided this was a good time to share their information. "There's a group of students from campus who went camping recently in that area, maestro. I was speaking with a couple of them earlier, and they believe they saw Yarozin and Hoanan."

Leongatti leaned forward over his desk. He looked surprised. "That's the first I'm hearing of such an encounter, Nujran. Are you sure? What exactly did they say?"

The prince proceeded to describe the specifics of the incident that Tryna and Klabe had related to Miriana and him earlier that day. As he spoke, Leongatti waved his pen in the direction of the whiteboard again, making notes to capture what he was hearing. When Nujran concluded his account, the dean turned to Amsibh. "I'll let Sarnoff know about this. He can pass the information on to the authorities in Foalinaarc."

"That's exactly what I was going to do," Nujran noted. "Just haven't had the chance yet, since I came right over to your office from the infirmary."

"Who's Sarnoff?" the maestro inquired.

"He's a detective investigating a case on campus," the dean replied.

"Maestro, he's a cousin of Pholtorimes," Nujran chimed in. "I think you'll enjoy meeting him."

There was a clicking sound as Leongatti pushed a small black button on the gold pen in his hand. He was pointing it toward the whiteboard, and Nujran could make out the faint outlines of a map that was starting to appear. As it came into focus, the prince recognized it as a map of the kingdom of Foalinaarc.

"Couldn't they just be heading to Cherstwine Castle, Amsibh?" The dean was pointing to an area in the mountains of Western Foalinaarc.

"Yes, indeed," Amsibh replied. "That was our first assumption when we heard the rumors. But then again, we cannot rule out that they are headed here."

"Why would they be interested in our school?" Nujran inquired.

"Because *you* are here, young man," came the maestro's reply.

"But why would they still be after me? They killed my father, my mother is not the ruler of the kingdom, and I am just a student going about his education."

"Yes, but as we have discussed before, Nujran, you are a symbol. Rababi was much loved by his people. You are a popular prince."

"So, that makes me a target?"

"Let's not jump to any conclusions," Leongatti cautioned, his tone reassuring. "I think Amsibh is speaking in hypothetical terms. But he's right in the sense that we cannot just sit back and be complacent. We take security on campus very seriously, so we need to hear what Queen Iolena's concerns are."

Amsibh nodded. "As we say when we go into battle, Nujran...we should hope for the best, while preparing for the worst."

"That's a clever statement, Amsibh," Leongatti observed. "Could apply to a lot of things in life. I'd like to use it in my classes...I'll give you credit, of course."

"No, it's not mine, Leon. I've heard Pelorius use it quite often, and I'm not sure where he picked it up." Amsibh grinned. "So, yes, feel free to use it, but just attribute it to an unknown philosopher."

Leongatti turned to the prince. "Amsibh will be staying on campus as a boarder for a few days, Nujran. There is a guest bedroom in my quarters. My wife needs a couple of hours to arrange everything, so perhaps you could show your teacher our beautiful campus in the meanwhile. That's assuming, Amsibh, that you're not too tired."

Nujran and Amsibh descended in the glass elevator and emerged into the garden in front of the building. As they walked on the paths among the plants and trees, Nujran was reminded of one of his early encounters with Amsibh, where the maestro had strolled with him through the palace gardens, explaining how plants were sources of various medicinal substances.

"Do you still have your herbarium in Narcaya, maestro?" the prince inquired.

"Yes, I do, Nujran. Tromzen helps me keep it going and always looks after it well when I am away. Under his influence, it's changed a bit though. You remember that he's a wonderful chef, always interested in trying out new things in his kitchen. So, he's transformed the garden from one where medicinal plants dominated, to one which generates fruits, vegetables, and the various leaves and herbs he needs for his cooking. I really don't mind…I know everything he grows gets used."

A thought struck Nujran. "Maestro, after Zhinso was shot, do you remember that we were heading back to Narcaya? Jozak wanted to make the antidote to the poison from herbs in your garden. Do you think he could have saved Zhinso if we had got back in time?"

"Beware of tying yourself up in knots with such hypothetical queries, Nujran. There's no harm in asking ourselves the 'what if' question in virtually any situation, as long as it's for the purpose of learning and perhaps not repeating mistakes. So, if that's the spirit of your enquiry, then yes, Jozak would have probably concocted the antidote, given that he knew what the poison was."

"Sorry, maestro, I don't understand…what's the downside to my posing the question?"

"Well, Zhinso has passed on, and we can't bring him back. So, it remains a hypothetical question. I guess I was just cautioning you not to get too upset about what might have been, had we reached the island in time. Do you understand the point I'm making?"

"Yes, maestro, I do understand." *He can be a tad harsh sometimes,* thought the prince. *All I was asking was whether Zhinso could have been saved. But I guess he's just trying to protect my feelings.*

"How are things in Typgar, maestro?" Nujran inquired, changing the subject.

"Iolena is doing an excellent job. She's given a lot of attention to education and healthcare, and she's continuing to support the technological revolution that your father foresaw and encouraged."

They turned a corner and wandered into a long corridor on the outer aspect of a building that housed classrooms and laboratories. A breeze greeted them as they sauntered through. A couple of female students walked past, greeting Nujran as they passed by.

"Are you in touch with Zaarica?" Amsibh asked.

"We haven't spoken in a while," answered Nujran. "She's studying at a school close to Loh'dis. When I left, and we said our goodbyes, we both understood that we were going in different directions. Although we didn't explicitly discuss it, I think it was implied that we were both free to see other people."

"Probably a good decision, Nujran. You're both still very young, so that makes sense. The university experience allows you to meet lots of people and explore friendships."

Nujran fell silent, his mind drifting back to the palace. He thought about Zaarica and his long friendship with her during their childhood, the start of their relationship just prior to his being sent away from the palace, and the surprising news that she was the daughter of the rebel leader Arondello. He realized that she had not entered his thoughts for a while, and wondered if that signaled he had moved on.

"Do you have a girlfriend now?" Amsibh's question interrupted his musing.

"Well, there's this girl, Miriana. She's a year ahead of me. We've been out on a couple of dates."

"That's nice. Is she interesting?"

"She's really friendly...and very smart. She wants to be a doctor."

As they entered one of the ubiquitous quadrangles at the university campus, another thought entered Nujran's head. "Maestro, is time travel possible?"

"A very interesting question, Nujran. Why do you ask?"

"I miss my father a great deal. I often regret the fact that he died before I really got to know him as a young adult. I often wonder if I could wander back through time and speak with him."

"Well, let's see. There are lots of memories of the people in your childhood stored in your memory banks. You can always delve into them and revisit your time with him. He may have passed on, but he lives on in your memories, your imagination, your thoughts."

"Yes, that's true…he used to appear a lot in my dreams in the days and weeks after his death. And off and on these days as well." Nujran paused, then turned to his teacher. "But I meant something different, maestro. I was asking if it's possible to really travel back in time…I mean physically go back. Or forward, for that matter, to a period in the future."

Amsibh fell silent for a while, pondering the question. A few moments later, he spoke. "In theory, yes, Nujran. It's definitely possible to go backward in time, but I'm not sure if travel into the future is possible. There are people who have spent their lives studying the space-time continuum. You have one of these brilliant men on campus."

"Who's that, Amsibh?"

"Your dean, my good friend Leongatti."

"Really?" Nujran had a look of disbelief on his face. "All I knew was that he taught physics, but I had no idea he was an expert in time travel."

"Well, you were in his office a short while back. Did you notice the clock on the wall above the sofa?"

"The one with the face of a man sporting an oddly-shaped mustache?"

"Yes, you probably didn't realize what you were looking at. It's one of Leon's inventions. He calls it a tempusmachina, or a time machine."

Chapter Seven

DISCUSSIONS WITH THE MAESTRO

It was late in the evening and Nujran found himself walking down one of the school corridors. He looked out across the adjacent quadrangle, noting that it was empty. This was unusual, as students usually took advantage of the mellow microclimate of the school at the twilight hour to be outside. Across from where he stood, the college steeple rose proudly into the sky, flanked by two bright celestial orbs, Handac and Iandic. His eyes searched across the indigo expanse for the third moon, Jovic, but it seemed hidden in bashful retreat. A chill breeze suddenly caressed his back, and he felt propelled down the corridor. In the dim light, he perceived someone approach from the distance. It was a broad-shouldered male, and the walk was distinctly familiar. As he approached, the man's unmistakable voice rang out.

"What are you doing outside your room? I thought you'd be studying for your test tomorrow."

"Just out for a walk, Dean Leongatti. Taking a break, just trying to get some fresh air."

The dean smiled but did not reply. All of a sudden, the ground seemed to tremble violently. A linear crack appeared on the floor and widened rapidly into an enormous crevasse. Large volumes of dust began to descend from the ceiling, temporarily obscuring the prince's view.

"Don't worry, Nujran, I've got you!" An arm grabbed him from behind and pulled him back from the brink, just as he felt he was losing his balance. The voice was comforting and distinctly familiar. He turned around and felt himself drawn into an embrace. Then, abruptly, he heard a staccato sound, as though bullets were raining down on him. He looked up to see Rababi, smiling at him, as blood emerged from the corner of his mouth, streaming down in bright red rivulets onto his jaw. As the prince's body started to shudder, he now heard a different voice, this time closer to his ear and considerably louder.

"Wake up, Nujran!" It was Tazloe. He was bending over the prince, shaking him back to consciousness. Nujran realized he had fallen into a deep sleep on the sofa in his room. He had returned after his meeting earlier in the day with Amsibh. After a couple of hours of study, fatigue had overpowered his attempts to remain awake, a likely consequence of his staying up quite late the previous night, working on an assignment. He was not sure how long he had been asleep. The dream had been quite vivid, a variation of many similar ones he had experienced. They usually started out quite routinely, often as a stroll in a familiar place. A dramatic, and frequently catastrophic, event would then ensue, at which stage Rababi would appear. The dream would end with the prince in his father's arms, gazing into the dying king's smiling eyes, a vivid and unsettling re-enactment of the final moments of his father's life.

There was a faint knock on the door. Neither the prince nor Tazloe moved from where they were. A few moments later, there was another series of knocks, this time more urgent.

"Can you get that, Taz?" the prince asked.

Tazloe ambled over lazily to see who it was. He opened the door partially and peeked out.

"What's up, Lincus?" Nujran heard Tazloe say.

"Is Nujran in?"

"Yes, he is, come on in and scooch down the couch."

Lincus wandered in, and Tazloe shut the door behind him.

Nujran hauled himself out of the sofa. "You looking for me, Lincus? Everything alright?"

Lincus' eyes darted around the room. He was clearly a little distracted. He remained silent, a quizzical expression appearing on his face, as though he was confused by something he had seen.

"Lincus, is everything alright?" Nujran repeated.

Lincus looked at him. "Oh yes, sorry...there's a lot of interesting stuff around here. I really like the way you guys have the room set up, with all the Plugarnican paraphernalia. I mean, I myself am a Mambozigan fan, but I respect the sportsmanship of your team."

"Lincus!" exclaimed Nujran, "What's up?"

"Right, well...the reason I'm here is that Sarnoff's back, and he's asking for you. He's with maestro Amsibh outside Leongatti's office."

"Alright, give me a second. Taz, have you seen my Zogo?"

Tazloe did not reply; he had collapsed on to the sofa just vacated by Nujran and was listening to music again through his earphones. *He spends a great deal of time with those earbuds in his ears*, Nujran thought. *I wonder what damage he's doing to his hearing. I must check with Miriana if there are any studies on that. If anyone would know, she would.*

Nujran and Lincus left the room together. On their way out, Lincus inquired, "Any new information on Shamirah's death? Is that why Sarnoff is here?"

Nujran wasn't sure how much he should share with Lincus. Not many on campus were aware of the facts that had emerged regarding

Shamirah. A reasonably tight wall of confidentiality had been maintained around the details.

After a brief moment of reflection, he answered, "Nothing much, really. I guess Sarnoff may have an update."

Lincus seemed disappointed but didn't say anything further. They parted company, and Nujran headed over to see Amsibh and Sarnoff.

It was late in the afternoon, and the rays of Yarus were beginning to lengthen. A few silvery clouds of various shapes floated around in an otherwise typically azure Foalinaarc sky. The maestro was seated cross-legged on a bench in the garden outside the building where Leongatti's office was housed. The bench was made of dark wood and had recently been polished to render it shiny, perhaps with an oil that protected it by making it resistant to weather-induced damage. Sarnoff was standing with his face to Amsibh, his back to a tree with low-hanging branches from which hung orange flowers, shaped like inverted cones. Nujran recognized it as an illowa tree, native to Typgar, and wondered if someone had introduced it to Foalinaarc at some stage. A gentle breeze was blowing in his direction as he entered the garden, bearing a pleasant assortment of floral and fruity aromas that greeted his nostrils. Sarnoff's back was to Nujran, but observing him approach through his rear-facing eyes, he swiveled around and addressed the prince.

"Hello, Nujran, maestro Amsibh was just talking to me about you. Your ears must be burning."

"What was the maestro saying?"

"Just how delighted he is to have watched you grow into a sensible young man."

Nujran looked at Amsibh and smiled. "Are you suggesting I wasn't always sensible, maestro?"

Amsibh chuckled. "Well, when I first met you as a young boy, you didn't know much about anything."

"That's true, maestro. I was both ignorant and spoiled. I have to thank you, and probably Zaarica as well, for helping to change that."

"You've obviously done something to impress the maestro, Nujran," Sarnoff chimed in. "Amsibh is a celebrated guru who has taught thousands of students over the years. I would assume that he is a discerning judge of character and does not lavish praise without reason."

Nujran now seemed somewhat embarrassed and decided it was time to change the subject. "Detective Sarnoff, do you have any further information on Shamirah's death?"

"Well, the investigation is still ongoing, so I cannot share very much at this point, Nujran. Rest assured that we are looking at her death from every angle, and we will get to the bottom of it."

"Was she murdered?" Nujran asked and then immediately wondered if he had been too blunt.

"Again, we're certainly looking at all possibilities," Sarnoff replied, politely side-stepping the question. "I have my theories, of course, but mine is a data-driven field, so I really need to wait for all the evidence to be analyzed before I can reach any conclusion."

"Shamirah sounds like an Ersipian name," said Amsibh. "Is that where she was from?"

Sarnoff nodded. "You're right, maestro. She was the university's first transgender student from there."

"Transgender?" Amsibh raised his eyebrows.

"Yes, so that's two reasons someone might have been prejudiced against her," Sarnoff pointed out.

"Two reasons?" Nujran asked. "What do you mean?"

"Well, one thing I've learned from all my years in the detective trade is that hatred comes in many forms. There's a lot of animosity to folks from Ersipia and Baariya. You were probably aware of that, growing up in Typgar."

Nujran winced. "Yes, Hoanan stirred up those sentiments. He was adept at making people turn against immigrants. Unsurprisingly, he loved talking about how Typgar was better before my father became king, and how he would revive those glory days. But an idiot like that, with such a paltry selection of words to choose from, I mean—what else could we really expect from him?"

"Yes, indeed," Amsibh responded. "He was a populist and attracted followers by promoting a xenophobic agenda. And he was against everyone…those from Aaltin, Baariya, Ersipia, and so on."

Nujran shook his head. "So, Shamirah may have been killed because she was transgender, or because she was Ersipian. Either way, it's just awful that she met such a tragic end."

There was a momentary lull in the conversation as they pondered the likelihood that Shamirah was the victim of a hate crime. Sounds of student chatter, from beyond the hedges surrounding the garden, interrupted the silence. Sarnoff waited till the chatter had faded into the distance before addressing Nujran directly. "Dean Leongatti informed me that some students on campus may have seen Hoanan and Yarozin."

"Yes, Tryna and Klabe were two of the students on a camping trip in the hills of Central Foalinaarc. They saw a couple of monks, and in retrospect, they're pretty sure they were the escaped prisoners." Nujran paused, then turned to Amsibh. "Maestro, did you know that Yarozin has the ability to levitate? Is it possible that he was once a monk?"

"I'm not sure, Nujran…Andron never mentioned it to me. I guess it's conceivable…he would not be the first example of someone with that kind of training, who then crossed over to the dark side. In our planet's checkered history, we do have several examples of monks and other spiritual leaders who have turned into despots."

"Amsibh is quite right, Nujran," Sarnoff acknowledged. "In the past, before democratic institutions were well established across Syzegis, there were often unholy alliances between kings and queens on the one hand and spiritual leaders on the other."

Amsibh nodded in agreement. "Yes, indeed…and religious institutions exerted a great deal of political influence. Needless to say, this was often quite unhealthy for those countries and governments."

"Unhealthy, maestro? How so?"

"Well, in my view, the spiritual dimension adds value in terms of encouraging introspection and contemplating the big picture, so to speak. But politics is a different business…by nature, it has to be pragmatic, rational, and based on rules and laws. Over the centuries, we've learned that religion and politics are best kept separate."

"This is a fascinating discussion, for sure!" exclaimed Sarnoff. "I would love to stay and chat further, but there are a million things I need to do." He turned to the prince. "Nujran, I'll be in touch… we will need to interview the students who believe they may have encountered the escaped convicts. Hopefully, you and Miriana can help me set up those meetings."

Sarnoff waved his hand in a gesture of farewell and walked away from them. Nujran noticed that his rear-facing eyes were still focused on them as he left, continuing to observe them as he withdrew from the garden.

"How does he process the visual input, maestro? He's got to look ahead to see where he's going, but his eyes were still trained on us."

"I'm not exactly sure, Nujran. But I would think that his bran has the ability to move back and forth between the images his front- and rear-facing eyes present. Since he's born with the ability, it probably comes to him quite naturally...he wouldn't even think twice about it, I would imagine."

"Wow...I was always intrigued by Pholtorimes...when I first met him, I stared at him a lot! He was the only one of his kind I had met before...and now, Sarnoff. What a unique type of individual!"

"Yes, indeed...and isn't it curious that the family seems to have dominated the detective profession? An example of using one's natural abilities to one's best advantage."

"Maestro, on a completely separate note, I've been thinking about the tempusmachina, the time machine in Dean Leongatti's office. Do you know how it works? Do you think we could use it?"

A mischievous look appeared on Amsibh's face. "What are you suggesting, Nujran? Should we go behind Leongatti's back and experiment with time?"

Nujran seemed embarrassed. "I don't want to break any rules, maestro. But I'll be honest, I'm really curious to see how it works."

"Well, it's late in the day, and both he and his assistant are likely to have left the office, Nujran. Let's go and have a look. Time travel is about the most fascinating thing there is."

They strolled up the cobble-stoned path to the old red brick building. Entering the atrium, they walked over to the glass elevator. Nujran remembered that he had to identify himself to gain admission earlier and wondered how that would work on this occasion. As he pondered the question, Amsibh waved his hands and clapped twice. The elevator doors promptly opened, and they entered. The doors closed, and they ascended toward, then through the ceiling. Leongatti's office was dark and devoid of any occupants. As they emerged from the elevator, Amsibh waved his hands once again and clapped twice. The lights in the office came on, and Nujran's gaze turned instantly to the clock, the dean's time machine.

"We may as well try it," Amsibh remarked, a twinkle in his eye. "I'm as curious as you are. Let's give it a whirl and go back in time."

Chapter Eight

THE DEAN'S TIME MACHINE

Amsibh ambled over to the clock on the wall, Nujran following tentatively behind. The shorter of the two hands was pointing downward and to the left; the longer one, upwards and to the right. The prince suppressed a desire to laugh, given the amusing appearance of the whiskered face.

"How does it work?" he inquired softly.

The maestro scratched his chin, his fingertips poking through the long wispy strands of his white beard. He pondered for a moment. "In other models that I have seen, you just fiddle with the clock hands, and we take a wander back through time. Now get ready, my boy, time is a vast expanse…like a colossal park with an unlimited variety of vegetation. You can so easily be distracted by the beauty of a single plant or tree that you'll forget which path you started walking on, and where you were headed to." He paused, staring intently at the clock. "As for how this one works, I'm not exactly sure. Hold on to my arm…I guess we'll just try it and see what happens."

Amsibh reached up and rapidly started moving the shorter hand backward, taking it through successive rotations. He kept his fingers on it, continuing the process for a short while. The lights in the room began to flicker, and the prince felt his surroundings start to spin around in a counterclockwise direction. Things became quite blurry for several moments, and then the room gradually came back into focus. Bright light was now streaming in through the windows, and from his vantage point below the clock, Nujran observed Dean Leongatti seated behind his desk. He looked like he was in conversation with someone settled in the armchair directly across from him. Initially, the words seemed to be coming at them from a distance, progressively becoming louder and clearer. Suddenly, the prince recognized Amsibh's booming voice, his words now coming through quite distinctly. There was then a sound to his left, the elevator doors opened, and someone sauntered into the room.

Nujran's jaw dropped in amazement…he was looking at himself walking into the dean's office. He realized that this was the scene from the previous day, when he had first come up to meet Amsibh on campus. The youth who had just entered said something to the dean, but Leongatti did not respond immediately. The youth then looked around the room, appearing to stare directly at the prince, then through him at the clock on the wall. It was at that point that Nujran grasped he was not visible to the people in the room, just an ethereal presence observing the proceedings from a future dimension. He tried to whisper something to Amsibh, but no words emerged. Suddenly, things started to get blurry again, and he felt the room spin, this time in a clockwise direction. When the spinning stopped, they were right back where they had started. He was standing beside Amsibh, it was dusk once more outside, and the lights in the room were back on.

Amsibh spoke in his usual booming voice. "Now, that was interesting! A short visit to yesterday, just at the point you entered Leon's office. What do you think, Nujran?"

"It was really strange looking at myself," replied Nujran. "I'm a bit shorter than I thought I was…and my voice sounded really high pitched."

"Yes, there can be some distortion, both visual and auditory," Amsibh explained. "But a nice window, nevertheless, into the past."

Nujran was silent for a little while, reflecting on what had just happened. It was his first experience of time travel. Albeit brief, it was both exciting and unsettling at the same time. *How exactly had the tempusmachina countered the laws of physics which dictate that time marches inexorably forward? I need to pay more attention to the dean's lectures. The man is a genius if he can manipulate time.*

Shortly thereafter, they exited the dean's office and entered the elevator. On their way down, Nujran wondered if they had violated some university rule, doing what they had just done. Not only had they intruded into the dean's office in his absence, but they had also used one of his inventions without his permission. Yet, Amsibh seemed entirely unconcerned. The prince assumed that either his relationship with the dean or his stature as a master teacher on the planet permitted him the luxury of these transgressions.

"How far back in time can one go?" Nujran asked as the doors of the elevator opened, and they stepped out into the atrium.

"In theory, there shouldn't be a limit," Amsibh replied. "But in practice, it's constrained by how many turns of the clock handle one can manage without stopping. So, I've never really had the experience of going back more than a few days, at the most."

The prince fell silent again, his brow furrowed in thought.

"I can guess what you are thinking, Nujran."

"What's that, maestro?"

"You want to go back in time and see your father again, correct?"

Nujran nodded. "You're quite right, maestro. That's exactly what I was wondering...do you think I could do that?"

"I don't see why not, Nujran," Amsibh responded. "We can plan that for another time. I think you need to be mentally prepared, though, or else you may emerge from the experience quite emotionally distraught."

"Honestly, maestro, I don't believe that would be a problem. Father appears not infrequently in my dreams. At first, it was a bit surreal, and I would awaken quite disturbed. But now, I think I'm getting used to it."

"Interesting," murmured Amsibh.

"Do you remember Ronanya, maestro? One of the monks on Flomo."

"Of course I do, Nujran. I remember her very well. A very interesting lady, a scholar in thanatology, if my memory serves me correctly."

"Thanatology? What's that?"

"The study of death, Nujran. The ultimate mystery, if you think about it. We know so little about what happens after, yet she has spent a lifetime thinking about it, studying it."

"Yes, we had some interesting conversations, for sure. She seemed to have the ability to communicate with the dead. I remember being quite skeptical, and yet strangely fascinated by her. I asked Andron about her abilities, and we had quite a lengthy discussion about her."

"What made you think about her just now, Nujran?"

"Well, it's interesting...Ronanya used to tell me that people visit us from the other side in our dreams."

"Ah yes, she's an expert on those topics."

"I'm not sure if you remember, maestro...you actually suggested that I seek her company after my father's death. And you were right... she was an incredible source of solace. I can't say that I completely believed everything she claimed. You know...the part about being able to communicate with the dead, feeling their presence, and so on. I just couldn't wrap my brain around all that...it was too abstract for me. But she was so warm and sympathetic and seemed to know exactly what to say."

They were now in the garden outside, walking between rows of plants. Amsibh would stop from time to time, bending over a shrub or inhaling the aroma of a flower. Nujran's mind again meandered back to the time they had wandered together through the palace gardens in Loh'dis. The maestro had patiently explained the intricate nature of various plants to him, expounding on the biodiversity found on Syzegis. The prince remembered being profoundly impressed by his teacher's knowledge right from those early days.

They continued their walk, and neither spoke for a short while. Amsibh broke the silence.

"Are you hungry, Nujran? I haven't eaten in a while. Perhaps you could take me down to your cafeteria, and I can have a taste of your regular cuisine."

"It's not that exciting, maestro. It's mostly generic, unseasoned meats. Occasionally, we get pasta...but even if you throw the pesto sauce on there from the salad bar, it's not really any good. Last week I found a bone in my meatloaf. Bone...ugh! Overall, though, it's acceptable, but I think they could do better."

"Well, it's unlikely to be anywhere near the gourmet cuisine you enjoyed at the palace growing up," Amsibh teased gently.

"Nowhere near it," agreed Nujran. "Those palace chefs...they were pretty talented."

"Nor would there be any comparison, I suppose, with the food produced by those remarkably gifted chefs, Tromzen and Baa'chirav," Amsibh continued.

"Yes, those were really wonderful meals, weren't they, maestro?" Nujran responded. His mouth had started to salivate as his thoughts drifted back. Tromzen was a friend of Amsibh on the island of Narcaya, and Baa'chirav was the chef on the floating ship, Flomo. During his adventures with Amsibh, he had been privileged to enjoy meals cooked by those expert chefs.

"Do you remember the banquets we had with the Monks of Meirar?" Amsibh chuckled. "Lots of food flying around...quite the spectacle!"

"I certainly do, maestro. They were able to turn any meal into an entertaining event. Some great memories of those days."

Having wandered down a couple of shaded corridors, they stepped out into the light. They were greeted by a hubbub as they approached a single-storied building with a triangular roof.

"This is the main cafeteria, maestro. Lots of food choices here, so I'm sure you'll find something you like."

They entered and looked around. Nujran headed to the food court, a large rectangular area with various stations around. There were groups of students at tables having their dinner, some seated quietly, others conversing animatedly as they did. Signs hanging from the roof indicated the multitude of food choices available. Amsibh's eye caught one of the signs in a corner, barely visible behind a large low-hanging chandelier. He walked toward it, Nujran following behind. As they got closer, the prince was able to read it clearly.

Meat for vegetarians, the sign read.

"That's interesting," Nujran murmured. "I've never noticed that before. I wonder if they used the same technology we saw on Flomo. Zoltar, the captain, gave us a pretty detailed account of how they did it when we toured the ship."

"Ah yes, taking a few cells from the muscle of an animal and then growing them in a laboratory environment. Cloning technology applied to the food industry...that was ingenious indeed!"

They advanced to the counter; a large man wearing a chef's hat had just emerged from a door behind it. "Can I help you?" he asked. "You're the first ones to visit this station today."

"I have a question for you, my good man," said Amsibh.

"Sure, go ahead."

"Your sign says, 'Meat for vegetarians.' Is the meat produced by cloning...you know, growing cells in a laboratory?"

The man looked puzzled and thought for a moment. "I don't believe so, sir," came his reply. "I was told that it's manufactured in a factory, from plant sources. Pea protein, I think, let me just check."

He disappeared through the door behind the counter, then re-emerged moments later, nodding.

"Yes, that's right. It's from a factory in Lustraa, from the kingdom of Andzale, actually. Apparently, they were the first ones to make meat from pea protein."

"That's remarkable," commented Amsibh. "I'd like to try some. What about you, Nujran?"

"Sure, why not," the prince replied, a little unenthusiastically. While he would have preferred to have his usual sandwich, he did not wish to offend the maestro. A part of him was curious too, as this was something novel in the food department. And in truth, the artificial meat he had tasted and enjoyed on Flomo, albeit generated through a different approach, had been an epicurean delight.

The prince tentatively dished out on to his plate small quantities of various meats from the counter, each of which simulated a different type of animal protein. By contrast, the maestro dove eagerly into each receptacle, spooning out substantial servings of individual dishes. They made their way over to an empty table, and as they approached to take their seats, a familiar voice called out from behind.

"Hi, Nujran, how's tricks?"

The prince turned around to see Miriana behind him, a plate in one hand and a glass of fruit juice in the other.

"Oh, hello Miriana. It's nice to see you." Nujran's voice had a genuinely upbeat tone.

"Who's your friend, Nujran?" Miriana asked, looking at Amsibh.

"This is the maestro Amsibh, Miriana. The person I've spoken to you so much about. You finally get to meet him."

There was a moment of silence.

"Oh my goodness, it's the great teacher himself." Miriana appeared genuinely impressed. "What an honor...it's such a delight to meet you, sir. Nujran constantly sings your praises."

"Maestro, this is my friend Miriana."

Amsibh smiled, extending one of his arms out toward Miriana. "So, you're the young lady this young prince speaks so fondly about."

Miriana blushed. "Really, maestro? He's spoken to you about me? I suppose I should be flattered." She then turned to the prince and asked in a mildly chiding tone, "So, why did you bring our planet's most celebrated teacher to this awful cafeteria, Nujran? Couldn't you have taken him off campus somewhere nice for dinner?"

Amsibh chuckled. "It can't be that bad, can it? I'm looking forward to this selection of vegetarian meats."

"Vegetarian meats? I've seen the sign a few times, but I haven't really sampled them."

"Do you know how they're made, Miriana?"

"Can't say I've given the subject much thought, maestro. But now that you ask, I'm intrigued. How exactly are they produced?" Miriana's curiosity appeared to have been piqued.

"Well, let's sit down at the table, shall we?" Amsibh suggested. "We can have a chat about the wonders of artificial meat." The maestro then proceeded to explain to Miriana how they had savored meat grown from animal cells on Flomo. "These dishes here appear to have been made with different technology, though," he pointed out. "The chef here told us they were made from pea protein."

"Can I have a taste?" Miriana asked.

"Help yourself," said Nujran, offering his plate to her.

Miriana scooped up a couple of chunks on the prince's plate and popped them in her mouth. "Not bad," she admitted. "Frankly, I'm surprised. Wouldn't have known this was from a plant source. Quite amazing, when you think about it. Technology has advanced to the point where we don't have to kill the animal for meat."

Amsibh nodded. "Exactly. And perhaps one day in the future, the large scale killing of animals for meat will be a thing of the past."

"But isn't it all processed food, maestro?" asked Miriana. "That can't be all that good for you, when you think about it."

The prince was getting a little tired of the discussion on artificial meats. "Miriana wants to be a doctor," he stated, deliberately moving on to another subject.

"I'm not a hundred percent sure," Miriana responded. "But it's the general direction I'm moving in. I really like studying anatomy and physiology."

"That's commendable," Amsibh noted. "We need more good doctors, that's for sure. There are still parts of Syzegis where healthcare is limited, and access to hospitals is practically non-existent."

Miriana nodded. "Yes, I'm certainly aware of that. In my home country Zilbaros, we have good medical care in the big cities, but once you move into the countryside, there isn't really much to speak of."

"That sounds more like a problem of non-uniform distribution, rather than a lack of medical professionals," Nujran pointed out.

"That's true," Amsibh commented. "I think it's a bit of both. An overall lack of good doctors, and the few good ones we have are concentrated in urban areas."

They fell silent for a few moments as they chomped down their food. Miriana broke the silence again.

"Maestro, you live on the island of Narcaya, right? What brings you to our university? And how did you get here?"

"I came to deliver a message to Nujran from Queen Iolena," Amsibh replied. "You perhaps know that she succeeded Nujran's father, King Rababi, as Typgar's head of state. I arrived here in a bubble, a form of transportation developed through research that Nujran's father supported. Nujran has actually traveled in one."

"Yeah, it was a fascinating experience," Nujran recalled. "That was my first visit to Narcaya."

"A bubble, as a form of transport?" Miriana asked. "How does that work?"

"Well, as the name suggests, it's a large transparent bubble," the prince explained. "You sit inside, and you get spectacular views of things below. It travels at a gentler pace than the aircraft we're used to."

"There's a local transport center not far from here," Amsibh said. "On arrival, I rented a personal drone to get here."

Nujran looked surprised. "A personal drone? Is that like Dean Leongatti's flying scooter?"

"Not quite," murmured the maestro. "It's a lot like the drones used in warfare, but there's a chamber below it, where a person can be seated comfortably. It's fully programmed, you see, and delivers you to your destination."

A short while later, after they had finished their evening meal, Amsibh and Nujran made their way back toward campus housing. Miriana had left earlier to finish an assignment that was due the following day.

"I'd love to try out the personal drone, maestro," Nujran remarked. "The concept is fascinating; I didn't know they existed."

"Well, we've used drones for many years now, first in warfare, then for aerial photography, and more recently to deliver objects to one's doorstep. It was only a matter of time before someone adapted them to transport people."

"How fast do they travel, maestro? Are they comfortable?"

"They're designed to travel pretty fast, but regulations require them to be operated at fairly slow speeds, comparable to the maximum velocity of a car on a road. So, not necessarily the ideal mode of transport for someone in a hurry. But yes, extremely comfortable, I would say."

They had reached the bottom of the stairs leading up to the floor on which Nujran's room was.

"Good night, maestro. I'll see you in the morning,"

"Good night, Nujran."

The maestro strolled back to the dean's quarters, and Nujran bounded up the stairs to his room. Tazloe wasn't in, and the prince wondered if he had been successful in getting a date. There was a faint odor of some aromatic herb that his roommate must have vaped earlier in the day. Nujran made a mental note to remind Tazloe to leave a window open when he smoked, else the scent lingered in the air. He ambled over to the refrigerator, grabbed a bottle of water, then strode into the bedroom. He decided he would do some light reading and grabbed a book from the shelf. However, just a few minutes later, he suddenly felt quite tired, and his eyelids grew heavy. Nodding off to sleep, he tumbled shortly after, as he usually did, into the world of dreams.

Chapter Nine

A MYSTERY ILLNESS

The sky was a bright cobalt blue, and an occasional white cloud floated by lazily. Yarozin's voice drifted from over the hill.

"We're almost there, Hoanan. I see the campus in the distance."

"So, what's the plan, Yarozin? We've come a long way."

"Well, I explained it to you several times, Hoanan! Weren't you listening? We walk in, grab the young man, and leave as soon as possible."

"What about campus security, Yarozin?"

"Don't worry, there's no one around."

"And what if we encounter any students or teachers who impede our way?"

"Just shoot them, Hoanan. And shoot to kill."

Suddenly, out of the sky, there was a buzzing sound, and what looked like a small aircraft came into view. As it drew closer, it appeared to be a drone with an elliptical chamber attached to it below. A side door popped open, and Amsibh's face appeared. He seemed to be carrying a weapon and, without warning, opened fire on Yarozin and Hoanan, who raced for cover. They were heading toward the guardhouse at the gates of the campus. Hoanan slowed down briefly and fired random shots in the air, all of which missed their target.

Yarozin then pulled something out of his pocket and hurled it toward the gates as bullets rained down from above. There was an explosion, then a big ball of flame, an intense brightness, and an incredibly strong sensation of heat.

Nujran awoke with a start, drenched in sweat, his head and torso suffused with a feeling of warmth. His bedroom window was open, and the rays of Yarus were streaming in, engulfing his body and temporarily blinding him as his eyes adjusted to the glare. He was a little surprised to note that he was fully dressed, his book lying next to him on the sheets. Realizing that he had fallen asleep the previous night without changing his clothes, he hauled himself off the bed, undressed, and jumped into the shower. The cool jets of water hit his skin sharply, sending messages to the alertness center in his brain, dispelling any residual somnolence. Reflecting on his dream, he wondered if Yarozin and Hoanan might, in fact, be getting closer to the university campus. After all, wasn't that why Amsibh had arrived, in effect, to warn him of the possible threat from the escaped fugitives? *Am I in real danger*? he wondered. *Would they be bold enough to enter the campus grounds and try to kidnap me?* He felt shivers run through his body and down his spine, then realized that the temperature of the water had decreased, suddenly rendering the spray rather chilly. He turned the knob to add more heat to the spray, and sure enough, the shivers subsided. But the angst lingered as he stepped out of the shower recess, and he made a mental note to discuss his concerns with Amsibh later that day.

Emerging from his bedroom in fresh clothes, the prince ambled into the living area. The window was open, framing the beams of sunlight pouring in. A gentle breeze wafted into the room, bringing with it the distinct scent of sycamund bushes. As he approached the light, a ruckus greeted his ears from the quadrangle below. He had a brief sense of déjà vu, his mind racing back like a Yarwonian sprinter in an Anendac Championship, to the day Shamirah's body was discovered. He looked out of the window and observed a crowd of students in the quadrangle. *What's going on*? he wondered. *Has another body been found? No, that's a really morbid thought. I always jump to the worst of presumptions, don't I? Unnecessary calculus.* He turned, letting his eyes wander around the room. Tazloe was nowhere to be seen, probably still asleep. *I'd better go and have a look*, he thought. *There's definitely something going on down there.*

He dashed out of his living quarters and down the corridor. Just before he got to the stairs, he stopped briefly to peer out over the ledge. The crowd had swelled, and the commotion had become even louder. He raced down the stairs, two steps at a time. Entering the quadrangle, he almost bumped into Lincus, who was standing on the bottom step, taking pictures of the scene with his Zogo.

"What's going on, Lincus?" Nujran inquired.

"Oh, hi Nujran. They're all waiting for Leongatti. Something weird is happening, and apparently, he's coming over to explain it to us."

"Something weird? What do you mean?"

"I'm not sure of all the details, but apparently, a mysterious illness has swept through the teachers' quarters. Many of them have collapsed, several have been rushed to the local health center. Someone said that it started late last evening and spread during the night. By the morning, there were already a large number of victims."

"You can't be serious!" exclaimed the prince. "And no one knows what this weird illness might be?"

"I guess we'll find out from the dean, soon enough. The rumor is that only a couple of teachers have escaped the outbreak. Looks like they will need to suspend classes from today. From what I have heard, there will be no one around to teach."

No classes…that might make a lot of students happy, Nujran thought. *Taz would be one of them…he could just hang out in his room, smoking whatever he smokes.* A whirring sound in the sky made them both look upwards. They spied Dean Leongatti's flying scooter appear from above and to their right. It made a slow descent into the quadrangle, its wings vibrating visibly as it approached the ground. The dean alighted gracefully, then turned to face the swelling throng of students.

"Everyone please calm down; I have something to say." He looked around as if expecting the undivided attention of the students, but to his chagrin, the din from the crowd continued, almost unabated.

"Quiet, please!" he bellowed, eliciting a startled reaction from the students closest to him. To his increasingly obvious displeasure, though, those standing further away persisted in their chatter. A frown came over his brow, and he scratched his head for a moment. He then delved into his pocket and pulled out a disk-shaped device that he placed on his right cheek. Pressing a button on it, he cleared his throat, a sound heard by the entire crowd.

"Silence, please!" he thundered, and this time, his voice projected to all four corners of the quadrangle, loud and clear. A hush descended promptly on the gathering as they ceased their conversations and turned their attention to him.

"A sizable number of our teachers have fallen ill," he began. "The symptoms appear to be nausea and vomiting; some have a fever too. Many have been transported to the health center in town; they're receiving treatment there as I speak. Our head nurse, Sheena, is attending to those with more minor symptoms in the school infirmary. We don't know yet what caused it, but the doctors are running tests, and I'm sure we'll find out the cause very soon."

Murmurs and whispers spread through the crowd as they digested the information they had just received.

"Is there anything we can do to help?" a female voice called out from the middle of the gathering.

"Thank you for the offer, young lady" replied the dean, "But not really. They need to be isolated until a diagnosis is made, so we don't want you going near them."

"So, what happens next?" a male voice inquired from the rear of the crowd.

"Well, given the number of teachers afflicted, we have to suspend classes at least for today, and possibly tomorrow as well. I would advise you to stay in your dormitories or rooms for the rest of the day. Obviously, we've closed the smaller dining hall used by the teachers, but the student kitchen and dining areas remain open, for now. The cooks and cafeteria staff are all well, fortunately. They have been examined and cleared by Nurse Sheena, so we believe it's safe to go there for your meals. Those who live close by are welcome to go home. I would encourage all of you to contact your parents or guardians and let them know that you are alright. News of the illness is likely to leak out, and it's best they hear from you before that happens. I will keep you all updated..."

He was interrupted by a humming sound above and a collective gasp from the students. Everyone was now looking up, and some of the students were pointing skyward. A small aircraft had appeared and was hovering above the quadrangle. It had a triangular body, two short wings, and a narrow chamber suspended beneath. It descended slowly, rocking slightly from side to side, then made a soft landing in a corner opposite to where Nujran and Lincus were standing. A hushed silence descended over the gathering as they waited for someone to emerge. A few moments later, a door on the side of the vehicle flew open, and the students observed a majestic elderly man with long white hair and four arms step out onto the grass.

"Greetings, Amsibh," said the principal, his voice now echoing in the quad, bouncing off the walls around.

The crowd parted, allowing Amsibh to walk over to where Leongatti was standing. *The drone looks a bit different from how I imagined it,* thought Nujran. It was smaller and had shorter wings than the one in his dream. The chamber was narrow and rectangular in shape, unlike the oval one he had visualized. *A cool way to get around, that's for sure. Only a matter of time before everyone is flying around in one of these. Traffic jams in the sky? Quite possibly, something that the future holds.*

The maestro was now deep in conversation with Leongatti. As he could not hear what they were saying, Nujran assumed the dean had turned off the microphone attached to his cheek. Discussions had started up again in the crowd. A group of students had moved over to the drone and were studying it from up close, evidently with great interest.

"Hello, Nujran." The prince turned as Miriana walked up to where he and Lincus were standing.

"Hi, Miriana. This is Lincus, a classmate of mine."

Miriana nodded at Lincus. "I just got out of the library…I was studying for a test. What's going on?"

"A mysterious illness appears to have stricken the teaching staff," the prince explained. "All classes have been canceled for the day."

"A mystery illness? That's so strange! What are the symptoms?" Miriana asked.

Nujran turned to Lincus. "She's going to be a doctor. Always interested in the medical angle."

Lincus grinned. "Yes, I see that."

"Fever, nausea, and vomiting…that's what the dean just said," continued the prince. "Many have been hospitalized. It sounds pretty serious."

"Your attention, please!" It was the dean; he had switched on his cheek microphone again. This time the crowd settled down quickly, waiting expectantly for him to speak.

"This is Maestro Amsibh," the dean announced. "A dear friend of mine for a very long time. One of the most renowned teachers on Syzegis. Let's welcome him to our school."

There was a muted round of applause. The prince observed that many in the audience were staring at Amsibh. He reflected on his first encounter with the maestro, when he had met him at the palace in Loh'dis. *What a majestic presence he had! I was blown away. No surprise these students are completely transfixed by his appearance!*

"That's a pretty weak welcome," complained the dean into his microphone. "Can I hear a more enthusiastic round of applause for this great teacher?"

This time there was a stronger ovation. Amsibh smiled and graciously took a bow.

"The maestro is just back from the health center," the dean continued. "It looks like the doctors are still waiting for a definitive diagnosis. We can assume our teachers will be convalescing there for a while." He paused and looked at Amsibh. "The maestro has made a generous proposition. Since the large majority of our faculty has been affected, he has offered to step into the breach. Starting tomorrow, he will conduct lectures and discussion sessions in Rababi Hall, our main auditorium in the political science building, at the north end of campus. We will work out the details and send out notifications. Just check your hand-held devices in a couple of hours."

While the prince knew that the university had named an auditorium after his father, this was the first time he had heard the name formally announced in this manner. Rababi's face flashed briefly across his mind's eye. *They honor you, Father. You are fondly remembered.*

"I was looking forward to some time off," Lincus remarked. "I guess it's back to class tomorrow."

"Sounds like the dean was talking more about an informal series of lectures," Miriana commented.

The prince turned toward his friends. "Well, speaking as someone with firsthand experience of the maestro's teaching abilities, let me say this: he is a brilliant teacher. He speaks with authority on just about every topic there is. I think we're all going to learn a lot…and be entertained while he's at it."

"How old is he?" Lincus was still staring at the maestro.

"Don't be rude, Lincus," Miriana spoke tersely.

"No, that's alright," the prince responded, smiling. "It's a fair question. I'm sure everyone's thinking it. As a matter of fact, he's well over four hundred years old."

"Wow, he's been around for a long time!" exclaimed Lincus.

"And if he was smart to begin with, imagine all the knowledge he has gathered over the centuries," Miriana pointed out. "I'm worried about the teachers and wish them well, of course, but perhaps this is a stroke of luck for us. What a great opportunity to learn from someone of his stature."

The crowd was gradually starting to disperse. Leongatti and Amsibh were still engaged in conversation, the dean's microphone now turned off.

"I'll see you both later, I'm heading over to the gym," said Lincus.

Nujran nodded. "See you later, Lincus."

The prince and Miriana wandered over toward Leongatti and Amsibh. They stopped a respectable distance away, to allow the maestro and dean to finish their conversation. A short while later, Leongatti strode off toward his scooter, started it up, and slowly ascended across the quad. Nujran and Miriana watched as he continued to gain height, disappearing shortly thereafter from view.

"A flying scooter…interesting device, isn't it?" Amsibh's booming voice interrupted their thoughts.

"Not as impressive as your personal drone, maestro." There was genuine admiration in the prince's voice.

"Come on over, I'll show it to you both." They followed the maestro briskly across the quad. Nujran noted that Amsibh was not wearing his hat, something he usually did when he stepped out. The vehicle was comfortably settled on the grass, still surrounded by curious students.

"Try and keep your hands off the windshield," the maestro called out as they got closer. A couple of students had their faces and hands pressed against the glass on the front of the vehicle, peering intently into its interior. Seeing the maestro approach them, they quickly stepped back. Some of the students began to walk away, a few stayed around the vehicle. Up close, it seemed larger than Nujran had first thought, about the height of a man standing up. Amsibh pulled a key fob out of his pocket, pointed it at the vehicle, and pressed a button. The side door from which he had emerged earlier slowly opened, like a bird unfolding its wing. There was a solitary high-backed cushioned seat inside the vehicle. In front of it was a large screen, on either side of which were a few levers and buttons. Amsibh stepped into the vehicle, leaving the door wide open so that the students could see what he was doing. He reached down to his left, picking up something from the floor. It was his trapezoidal hat, the one that Nujran had become accustomed to seeing him wear. Placing it deliberately on his head, he touched the screen in front of him, causing it to light up.

"In essence, this drone flies itself. I just have to program in my destination, and it takes me there."

"Is it completely safe, maestro? What if the controls fail?" It was Miriana who had posed the questions.

"Fortunately, the likelihood of that happening is low," Amsibh answered. "Although these vehicles are relatively new to the public, the air forces in Foalinaarc and Typgar have been using them for a while, mainly for aerial reconnaissance. Not surprisingly, they've been fully safety tested over the last several years. Still, your question is a good one. There is a built-in manual override. You see these levers and buttons on either side of the screen? They are the backup in the event of catastrophic instrument failure. They would enable the occupant to fly the drone manually and bring it down safely."

"How high can it fly, maestro?" The question came from a short dark-haired girl standing close by. She had edged closer to the door as the maestro was speaking. The prince did not recognize her.

"Well, they're designed to stay above the height of our tallest buildings," replied Amsibh. "They have a maximum height of a few thousand feet, that's about it. So, they don't have to be pressurized."

"And how fast can they go?" This question came from a tall lad standing beside Nujran.

"We're only allowed to fly them at around the same speed as that of a car on the ground," came the reply. "These new models are capable of much faster velocities, of course. They can travel so swiftly that you'll have to hold on to your grandad for dear life, while he clutches his toupee when they zoom past!" Amsibh chuckled, then continued. "But you see, the Transport Ministries have imposed strict speed restrictions in civilian settings. And that's understandable, since we're in the early stages of the technology."

There was a brief silence as the crowd lapped up the information they were receiving.

"I have to head back to the dean's quarters now," Amsibh declared. "It was fun meeting all of you. I guess I'll see you all tomorrow in Rababi Hall. In case you didn't know, Rababi was Nujran's father. He was a great king, loved and revered by all across Syzegis." He winked at Nujran, then pressed a button to the right of his screen, causing the side door to slowly descend until it was fully shut. They watched him press the screen, and the drone's engine roared instantly to life. The students stepped back as the hum of the engines picked up in intensity. The aircraft wobbled gently from side to side, then slowly ascended from the grass. As the students waved from below, the drone headed up vertically all the way to the height of the building surrounding the quad. Bombinating softly, it moved diagonally across the quad, gaining a little height to clear the structure, and slowly retreated from view.

Chapter Ten

THE RABABI HALL LECTURES

Amsibh's lectures in Rababi Hall started the following day. The maestro was an iconic figure in educational circles, his teaching prowess legendary across the planet. Word had quickly spread across campus. So, at the appointed hour, students arrived in droves to listen to the initial lecture, curious about what the learned scholar had to say. The theater was packed, every seat occupied. There were students perched on the steps that ascended the middle of the hall, others gathered along the side walls and at the back. The class was scheduled to start at mid-day, just when Yarus was at its zenith. Close to the podium, adorning one of the walls, was a circular clock, enormous in size and ornate in design. As its hands approached the hour of noon, the hubbub of students conversing began to die down, an expectant hush gradually permeating the room.

Nujran and Miriana were seated about halfway up the hall, close to the aisle. Wondering why the room had abruptly fallen silent, the prince looked around. A lot of heads were turning toward the rear entrance. All of a sudden, the doors swung open in an outward direction, and a majestic figure entered. It was Amsibh, dressed in flowing maroon academic robes, a yellow sash draped around his waist. His trapezoidal hat was perched on his head as usual, at a slight angle. But what fascinated the students the most was the fact that his feet were several inches off the ground, as he levitated down the middle aisle. The throng seated on the steps parted down the center as he descended, students angling their bodies to create a breach sufficient for the maestro to float through.

Approaching the front of the hall, his feet slowly hit the ground. He walked around to take his place behind the podium. Pushing a button, he triggered the rapid drop of a microphone from the ceiling; it came to a standstill just in front of his face. He pressed another button, and an image of him appeared on the massive screen at the front of the room. Reaching into his cloth bag, something he almost always carried, he then extracted a cubical device that he placed on the desk beside him.

"That looks like his cephavid," Nujran whispered softly to Miriana.

"What's that?" she asked.

"A device he uses to read people's minds."

"No, that's impossible...such things don't exist."

"Trust me, it exists...he's used it on me. I think he invented it."

"The maestro read your mind with that machine? Incredible!"

Amsibh then extracted a helmet from his cloth bag and, to Nujran's surprise, placed it on his own head. The prince could not recall having seen him do this before. The audience was now watching the maestro's every move on the big screen, completely transfixed by what he was doing.

He's managed to grab the attention of pretty much everyone in the room, Nujran thought. *Assuming there are about five hundred students in this auditorium, that's quite a feat!*

"Today's lecture will be on our solar system, and its place in the universe," Amsibh began, his booming voice resonating through Rababi Hall. "Let's start with our own planet, Syzegis."

Nujran's mind drifted back to a time many years prior, shortly after he had first met the maestro at the palace in Loh'dis. They had taken a walk to the nearby lake, and Amsibh had discussed exactly the same topic with the young prince. It was a scene that he had frequently revisited in his mind's eye, each time with a similar degree of enjoyment as the first. In fact, memories of his childhood interactions with Amsibh served as an emotional anchor for Nujran. They were a persistent reminder that the maestro would always be there for him: a guide, coach, and teacher, constantly willing to share his knowledge and wisdom with the young prince.

As Amsibh continued to speak, Nujran observed that the cephavid on the desktop beside him had started to wobble. Multiple serpentine tubes emerged from the surface of the helmet on the maestro's head. A ray of bright blue light from one of the tubes emanated upward, in the direction of a projector suspended from the ceiling. As the light beam aligned with the projector, Amsibh's image slowly faded away from the screen and was replaced by one of Syzegis, spinning in space.

Nujran leaned over to Miriana. "He's using the cephavid to project his thoughts on to the screen."

"Wow, that's so cool. I've never seen that done before."

Seated immediately in front of Nujran, Lincus had overheard what the prince had just said. He turned around and made a gesture, touching his forehead and pointing to the screen. His lips mouthed the words, "*His thoughts?*"

Nujran nodded. A buzz of hushed whispers dispersed through the auditorium. As the word spread rapidly, most of the class soon realized that they were witnessing an astonishing demonstration. They were reading their teacher's mind on the big screen in real-time, visualizing each element of the lecture as it was being delivered in its intricate detail.

In front of them, the screen was now lit up from end to end, displaying the ten planets in their solar system. Amsibh's voice reverberated in the background, his various thoughts illuminating different parts of the screen. Moons appeared around the planets as smaller dots and spheres. Every student was now listening with rapt attention, many on the edge of their seat.

About a half-hour later, after unraveling the basic structure of their solar system, Amsibh paused briefly, peering out into the audience. "Are there any questions?" he asked.

Several hands promptly shot up from various parts of the hall. The maestro pointed to a student in the front row.

"Are we really seeing your thoughts on the screen in real-time?" she inquired. "How are you doing that?"

Amsibh chuckled. "I thought your question was going to be something about our solar system."

"I'm sorry, maestro." The girl who had posed the question now seemed a tad embarrassed.

The maestro held up one of his hands. "No, that's perfectly alright; there's no need to be apologetic. I welcome all questions." He turned and pointed to the cubical box on the table beside him. "That's a cephalovideograph," he said, "Or a cephavid for short. It's a machine I designed that can read a person's thoughts and then display them as images in the air or, as in this case, project them on the big screen so that you all can see them."

Another hand went up toward the back of the room. As the auditorium was still dimly lit, Nujran could not make out who it was.

"Maestro, it is widely rumored that you might be an alien." It was a male voice, with a distinctive Lustraanite accent. "Is that true, and if so, are you from another planet in our solar system, or from outside it altogether?"

There was a stunned silence in the auditorium. Nujran's mind went back to a time as a teenager, when he had been very curious about his teacher's origins. But he had hesitated for a long time before plucking up enough courage to ask Amsibh the question. He had finally raised it when they were on the Floating Monastery. The prince wondered how the maestro would respond on this occasion. Amsibh did not answer immediately. He was stroking his long beard and peering into the audience, as if trying to pick out the student who posed the query.

"Well, I did say that I welcome all questions. I didn't realize that you'd take my advice to heart so seriously." He smiled, and a ripple of laughter spread through the hall, dispelling any tension the inquiry appeared to have created. Amsibh waited patiently for it to subside, then continued. "The answer, young man, is simply this: I wish I knew. I was discovered as a baby in a capsule that was found in the ice cap at Syzegis' north pole. There were some others they found at the same time as me, and apparently, our genetic makeup is unique. We may well be aliens; in fact, you only have to look at me to arrive at that assumption. I'm sure it's pretty obvious to everyone here that I appear different. That said, differences can be deceiving, as they might mask the similarities that bind us to one another." Amsibh paused, and a few moments of silence ensued as the audience pondered his profound statement. Then, quite unexpectedly, he began to slowly wave his four arms in various directions. "How many of you can do this?" he asked, a grin on his face. In response, there was another wave of laughter, now louder and engulfing the entire audience. Clearly, the students were enjoying the unorthodox teaching style of this very unusual teacher.

By this time, several hands were raised again. Amsibh pointed to one not far from Nujran, and this time it was Tryna, the blonde girl with tattoos, who Nujran and Miriana had interacted with in the infirmary.

"Maestro, if you're an alien, then that's recognition of the fact that there's life elsewhere, not just on Syzegis. Can we conclude that we are not alone?"

Amsibh was now beaming. Nujran recalled having a similar discussion with the maestro while sitting by the lake behind the palace. They had just made each other's acquaintance, and the prince was going through a phase when he constantly asked questions. As he pondered how the maestro would address the query this time, he was surprised by the reply.

"That's an excellent question, young lady. I remember deliberating this with Nujran many years ago. Perhaps we can ask him." The maestro shielded his eyes from the bright light over the podium with one of his hands, peering once again into the audience. "Nujran, are you out there?"

Somewhat reluctantly, the prince raised himself to his feet. "I'm here, maestro."

"Ah good, I see you now. The floor is yours."

"Let me see if I can recall our discussion correctly, maestro. I believe you made the argument that there are many billions of stars out there. And with so many planets revolving around each of those stars, the chance of finding another Syzegis-like planet must be pretty good. Syzegis is just at the right distance from Yarus. It's not too hot, nor too cold, and has liquid water that's essential for life to exist. The probability of such conditions existing elsewhere is high. So, it's realistic to conclude that there's life somewhere else. In fact, I believe your contention was that it would be arrogant to assume we are the only life forms in the universe."

Miriana started to clap and a few others followed suit, resulting in scattered applause around the auditorium. Feeling quite pleased with his response, as well as the impression it seemed to have made on the audience, Nujran quickly seated himself.

On the podium, Amsibh was nodding vigorously. "Precisely, Nujran. That's a good summary of our discussion. There is indeed a very high chance that life exists elsewhere…it's not just the prerogative of this planet. That said, we must recognize that the search for alien life is expensive, and plagued by challenges of time and distance."

At this juncture, Miriana raised her hand. Then, unsure if the maestro had seen it, she stood up to get his attention.

"Yes, Miriana...you have a question?"

"Maestro, have you met people who have visited other planets?"

"Indeed, I have," came the reply. "The Lustraanites are the most adventurous travelers on our planet. I've encountered many who have traveled to the edge of our solar system, but there are very few who have ventured beyond. As you can imagine, a single journey can involve many years of travel, and the voyages take a huge physical and mental toll on those explorers."

"What kind of toll, exactly?" asked a student seated near the front of the class.

"Well, the emotional impact is easy to understand," Amsibh responded. "For a start, there is the social isolation that lasts for the duration of the journey. Even though there are usually multiple passengers, it is extremely stressful to be cut off from home and all that is familiar. These travelers leave their families, friends, and neighbors behind on Syzegis. Thanks to the wonders of modern communication, they can interact via videophones with their loved ones, but with the caveat of a huge distance between them. A little child they bid farewell to, might be a teenager or young adult when they return. Some might feel tremendously guilty about missing the formative years in a son's or daughter's life.

"And if that's not enough, there's a significant physical toll as well," the maestro continued. "Initially, in the first few days in space, there is a great deal of disorientation. Since there's no gravity out there, and nothing pulling you downward, the body's sense of position is lost. Blood gets redistributed to the upper part of the body and the face. The head congestion causes a feeling like one has a cold all the time. Over the long duration of the voyage, there is a substantial loss of muscle and bone. Our spacemen and women have to focus hard on physical fitness, working out several times a day to conserve musculoskeletal mass."

"Have you ever been in space, maestro?" The question came from the rear of the room.

"Indeed, I have," Amsibh answered, with a smile. "A year ago, I was offered a seat on a scientific expedition to our neighboring planet Imogezis. It was a brief trip, in space travel terms, just under a month. But it was a fascinating voyage, and I learned a great deal."

Amsibh's response came as a complete surprise to Nujran. He had no idea that his teacher had traveled into space. That said, he had now been out of touch with the maestro for at least a couple of years, and they really had not had a chance to catch up on all that had happened during that time. *At his age, that could not have been an easy trip*, the prince thought. *But then again, Amsibh is always incredibly fit, and knowing his passion for exercise, he would have surely trained twice as hard as everyone else.*

Nujran's mind wandered back to the time just before the battle to take back Typgar, when they had spent a few nights at the Castle of Mirrors. He had had the opportunity to train with Amsibh while waiting for the battle plans to unfold. They had performed several intense combat drills together and the old teacher's endurance was striking. The voices in the auditorium had temporarily receded to a distant drone in a remote corner of his consciousness, as he was quickly transported to that moment. *I'm traveling back in time... there's no need for a machine,* he realized. *The past is presenting itself with such clarity...I might well be back there.* Then, abruptly, he felt a hand on his arm and was instantly returned to the present.

"Who's that asking the question?" It was Miriana who had dragged him back to the moment. She was pointing to the front row, in the direction of a young man with long straight black hair. Nujran craned his neck, noting that the youth was in a wheelchair.

"Oh yes, that's Gin'kwah...he's in my year. I think he's from Inchea, or at least from that region."

"He's just posed an absolutely brilliant question to the maestro. Did you hear it?"

"I missed it, Miriana. What was it?"

"He asked about the origins of our universe, then suggested that the maestro do a thought experiment...to go back in time...all the way back to the beginning."

On the screen, Amsibh was starting to project his thoughts in a rapid sequence. There were galaxies and suns and planets flying around on the screen. And then the whole universe began to contract in front of their eyes, gradually becoming smaller. Various parts of it appeared to implode, and a few minutes later, it was down to a bright white dot...and then finally...nothing.

"And that, presumably, was the start of time, the origin of the universe," Amsibh was saying. "On that exciting note, I think we should end today's lecture. I've enjoyed it, and I hope all of you have too."

There was a round of applause from the audience, a genuine display of appreciation for the maestro's lecture. Nujran turned to Miriana. "I'd like to have a quick chat with the maestro, if that's alright with you. You're welcome to come along, of course."

The students began to file out of the auditorium through the exit doors at the side and the rear. Nujran and Miriana made their way to the front of the hall. They reached the podium where Amsibh was engaged in conversation with Gin'kwah, a few other students gathered in a circle around them.

"Everyone assumes it started with the big bang," Amsibh was saying. "Was there a time before the big bang? I don't really know. Perhaps you will explore this question."

Gin'kwah adjusted his wheelchair slightly with a flick of his wrist so that it turned left a few degrees. "It's certainly one that fascinates me, maestro. I especially enjoy working on the mathematics of it all. It's a subject I have been interested in for as long as I remember."

"That's wonderful, young man. I would love to spend more time with you, discussing the topic. It's nice to see your passion for a field many would consider abstract, and perhaps too difficult. Keep going with that inquiring mind, and one day you may well unlock the mysteries of the universe."

Gin'kwah thanked the maestro and guided his wheelchair unhurriedly toward the exit. The other students followed him, chatting with him as they left the hall.

"Incredibly sharp young man," Amsibh commented to Nujran and Miriana when they were out of earshot. "He will go far…mark my words. What's his name?"

"That's Gin'kwah, maestro. I've heard he has a disease that progressively paralyzes his muscles…hence the wheelchair."

"A brilliant mind. And certainly not held back by his physical challenges."

"I've noticed him around campus, but I've never spoken to him," Miriana chimed in. "Nujran, we should get to know him better."

The prince's mind briefly flashed back to Zaarica, his girlfriend back at the palace. She had been born with no limbs and had artificial ones implanted when she was young. Yet, she had never complained about her disability, always impressing Nujran with her positive attitude to life.

"Nujran, I have some news." The maestro's booming voice interrupted his thoughts.

"Yes, maestro?"

"Leongatti feels that it might be a few weeks before all the teachers are well enough to return to work. He is looking for temporary alternatives. I suggested something to him, and he readily agreed. I think the solution I offered him will be of interest to you."

"What's that, maestro?"

"Flomo just happens to be moored off the southern coast of Foalinaarc. I've sent a message to Andron, inviting the monks to the campus. Just prior to this class, I received a message of acceptance from him. His monks will arrive at your campus shortly and serve as substitute teachers for as long as the school needs them."

Miriana looked puzzled. "I'm sorry, maestro…I'm a little confused. Who are these substitute teachers arriving here?"

The prince turned to her. "Miriana, this is sensational news. We are going to be taught by the Monks of Meirar."

Chapter Eleven

THE MONKS OF MEIRAR

Nujran and Miriana left the auditorium and found their way to a small café at the north end of campus. It was owned and operated by a family from Inchea, who had immigrated to Foalinaarc. It was Nujran's favorite spot on campus for completing an assignment, or for an hour of quiet reflection, always less noisy and crowded compared to the university cafeteria. The prince ordered hot beverages for them both, a brew of leaves from central Inchea, spiced with special herbs that gave it an interesting flavor.

"So, tell me more about the Monks of Meirar," said Miriana. "I must confess I don't know a lot about them."

"But you've heard of them before, right?" Nujran asked, now barely able to conceal his excitement at their imminent arrival.

"Yes, indeed, Nujran…we started to talk about them while watching jet hockey in the Briztanga, remember? You explained to me that they have the ability to levitate."

"Yes, of course…and that's just one of the many skills they have. They really are an extraordinary group of monks. They spend their time traveling around Syzegis." Nujran was clearly enjoying himself as he described his friends. "They live on a ship called Flomo…that's just a nickname for Floating Monastery. They are led by a colleague of Amsibh's, a brilliant blind monk named Andron. Each monk on the ship tends to have a special talent, developed over years of practice. I first met them when they came to visit Narcaya a while back. I was on the island with Amsibh at the time, and we decided to leave on Flomo together. It was an eventful voyage, during which I got to know many of them quite well."

"Eventful? How so?"

"We were attacked by intruders, who arrived on an aircraft sent by Hoanan and Yarozin. They came to kidnap me, but under instructions from the maestro, I was protected by a monk named Kalimo. He's someone who is skilled in the art of camouflage and can effectively blend into his environment. He concealed me behind him, and the intruders couldn't find me despite their extensive search of the ship. However, there was an altercation with the pilot, and sadly, we ended up losing Zhinso, one of the monks who I had got to know really well by then. It was my first close encounter with death. I attended his funeral and participated in the ceremonies and rituals the monks performed to bid him farewell."

Nujran's voice had become somewhat tremulous. His eyes were moist as he sorrowfully recalled the passing of his friend. Miriana put a comforting hand on his arm. She spoke quietly.

"It's never easy losing someone you're close to."

"No, it isn't. I wonder if Tyora is still with them."

"Who's Tyora?"

"She was Zhinso's girlfriend. She was also a monk."

Nujran dried his eyes on the sleeve of his shirt. He turned to Miriana and forced a smile. "I was thrilled when Amsibh told me they were coming," he continued. "They're truly special individuals, each unique in his or her own way. And they're all such nice people, humble and easy to interact with. I think you will really enjoy meeting them."

Later that night, when Nujran was lying in bed, sleep did not come immediately. He stared at the ceiling, his thoughts drifting to the time he had spent on Flomo. He vividly remembered being carried out over the water with Zhinso and Tyora, when they had levitated from the sandy beach back to the ship. He recalled how Zhinso had been asked to join Pelorius, Tromzen, and Manolos when they boarded the hostile aircraft hovering above the ship. He thought of how distraught Tyora had been when the injured Zhinso was brought down after being shot. The prince had accompanied him when he was taken to the sick bay where the ship's physician Jozak had treated him, but unfortunately, Zhinso quickly slipped into a coma caused by the poison on the bullet. Then there was the surreal experience when Zhinso seemed to be trying to communicate with him, while still unconscious. And finally, after Zhinso died, and just after they had cremated him, the prince was sure he had seen him float by, a seemingly impossible feat that left him wondering later if he had just imagined it.

When sleep finally came, it was not surprising that Zhinso visited him once again in his dreams, this time speaking directly to him. "You're going to see Tyora again soon," he said, a smile on his face. "Tell her that I love her."

The next morning, Nujran awoke, his continued exhilaration about the impending visit of the monks uppermost in his mind. He decided he would try to have breakfast with Amsibh so that he could get more details about their arrival. He had no doubt that Andron and Glyoptula would make great teachers, given their vast experience, but wondered if the others like Yin'hua would take to it with the same ease. And then his thoughts drifted to Maaya, the young novitiate he had befriended. He remembered being drawn to her but then feeling guilty that he was being disloyal to Zaarica. As a result, they had ended up just being friends.

Nujran found Amsibh in the cafeteria, having a bowl of vegetable soup. Seated across from him was Miriana. The prince was able to overhear the last few words of their conversation. She was plying the maestro for more details on the monks.

"So, how long have you known Andron?" she asked, just as Nujran seated himself on a chair beside her.

"Hello, Nujran," said the maestro, acknowledging the prince's arrival before responding to Miriana. "Andron? I've known him for a really long time. We were actually children together in Nadii and ended up befriending each other."

Nadii was a kingdom on Angawunde, on the opposite side of the planet from Typgar. It shared a common border with Inchea. Both Nadii and Inchea had been homes to ancient civilizations, dating back several thousand years. With the advent of new technologies in Foalinaarc and then Typgar, the ancient kingdoms had lost some of their influence over time. However, in recent years, with the emergence of strong leaders and a commitment to modernization, both nations had started to make their presence felt on Syzegis once again.

"I did not know that you had grown up in Nadii," Nujran remarked. Amsibh was always full of surprises.

The maestro chuckled. "Well, I've lived for many centuries and traveled to a lot of countries. It would take a long time for me to list all the places I have been in."

"Maestro, if your lectures were just on the experiences you've had over your lifetime, you'd keep us engaged for many months," Miriana commented, genuine admiration in her voice.

"Age does have its advantages," Amsibh agreed. "One gathers a lot of knowledge along the way, and if the mind stays fresh, one can actually recall and share what one has learned. The challenge, my young friend, is finding a willing set of ears to listen. To capture a droplet of wisdom, there must be a goblet eager to receive it."

"For a person of your advanced age, your mind is remarkably clear, maestro," Miriana added. "What is your secret?"

"That's an odd question, Miriana," Nujran said, his tone chiding.

Miriana blushed, now looking embarrassed. "Sorry, maestro...I didn't mean to imply that you're an old man. What I really meant to ask was...you've had the privilege of a long life on Syzegis...how have you kept your mind fresh?"

"Much better, Miriana," the prince murmured.

Amsibh was smiling. "It's perfectly alright, Miriana. At my time of life, I routinely hear comments about my age. They don't bother me at all. But in answer to your question, there are a few things one can do to keep the mind active into our senior years. There's been a lot of research at our Institutes of Aging, especially at the one your father established in Loh'dis, Nujran."

"And what has the research demonstrated, maestro?" Miriana asked.

"I like your curiosity, Miriana," Amsibh replied. "It will serve you well in a career in medicine, should you choose it. In essence, a key to staying mentally alert appears to be sustained physical activity. I exercise every day, as you know, and research has shown that this slows down age-related degeneration of the brain. Staying socially connected is another one...being an active part of our communities has many advantages. Having a close circle of friends, whom one can rely on, is hugely beneficial; conversely, being isolated hastens our decline. Some folks are lucky enough to be professionally active till a ripe old age; obviously, that helps greatly in the quest to stay engaged and energetic. Others like me might retire but actively pursue a hobby...in my case, it was tending to my garden, until Nujran's parents brought me out of retirement and sent me off on various adventures."

"Do you remember much about Nadii, maestro?" Nujran inquired, changing the subject.

Amsibh smiled. "From my childhood? That was over four centuries ago! I do have many recollections of those happy days, but they're gradually starting to fade. That said, I've been back many times as an adult and seen it change quite dramatically, over the years. In the recent past in particular, and especially during the last couple of decades, their wholehearted embrace of technology has greatly helped them. As you may know, the cost of labor is a lot cheaper in that part of the world, compared to our side of the planet. So, both Nadii and Inchea have started to be key players in the technological and industrial sectors. A lot of jobs in the service industry have been outsourced to Nadii, while Inchea has emerged as a key nation in manufacturing."

"That's a good thing, isn't it, maestro?" It was Miriana this time who had posed the question.

"Depends on whom you ask," came Amsibh's reply. "For those nations, it's been generally good. Improved economies have meant more jobs and an overall improvement in living standards. There's generally less poverty and an expanding middle class that is able to participate in the consumer economy, with the ability to provide good education and healthcare for their children. But for our hemisphere, many would argue, it has meant the loss of our dominance. When Hoanan opposed your father in Typgar's election, he focused his attention on immigration from Aaltin. It's easy to see how a future candidate, a challenger to Iolena for instance, might use the loss of jobs to Nadii and Inchea as an election issue to stir up nationalistic and isolationist sentiments just as Hoanan did."

As usual, Nujran was amazed by the maestro's encyclopedic knowledge and his ability to discuss any subject with ease. "So, did Andron also grow up in Nadii, maestro?"

"He was actually born there. For a while, I lived in his home in a town called Dramsa, with his parents. They looked after me as one of their own. I've mentioned to you that I was discovered on this planet, as a baby, in a capsule of some kind, and never knew my parents. Andron's family was the closest I had to having one of my own."

We rarely think to ask old people about their families and least of all about their parents, Nujran thought. The maestro had never discussed the subject before, and the prince wondered if he should feel sorry for him. *I can't imagine growing up, never having known my parents. It must have been a difficult childhood for the maestro.*

"When are the monks arriving?" Miriana's voice interrupted his thoughts.

The maestro thought for a moment. "Shouldn't be long now. They're traveling inland as we speak and should arrive on campus by nightfall."

Nujran wanted to ask if Amsibh thought about his parents, individuals whom he had never met. However, he ended up asking another question. "What was it like, maestro, growing up in Dramsa?"

"It was a lot of fun," Amsibh answered. "It's a hot and humid city, but the people embrace culture, music, and learning. Andron and I spent our first ten years or so there, and it was a wonderful time in our lives. We knew our neighbors well, dropped into their homes unannounced all the time, and roamed the streets unrestrained. Of course, at that age, we were cheerful and carefree all the time, so our memories of the place are naturally quite pleasant, to say the least."

"And you left when you were still a child?" Miriana asked.

"Andron's parents had the wanderlust, so when we were in our teenage years, we left Dramsa. We moved around Nadii a bit and then ended up emigrating. We wandered through several different countries and eventually arrived in Typgar. After that, we stayed put, making Typgar our new home."

Amsibh then got up, preparing to leave. "I'd love to stay and continue our chat, but I have to see Leongatti. There's a lot that we have to do. We must plan the classes for the next few days. He needs to understand the capabilities of each of the monks before he can draw up a schedule. Hope I'll see you both at my noon lecture tomorrow."

Shortly thereafter, Nujran and Miriana also left the cafeteria, heading toward their respective apartments. As they were about to part company, Miriana asked, "Dinner later this evening, Nujran? We haven't been out in a while."

"Sorry, Miriana, I'll need to welcome the monks tonight. You could join me, of course, if you like."

"No, that's alright, Nujran. You should catch up with them. You were close to them, and you haven't seen them in ages. Dinner can wait, no problem."

The prince was pleased that Miriana wasn't particularly pushy in this regard. They had only been out on a couple of dates and had certainly enjoyed each other's company. They had also found themselves seated next to each other during the classes they shared. However, since Amsibh's arrival on campus, and the mysterious illness that had afflicted their teachers, they had not spent a great deal of time together. Miriana had not complained, and for that, Nujran was grateful. He had only been in one relationship earlier, with Zaarica, and that had developed over several years, starting as childhood friends. The brief flirtation with Maaya had not amounted to anything serious. *I'm comfortable with Miriana, and we'll probably go on dates more regularly. At what point does a relationship commence?* he wondered. *Is there a certain number of dates after which that is just assumed? Is it official after the first kiss? Or do we have to sleep together before the label is applied?*

The prince found himself at the door to his apartment. While deeply engrossed in his thoughts, he realized he had walked through a corridor, crossed a quadrangle, and climbed a flight of stairs, all without being aware that he had done so. As he fished in his pocket for his key, he marveled at how automated the mind could be, guiding him back to his destination without so much as a conscious thought about which direction he was taking.

Consulting his schedule, he found he only had one class that day. It was to be a lecture by Leongatti on gravity. Until the Monks of Meirar arrived on campus, there was an acute shortage of educators available to teach. The workload was, therefore, being shared between the dean, Amsibh, and a couple of teachers who had managed to avoid the illness. The lecture was in "The Cube", an auditorium on the south side of campus, named for its shape. It was an impressive cubical structure, striking in appearance even from a distance. Approaching it, one could observe that the walls had dozens of cubes in them, and each of these cubes was of a different color. That made its appearance similar to one of the toys Nujran had played with as a child. It was called a Kiburk's cube. He recalled that one had to rearrange the sides of the cube so that each face was a certain uniform color, something that he had always struggled with. Zaarica had been quite adept at it, insisting that there was a system to it, and had patiently shown him on several occasions how it worked. Despite a lot of practice, he never mastered it fully, but since it was such a relaxing activity, he never really gave up on it.

Each time he approached The Cube on campus, his mind flashed back to that brief period of childhood when he had carried around the Kiburk's cube, a possession that had quickly become an inseparable part of his life. And invariably, that brought back memories of Zaarica and a smile to his lips.

Entering the auditorium, Nujran noted that it was only half full. Leongatti was at the podium, his opening slide adorning the large screen. He seemed to be waiting for a few more students to arrive. The prince looked around for Miriana but did not see her in the room.

For a split second, he wondered if he had offended her by declining her invitation to dinner, but quickly dispelled the thought. The dean started to speak, and then the screen lit up with a brief video presentation. *No helmet on his head,* Nujran observed. *So, these are not his thoughts being presented. That's Amsibh's signature. Why can't every lecture be presented that way? Couldn't all teachers use a cephavid? That would certainly make classes so much more stimulating.*

The topic of the dean's lecture turned out to be quite thought-provoking. "Gravitational forces vary from planet to planet," Leongatti was explaining. "The size of a planet, its density, and many other factors can influence its gravitational pull. Satellites that orbit around planets also exert such forces. One of the reasons we have very high tides on Syzegis, especially after midnight, is the collective influence of our three moons."

The lecture went by quickly, and at its conclusion, the dean asked if there were any questions. Nujran decided to ask one, raising his hand.

"Lights up, please," Leongatti called out. An unseen hand at the controls somewhere at the back of the room responded; bright lights swiftly bathed the auditorium. The prince wondered momentarily who the person was. *There are so many employees of the university around campus who make things work, keep things going, repair things when they are broken. The unsung heroes…loyal unknown workers who are always there. Sadly, I don't know any of their names.*

"Yes, Nujran?" The dean's voice cut through his thoughts.

He realized his arm was raised, and for a brief moment, he forgot what he was going to ask. "Ummm…" he began, stalling for time. His arm started to sag with its own weight, and then he remembered… the topic was gravity.

"Professor, the Monks of Meirar are arriving shortly at our school. I had the privilege of meeting them a couple of years ago. They can levitate, in essence, defying gravity. How do they do that?"

"Great question, Nujran," came the dean's response from the podium. "It's not something I'm an expert on, and perhaps it's a question more appropriate for Amsibh. Or better still, for one of the monks themselves, since they will be here very soon. My understanding is that they have learned to counter the force of gravity through training. While I have observed the phenomenon firsthand, it is not entirely clear to me how this is accomplished."

The prince did not find the response very satisfying and decided that he would ask Andron or Amsibh the question some other time.

There was not much to do for the rest of the day. Later that afternoon, the prince spent an hour working out in the gymnasium. He recalled the conversation with Amsibh about how the maestro had managed to stay alert and fully engaged, even at his age. *I'd better keep exercising throughout my life. It would be great to end up with the maestro's clarity of thought when I'm as old as he is.*

On his way out, he walked past a group of people who were playing jet hockey in a small field adjacent to The Cube. His eyes scanned the group for a blonde girl with tattoos on her arms and a boy with a single earring, but neither Tryna nor Klabe was there. He meandered around the outer perimeter of the building and began to cross a quadrangle on his way back to his apartment. And that's when he heard the chanting. At first, it was soft music in the distance, but then it gradually increased in intensity. It seemed to be coming from the center of the campus, from the direction of Reinhart's Green, a well-manicured field next to the library. Students often basked there directly under Yarus' rays or in the shade of trees scattered randomly across it.

The prince bounded toward the sound, his ears guiding him in the right direction. Two more corridors, a quadrangle, and then suddenly he found himself at the entrance to the library. He looked out to the field and immediately saw them. A bunch of hooded figures, chanting in perfect harmony, slowly floating across the field, feet several inches off the ground. As he was about to approach them, he felt something grab his right leg and hold him back. He looked down, then turned his head to see what was restraining him. To his astonishment, a pair of small dark eyes adorning a cherubic face stared right back at him from about knee level.

"Nujran!" a voice called out from behind and to his left. He turned once again, this time twisting his torso the other way, and immediately saw Tyora. Her hair was different, but otherwise, she looked just the same as when he had bid her goodbye in Narcaya. Embracing the prince, she continued, "Meet Miko…she's my daughter."

Chapter Twelve

A REUNION WITH OLD FRIENDS

Dean Leongatti had arranged a welcoming dinner that evening in the cafeteria for the monks. It was widely advertised across campus on noticeboards, and the student community also received notifications of the event on their Zogos. Nujran arrived early, hoping to get in ahead of the crowd. He had really been looking forward to catching up with his old friends. Upon entering the cafeteria, he looked around, systematically surveying the scene. Although he recognized most of the monks there, there appeared to be several new faces as well. Tyora accosted him; she was holding Miko's hand.

"Let me take you around, Nujran." As the prince followed her, Miko turned back a few times, stealing furtive glances at him. Each time, Nujran smiled at her and on one occasion made a funny face, which caused her to giggle. "You remember Glyoptula," Tyora said, tilting her head in the direction of a woman with wavy silver hair. The prince noticed immediately that she had long braids, ending in small multicolored beads.

Glyoptula looked up. "Oh, hello Nujran. Nice to see you again. Teyi aha na hoi."

"Teyo aha na kum," responded Nujran. This was a dialect that was used only in Loh'dis. Glyoptula was an expert linguist, a polyglot who could speak fluently in multiple languages. She had picked up the Loh'dis dialect when she visited the palace there a long while back. During her sojourn in Typgar, she had befriended Queen Roone, Nujran's mother, translating texts and passages for her from other languages. Roone had spoken to King Rababi about her talents, and together the royal couple had convinced her to stay. She had established an internationally acclaimed Institute of Languages, which ended up being named after her.

"What languages are you going to teach us?" Nujran inquired politely.

"Hmmm, not sure yet," Glyoptula replied. "I've been retired a long while now. Honestly, I haven't taught students in years. Looking at a syllabus and creating lesson plans is a distant memory. But it will be fun to jump back in and educate all the eager young minds here. I just need to discuss with your dean where he'd like my focus to be."

Feeling a gentle tap on his shoulder, the prince turned around to see a monk with a partly shaven head and a ponytail.

"Yin'hua, it's so good to see you! You look different..."

"Nice to see you too, Nujran. The beard's gone...it was starting to itch a bit." Yin'hua was grinning from ear to ear, obviously pleased to see the prince.

Yin'hua was a geographical seer, with the unusual ability to pinpoint an exact location on the planet in his mind's eye and then visualize exactly what was taking place at the scene. He had provided huge support to Rababi's team during the conflict with Hoanan, leveraging his unique skill to supply detailed topographical knowledge in advance of planned military action. On occasion, he had also guided teams during their actual missions. But Nujran had often wondered if that had been a misuse of his special talent. For a peaceful monk, dedicated to a life of reflection and contemplation, the act of being drawn into military strategy understandably presented a contradiction of purpose. Apart from physically draining the monk, it had greatly troubled him and caused significant emotional strain, particularly since he had witnessed substantial and bloody violence. And it was Nujran who had first suggested the use of Yin'hua's abilities to help with the political conflict. Ever since, he had felt guilty that he had implicated his friend in matters both unfamiliar and distressing, even though the outcomes had been spectacularly beneficial to Rababi's side.

"Hey, Nujran!" A voice sounded out from his left, but when he turned around, all he saw was a vending machine. And then he noticed a shimmering play of light and shadows, gradually revealing the outline of a man.

"Kalimo!" Nujran exclaimed. "It's great to see you!"

Kalimo had an uncanny and innate ability to blend into his surroundings, effectively disappearing from sight. This talent had saved Nujran once from capture on-board Flomo, when intruders had boarded the ship, seeking him out. The prince had often thought that Kalimo's skill was perfectly aligned with his personality: a quiet individual who remained largely unnoticed by others in the room.

I owe so much to these monks, Nujran thought. *They've been more than friends; they've been my protectors. And I have learned so much from them. What was it that Amsibh used to say? 'Making friends comes easily, forming alliances is difficult, but finding mentors is a gift'.*

Nujran's reflections were interrupted by a soft tap-tap behind him. It was a familiar repetitive sound, one that evoked warm memories. He turned around to see an old blind monk approach with a cane. "What a pleasure to see you again, Master Andron!"

Andron embraced the prince. "I trust you're enjoying your education here at the university. From everything I've heard, Leongatti runs a great school…its reputation has traveled far and wide. A real pity, this illness that has taken down so many teachers. We are here to help. We'll do what we can to ensure that learning continues."

As the prince was about to respond, he was interrupted by the sound of clapping behind him. It was Dean Leongatti, trying to get the attention of everyone in the cafeteria. By this time, a large number of people had gathered within, a motley crowd of students, teachers, and monks. Against the noisy backdrop of loud and animated conversation, the dean's first attempt to get everyone to listen was largely ineffective. As he had done before while addressing students in the quad, he then fished out his disc-shaped microphone from his pocket, placing it on his right cheek. Pressing a button on it, he coughed gently, a sound that now projected noisily across the room, finally succeeding in drawing the attention of his audience.

"Please find your seats at the tables, ladies and gentlemen."

Over the next few minutes, students and monks took their places at the cafeteria tables, seating themselves on the long benches on either side. Nujran found himself between Tyora and an older woman, small in build. The woman had a prominent chin and long, wavy hair that flowed down her back in black and white stripes. Around her shoulders was draped a colorful shawl. She turned to Nujran, upon which he immediately recognized her.

"Ronanya, it's been a long time."

"Yes, it has, Nujran. I hope you are well." She stared at him, her transparent green irises now fixed on his face, making him feel somewhat uncomfortable. *Her gaze is always a bit disturbing…it's like her eyes are staring right through me.*

"I'm well, thanks, Ronanya," said the prince.

"Are you still receiving visits from the other side?"

The prince was perplexed. "What do you mean, Ronanya?"

"Have Rababi and Zhinso been visiting you…you know…in your thoughts and dreams?"

From being initially skeptical about Ronanya, Nujran had come to accept that she perhaps did have unusual skills. In truth, he was still unsure if she was actually able to communicate with the dead. But at the very least, she was an incredibly perceptive individual. As her eyes seemed to search his face, the prince wondered if she was reading his thoughts.

"How did you know that, Ronanya?" he responded. "You're absolutely right, my father visits me quite frequently in my dreams. I had one just the other day, where he rescued me from a catastrophic situation. It's been a couple of years since his passing. I thought the frequency of these meetings would decrease over time, but they haven't really."

"Do you think about him much during your waking hours, Nujran?"

"I guess I do, Ronanya. I still miss him a great deal. I wish he were around so that I could have daily conversations with him. I should have spent more time with him when I was growing up...but it wasn't that easy. You know, as the king, he was always busy with matters of the state. I'm just starting to appreciate what an extraordinary individual he was and the enormous contributions he made, not just to Typgar but to the entire planet. And I regret the fact that I didn't get to know him as well as I could have."

"Don't be too hard on yourself." Ronanya's tone was gentle. "You were just a teenager. Even with adults, it's certainly not unusual that the value of our relationships with the ones we love becomes obvious only after they have left us."

Nujran fell silent and pondered Ronanya's statement. For a short while, neither spoke.

"And what about Zhinso?" Ronanya inquired, breaking the silence and changing the subject.

"Well, actually, I dreamed about him quite recently. It happened last night, as a matter of fact. He asked me to tell Tyora that he loved her."

"Did he mention Miko?"

"No, he did not. How could he? He wasn't even aware that Tyora was pregnant when he died."

Ronanya did not respond. She was now looking up, staring into space. A few moments later, she spoke again.

"Well, you never know. He might be observing our world from another dimension."

Nujran was about to comment, but his thoughts were interrupted by the dean speaking into his microphone.

"It gives me great pleasure to welcome our very special guests, the Monks of Meirar, to our campus," he announced. "Their offer to assist us in our hour of need was an act of great generosity, for which I am very grateful to my dear friend, Andron. They have arrived at an extremely difficult time for our school, and we greatly appreciate their presence here. They are an enormously gifted group of individuals, each one skilled in his or her own special way. I am positive that the entire student community will benefit from their knowledge. This is a temporary measure, until our teachers recover, and allows us to move forward with our curriculum, as best as we can. Let's open our minds and hearts to what they have to offer. Students, I know you will not be disappointed!"

There was a round of applause, as the dean sat down at one of the tables. Next, Amsibh arose to speak. The prince noted that he did not use the dean's microphone. His naturally booming voice reached all corners of the room.

"I echo the dean's words," he began, looking around the room as he spoke. "I welcome Andron's band of wandering monks, whom I have known for a very long time. Yes, I am an old man, as you all can see…" He smiled, and there was polite laughter around the room. He then continued, "They are wonderful people, with abilities that can only be described as extraordinary. Their gifts have been finely honed through years of training and practice. Their teaching methods are likely to be unorthodox, but those of you who have come to my lectures are already used to that." He paused again briefly, as more ripples of laughter spread through the room. "I have no doubt that you can learn a great deal from them in the short time they are here. It is indeed unfortunate that most of your teachers have been taken ill, and I wish them all a speedy recovery. I am sure they will rejoin us soon; indeed, some are on the mend already. Nevertheless, the universe has presented the student body here with a unique alternative…being taught by these amazing Monks of Meirar. Make full use of this opportunity, and I guarantee you will remember the experience for the rest of your lives!"

Robust applause followed as Amsibh took his seat. As dinner started, the monks made their presence felt. In no time, food items were moving around in the air, rising from dishes in the center of the tables and guided by the monks in various directions toward their destinations on their plates. Nujran had seen this spectacle before, when he first interacted with them at Amsibh's place in Narcaya and later again aboard Flomo. But to the students in the cafeteria, watching it for the first time, it was a novel and fascinating experience. Noisy banter morphed into giggles, squeals, and shouts of surprise, interspersed with rounds of appreciative handclapping when flying morsels of food found their targets. Nujran looked around, smiling as he did, thinking back to the time he had first observed this feat. It was then that he noticed a young lady in monk's robes standing at the entrance to the cafeteria. Her eyes met his, and he immediately recognized her. He got up from the table and walked over to the entrance. Approaching her, he raised his arms and hugged her warmly.

"Maaya, it's so wonderful to see you!"

"Likewise, Nujran, likewise."

Just then, the prince realized that someone was standing a few paces behind Maaya, outside the cafeteria. He looked up to see Miriana, staring at them. The intensity of her gaze made him feel uncomfortable, and he felt he had to explain himself.

"Miriana, this is Maaya, one of the Monks of Meirar. Maaya, this is Miriana, a friend of mine."

There was an awkward pause. The prince was unsure if he should say something more about either one of them to the other. The undeclared nature of his relationship with Miriana made it difficult. She wasn't officially his girlfriend, but they had been on two dates. And they had spent a lot of time together. Hopefully, introducing her as a friend was the right thing to do.

Maaya spoke first. "It's nice to meet you, Miriana."

Miriana smiled and nodded.

"Perhaps we should all go in," Nujran suggested. "Everyone's having a great time inside. The monks have been entertaining us by making their food fly."

"Flying food?" Miriana looked puzzled.

"My colleagues have all developed the ability to mentally lift objects and move them around," Maaya explained. "It would appear that they're up to their usual antics at the dinner table."

"I've got to see this!" exclaimed Miriana, entering the cafeteria.

While Maaya seemed unimpressed, the prince observed Miriana's jaw drop as she took in the scene. It looked like one of organized chaos, with servings of food traveling in various directions above the tables. Meats were moving one way, vegetables in another. Rolls of bread seemed to be jumping haphazardly from one table to the next. Occasionally, a monk would stand up to get a better look at what was on the table further down from where he or she was seated. The arrival of food was usually greeted by the receiving monk with a shout of approval, prompting raucous laughter from the others.

Nujran walked Miriana and Maaya over to one of the tables where there appeared to be some seating still available. He was debating whether to sit down with them or return to his original spot with Tyora and Ronanya. Deciding that the latter was the more polite option, he turned around to head back. It was then that he noticed Amsibh stand and look around. Seeing the prince, the maestro beckoned to him, inviting him to come over to where he was.

Nujran turned back to Miriana and Maaya. "It looks like Amsibh would like to have a word with me. I'll see you both a little later."

Approaching the table beside which Amsibh was waiting for him, Nujran noted that the maestro seemed worried. His brow was furrowed, and he was repeatedly stroking his long beard, a classic gesture the prince had observed him perform when in a pensive frame of mind.

"Something the matter, maestro?" the prince inquired.

"I'm not sure, Nujran. But we need to talk. Let's step outside."

They wandered between tables, ducking occasionally to avoid a bread roll that soared overhead. Nujran wondered if people would think he was flaunting his association with the maestro, who after all was one of the most renowned teachers on the planet. The prince waved to a couple of students he recognized, and they waved back enthusiastically. *That's reassuring,* he thought. *No one seems envious... why should they be? Everyone here knows Amsibh and I go back a few years.*

A few moments later, when they were both outside the cafeteria, Amsibh spoke. His voice was soft, his tone serious. "Nujran, there's been an update from the palace in Loh'dis. Apparently, Yarozin and Hoanan did not go to Cherstwine Castle. Our best intelligence suggests that they are heading here."

Chapter Thirteen

CAFETERIA KARAOKE

Nujran and Amsibh went back into the cafeteria. The meal was still in progress, the scene energetic, the laughter lively. Tyora and Ronanya had finished eating and were deep in conversation with each other. *Is she asking Tyora if she's seen Zhinso lately*? he wondered. The lack of separation, in Ronanya's mind, between the living and the dead was always something that had both fascinated and annoyed the prince. *While many intelligent minds have spent lifetimes agonizing over what happens to people after their death, Ronanya seems to have all the answers there.*

He felt someone grab his leg. He looked down to see Miko seated on the floor, grinning up at him.

"Oh, hi Miko! Have you finished eating?"

Miko nodded, pointed at her mouth, then made a movement with her thumb and forefinger like she was spooning something out of a bowl.

"She wants ice cream, Nujran," Tyora explained, a smile on her face. "I don't think it's on the menu for tonight. I tried to tell her that, but she seems persistent."

Nujran winked at Miko. "I know exactly where I can get you some. Come with me."

Miko looked at Tyora, unsure of what she should do.

"It's alright," Tyora said reassuringly. "You can go with Nujran. He'll find you some ice cream."

Miko extended her tiny hand upwards. For a brief moment, Nujran's mind flashed back to when Miko's parents, Zhinso and Tyora, had levitated across the water to where Flomo was anchored. *I was holding their hands as they guided me across the water,* he thought. *Now their daughter is extending hers toward mine.* The prince bent down to grasp Miko's hand gently, then led her toward the far side of the cafeteria, where there was a large counter. The lights were switched off behind it, and there was no one to be seen. There was, however, a large black button prominently visible on the counter. An arrow dangled over the button, daring visitors to press it. Nujran thought it would be something entertaining for Miko to do. He lifted her up with one arm and pointed to the button with the other.

"Push," he said encouragingly.

Miko pressed it, but nothing happened.

"Try again, maybe push a little harder."

She pushed once more, and they waited a few moments. This time, they were rewarded with the sound of heavy footsteps advancing toward them, one thump at a time. A light flickered behind the counter for an unreasonably long period of several seconds, seemingly hesitant as to what its next move should be, and then finally came on. A large man wearing a chef's hat emerged from the shadows and stepped into the spotlight like a seasoned thespian making his entry on stage. The prince recognized him instantly as the same individual who had talked to Amsibh about vegetarian meat during the maestro's first visit to the cafeteria. The man seemed tired, making his way over to the counter, taking slow and deliberate steps. As he approached, Nujran observed that his face was flushed, and he seemed slightly short of breath. He looked at Nujran and then at Miko, who was now seated on the counter. The prince noticed he wore a name badge on his gown that stated 'Eramsen, Head Chef.'

Nujran spoke, his tone apologetic. "We're so sorry to bother you at this late hour. This little one would like some ice cream. I was wondering if you had any."

Quite unexpectedly, the stressed look on Eramsen's face dissolved into a big grin.

"You're just like my granddaughter!" he exclaimed. "She's always asking for ice cream!"

Miko tossed her head back and laughed. "Ice cream," she said, her eyes darting eagerly toward Nujran and then back to Eramsen.

"Just wait here, my dear. I'll be right back." Eramsen retreated from the counter, faded into the shadows, and turned on another light. He then flicked a few switches on the wall, and a machine with flashing light bulbs of varying colors lit up the area. He bent down and picked up something from a box on the ground. Pressing a lever on the machine with one hand, he made a small swirling motion with the other. A few moments later, he traipsed back to the counter, bearing a large beige cone filled with ice cream of three different shades. Leaning down behind the counter, he pulled out a jar, deftly shaking a few colorful sprinkles over the top. His countenance even more flushed than earlier, but now adorned with a broad smile, he extended his arm, offering the treat to Miko.

"There you go, sweetheart. Hope you enjoy it."

Miko clapped her hands, then gleefully accepted the cone. She slurped it contentedly as Nujran walked her back to where Tyora was seated. His eyes searching the room for Miriana and Maaya, the prince was pleasantly surprised to spy them enthusiastically chatting with each other. Maaya looked radiant and happy. For a few moments after he had introduced them to each other, he had wondered why Miriana seemed irritable. *Is she annoyed that I did not tell her earlier about Maaya? Was she resentful…would she perhaps consider her a competitor for my affection?* Now, observing them at the table, they seemed to be getting on like a house on fire. Realizing that he was worrying himself about something that might not exist, he sat down at the table between Tyora and Ronanya.

"No need to tie your mind into knots," Tyora said. "I don't think they are talking about you. They're just getting to know each other."

"What do you mean?" Nujran asked, his face reddening a bit. He had not said anything aloud, so he wasn't exactly sure what Tyora was referring to.

"Didn't you know?" Ronanya's voice had a mysterious tone.

"Know what?" Nujran was trying not to sound cross. He respected Ronanya a great deal, but she sometimes got under his skin by the manner in which she spoke.

"She reads minds. That's her talent."

"Tyora reads minds?" The prince was clearly startled by Ronanya's revelation.

"She may not have been an expert when you knew her earlier, but she's worked hard at it and mastered the art now. And she's a better exponent than anybody I know."

"You flatter me, Ronanya," Tyora interjected. "It's true, Nujran…I can read minds. But I still have a long way to go and a lot to learn."

"That's amazing, Tyora! It's a skill I'd love to have."

Their conversation was interrupted by the sounds of furniture being dragged across the floor behind them. Looking around, the prince observed that tables and benches were being moved to the perimeter of the cafeteria. Just as he wondered what was happening, Leongatti's voice came through stridently over the microphone that he once again had pressed to his cheek.

"It's time for Cafeteria Karaoke!"

Nujran had heard that this event took place from time to time on campus, but he had never attended, nor participated in it. *This is a great idea*, he thought. He looked around and noticed that the monks also appeared excited by the idea. *Do they like to sing, or are they just looking for some entertainment in their semi-inebriated state*? he wondered.

Giant screens slowly descended near the middle of each of the four walls of the cafeteria. The rearrangement of furniture continued for a few more minutes, the resulting screeching sounds causing some of the students to cover their ears. The task complete, monks and students started gathering around the screens.

"Dean's choice for the first song!" Leongatti's voice came through again over the microphone. He was holding up a box, displaying it to the occupants of the cafeteria. He then punched in a few numbers, and the screens lit up. A few notes rang out, prompting a rousing cheer from the students in the room.

"That's our school anthem," Nujran explained to Tyora and Ronanya, who were now standing beside him.

As the words appeared on the giant screens, students started to sing. At first, it was just a few, but a couple of lines into the song, more joined in. Very soon, all the students were active participants, shouting out the words, dancing gleefully, shedding their inhibitions. The prince joined in as well, locking arms with Tyora and Ronanya and encouraging them to rock on from side to side with him, to the rhythm of the anthem. Tyora swayed happily to the music, while Ronanya smiled but didn't move very much. The singing gradually increased to a crescendo as the crowd belted out the last lines of the song. Tumultuous applause broke out, lasting an entire minute.

"There are control boxes beneath each screen," Leongatti announced. "Feel free to select the songs you'd like to sing."

Students converged on the boxes and began to enter their selections. The screen lit up as the first of these appeared, mellifluous music filling the hall. As students began to sing and dance again, Nujran's eyes searched the room for Miriana and Maaya. He located them near the screen on the far side of the room.

"See you in a little while," he called out to Tyora and then started to make his way across the room. He walked past Tazloe, who had his arm around a girl whom he did not recognize. Both were sashaying to the music, though neither appeared to be mouthing the words of the song running across the giant screens. He reached Miriana and Maaya, who appeared to be enjoying themselves, singing along with the others around them.

"Should we choose a song?" the prince asked.

"Sure, sounds good," Miriana responded. Maaya nodded.

Nujran walked over to the control box that was hanging by a cord from the bottom of the screen. He flicked through a few songs, then selected one that he liked. Maneuvering his way back through the crowd, he found the girls once again and informed them of the song he had chosen. It was a ballad of love from about thirty years prior, one he knew that his father, King Rababi, had enjoyed listening to.

"Good choice," Miriana murmured.

After a few more songs, the prince's selection came up on the screen. He grabbed a microphone from a stand nearby and started to sing into it. He beckoned to Miriana to join in. Maaya remained a short distance away, eyes closed, listening to the melody. As it progressed, Nujran put his arm around Miriana, and they swayed gently from side to side. The romance in the words was beginning to influence Nujran. His heart had started to quicken, and beads of perspiration appeared on his brow. He turned to Miriana and looked directly into her eyes as they sang the last couple of lines. Then plucking up courage, as the song concluded, he planted a kiss firmly on her lips. A loud cheer went up from his fellow students, and many of the monks standing around were smiling. Miriana blushed, then gave Nujran a bear hug.

They remained where they were, holding hands, surrounded by a group of students.

Meanwhile, the next song had started. Maaya had made her way over to the control box and appeared to be making a selection. Observing this through the corner of her eye, Miriana inquired, "Do you know if Maaya is a good singer?"

"No idea," Nujran replied. "We'll find out in a short while."

Shortly thereafter, Maaya's song came up. It was an unusual tune, one that Nujran had not heard before. And then as she started to sing, the entire crowd fell silent. Her voice was rich and melodious; it reached every corner of the room. Jaws dropped and eyes widened, as the audience was completely captivated. She started to move to the music, her body gently swaying at first, then speeding up with the song until, finally, she was dancing with wild abandon, hips gyrating, her voice in complete command of the room. When she finished, the students and monks alike erupted in an exuberant ovation that seemed to continue for several minutes. Nujran felt a touch on his sleeve and turned around to see Ronanya standing behind him.

"Music and dance," she said. "Those are Maaya's talents."

"She's incredible!" Miriana exclaimed.

"I had no idea," Nujran commented.

Just then, there was a whirring noise at the entrance to the cafeteria. It sounded as if a small plane had entered the building. Someone paused the music, and everyone turned to look. An object had appeared in the doorway and was moving slowly into the cafeteria, above the heads of the people within.

"It's a drone," one of the students called out.

The prince heard a voice behind him. "Get down, Nujran." The tone was urgent. He recognized Amsibh's voice. He felt himself being pushed down to the ground. As he descended to the floor, he heard the maestro's words in his ear. "Concentric rings…on the underside of the drone…the insignia of Hoanan's rebels."

Chapter Fourteen

DRONE INTRUSION

As Nujran lay on the floor, the drone slowly circled overhead. A light flashed down from its hull. It seemed to be probing the crowd below, moving systematically from one face to the next. Students looked at it nervously, unsure about what to do, wondering if it was part of the Cafeteria Karaoke arrangements for the evening. *Perhaps Leongatti arranged for the event to be photographically recorded*, some of them were thinking. As the drone circumnavigated the room, Tyora made her way quickly over to Andron and described to him what was going on. Having observed Amsibh's reaction to the intruder when it first entered, she had realized immediately that something was wrong. Andron listened carefully, thought for a moment, then turned his face toward Tyora.

"Is Brenlo here?"

"Yes, I saw him earlier in the evening," Tyora replied.

"Find him and bring him to me." Andron's tone was urgent.

Tyora quickly scanned the crowd but was unable to locate Brenlo. She did notice, however, that Leongatti was standing nearby, keenly observing the drone. She hurried over to where he was standing.

"Dean Leongatti, can I borrow your microphone for a second?"

Without waiting for a response, Tyora peeled the device off the dean's cheek and placed it on hers. Running over to a chair nearby, she quickly stood on it. Then, pressing the button on the microphone, as she had seen Leongatti do earlier, she announced, "Your attention, please…Brenlo, if you're still here, can you make your way over to where I am?"

A moment later, an extremely tall dark monk, with a shaven head and a muscular physique, emerged from the shadows in the corner of the room. With great alacrity, he made his way over to where Tyora was perched. He was about the same height as Tyora standing on the chair. As he approached Tyora, both had to duck, to avoid the drone as it darted over their heads.

"Andron wants to speak to you." Tyora nodded toward where the blind monk was standing. Brenlo took a couple of quick steps and was alongside Andron in an instant.

He bowed down and spoke in Andron's ear. "What is it, maestro?"

Andron beckoned to him to bend a little further and whispered something in his ear. Brenlo smiled, then looked at the drone.

"Make room," he bellowed, spreading his arms apart, then pointing to the drone. The crowd split down the middle, creating a path for him that led to the intruder. Taking a couple of steps, Brenlo then broke into a run. Approaching the drone, he launched into a massive leap, his right arm in the air, rising several feet off the ground. The searchlight from the drone was now shining on him, giving the occupants in the hall a spectacular view. Brenlo's hand then locked on the drone, and as he descended, his grip tightened to ensure that he maintained his grasp on it. He landed on both feet, the drone now wriggling around in his hand, like a bird trying desperately to break free. Bringing his other arm up, he wrestled it to the ground, pinning it down with his massive frame. Tumultuous applause went up from the spectators in spontaneous admiration of this impressive athletic feat.

By this time, Amsibh had arrived beside him. "Keep holding it down, but let me have a look," the maestro instructed.

Maintaining his prone position, Brenlo turned his body a few degrees sideways so that Amsibh could get closer. The maestro reached down to the hull of the drone, feeling under it for a moment or two.

"Found it!" he called out, appearing to flick a switch. One last shudder emanated from the drone, as it was trapped beneath Brenlo's giant frame. It then went still, as a hush descended on the cafeteria.

Nujran was standing up now, and he made his way over to Amsibh and Brenlo. They were joined by Tyora and Andron. A small crowd curiously gathered around the captured drone.

"Well done!" Amsibh was appreciative as he shook Brenlo's hand. Andron slapped him on the back a couple of times, nodding in agreement. Nujran was looking up at Brenlo, amazed by his giant physical stature.

"He's a magnificent athlete," Tyora explained to the prince *sotto voce*. "Endowed with a towering physique, he's mastered the skills of running and jumping. He was a professional athlete during his university days but sought a different life and joined us somewhere along the way."

"Yes, that's an incredible talent," Nujran remarked. "I don't recall meeting him on Flomo though."

Tyora nodded. "That's right, he wasn't on that voyage when you were with us. He had gone home to Krifaca to visit his family."

By this time, Dean Leongatti had walked over. He politely requested the crowd to disperse. Students started to leave the cafeteria in small groups. A few of the monks remained, waiting for further instructions from Andron.

The prince looked at Amsibh. "What do you plan to do with the drone?"

"Let's turn it over to Detective Sarnoff," the maestro suggested. "He can have it examined and confirm whether it is connected to Hoanan or his men."

"Good idea," agreed Leongatti.

"What do you think the drone was doing in the cafeteria?" asked the prince.

"I think we should determine where it came from first," Amsibh replied. "Not much point in speculating what it was doing here until we establish that fact."

"Was I in danger, maestro? Is that why you pushed me down?"

"Just an abundance of caution, Nujran. Never hurts to be careful."

As they made their way out of the cafeteria, the prince reflected back on the evening. It had certainly been an exciting one—one for the ages, in his mind. Or at the very least, it was an event worth recounting to friends at dinner, for years to come. Just kissing Miriana would have made it memorable. Maaya's incredible singing and dancing had left an impression on all present. And then the drone intrusion, completely unexpected, had caught everyone off guard. Brenlo's display of his athletic prowess, leading to its capture, had been the stunning climax.

"Are you alright, Nujran?" It was Miriana, who was waiting for him by the doorway.

"Yes, I'm good." Nujran raised both thumbs to indicate all was well.

"Why did Amsibh push you to the ground?"

Nujran lowered his voice to a whisper. "He recognized Hoanan's insignia on the underside of the drone. He was protecting me."

"I suggest everyone retire to their rooms," the dean called out as the remaining students and monks filed out of the hall.

Amsibh came over to Nujran and Miriana. "Nujran, we're meeting in the dean's office tomorrow morning. We'll discuss what to do... what precautions to take, if any. I've sent a message to Sarnoff, asking if he can join us. Hopefully, he can make it."

Nujran held Miriana's hand as they walked back toward their apartments. They reached Miriana's building first.

"You're sure you're alright?" There was concern in Miriana's voice.

"Absolutely," came the prince's reply. "The campus is safe. Amsibh is here. My friends, the Monks of Meirar, are here. I'm not worried."

"Well, I am," said Miriana. She gave Nujran a hug, holding on to him for a few seconds. Releasing him, she planted a kiss on his lips. "Goodnight, Nujran," she whispered in his ear, then walked through the doorway of her building. Nujran waved goodbye and started to walk back to his room.

A few steps later, he was joined by Tazloe. He must have been right behind them. "She's your girlfriend now, Nujran?"

Nujran smiled but did not respond. He was feeling good about Miriana, and the kisses had taken their relationship to the next level. Yet, there was something in the back of his mind that seemed to be holding his spirits back. *Was Hoanan watching me through the camera on that drone?* he wondered. *What are he and Yarozin up to?* Then, realizing that he didn't have the answers to these questions, and there was no point in causing himself anguish, he turned to his companion.

"And you, Taz? That girl you were with earlier this evening... anything serious there?"

"Nah, just a friend," Tazloe replied. "Not sure if we'll hook up again."

Nujran marveled at how easily Tazloe could befriend female students and then just move on, not seeing them again. *We're so different,* he thought. He resisted the temptation to label Tazloe as shallow. *I don't want to be judgmental. That's just who he is.*

They walked back to their room in silence. At one point, Tazloe seemed a bit unsteady on his feet. Just as the prince was about to ask him if he felt alright, Tazloe's gait returned to normal. *He's probably been smoking some of that stuff he leaves lying around the apartment*, Nujran thought. Aloud, he commented, "Now that the monks are here, I guess Leongatti will post fresh class schedules." Tazloe made a sound that resembled a grunt but said nothing. They reached their room, and the prince retired to his bed.

The next morning, Nujran rose early and headed over to the gym. Probably as a result of the preceding late night in the cafeteria, it was largely empty. The prince joined a small handful of students engrossed in their exercise routines. He worked out for about an hour, then showered, and headed over with his gym bag to the dean's office. He ascended in the elevator and found Leongatti already in the office with Amsibh and Detective Sarnoff. Entering the room, he realized that he had walked in on something important. Both the dean and the maestro had grave looks on their faces.

"Something the matter?" he inquired.

Amsibh turned to him. "The detective just gave us the report on Shamirah's autopsy. Based on the findings, it would appear that she had an extreme case of whatever has afflicted our teachers. Sadly, it took her life."

"But…that was a while before the teachers were taken ill," Nujran pointed out.

"Yes, quite right," Leongatti chimed in. "It might have been a test run."

Nujran looked bewildered. "A test run? I don't understand."

"Wait a minute," Sarnoff interjected. "Should we be discussing this matter in front of a student?"

"I can vouch for Nujran." Amsibh spoke in an emphatic tone. "He's been through a lot with me, and we can trust him to keep this information confidential. I'm sure he understands its sensitive nature."

Nujran recalled that Sarnoff's cousin Pholtorimes had expressed the same concern during the early days of Hoanan's attacks on Typgar. Not surprisingly, given the prince's tender age and lack of experience, Pholtorimes had been reluctant to include him in the investigations. At that time as well, it was Amsibh who had reassured the detective that Nujran could be taken into confidence.

Sarnoff took a deep breath, then began. "There are two investigations going on in parallel here. We have been looking into Shamirah's death, and more recently, we were called in by the doctors in regard to what affected the teachers of this university."

The prince had a frown on his brow. "Hmmm, didn't realize that there was anything sinister about the teachers' illness."

"Neither did we," Leongatti remarked.

"So, here's what we have discovered," Sarnoff continued. "The teachers were poisoned with a toxin that induces gastrointestinal symptoms in low concentrations. The toxin is called 'licroin' and comes from a plant source. It's relatively rare, but highly dangerous, nonetheless. In the past, criminals have used it on occasion to incapacitate victims, but in recent times, terrorists have weaponized it, deploying it in attempts to advance their sick and twisted causes. When purified and concentrated, and then ingested or inhaled, the toxin is lethal. That's what we think happened to Shamirah."

The prince seemed flabbergasted. "So, Shamirah was poisoned first to test the compound?"

"That's our current theory," came Sarnoff's reply.

"By whom?" Nujran asked.

"We don't know. We have some leads that we are following up on, but it's too early to say."

"I have to ask," Nujran continued. "Was Shamirah murdered because she was transgender?"

"It's possible that it was a hate crime," answered Sarnoff. "The killer may have targeted a member of the student community who was in a minority to make a point. Or perhaps she was chosen because she didn't have many friends and was solitary most of the time. She was thus easy prey for someone with nefarious intentions."

Nujran was shaking his head. "I'm still confused. Shamirah was killed to test the poison. But it was then administered in a lower dose to the teachers, just to make them ill?"

"The killer or killers may have changed their strategy," Amsibh suggested. "Or perhaps, they did not intend to kill Shamirah... something went wrong and their experiment yielded a fatal result."

"Those are all possibilities," agreed Sarnoff. "For now, suffice it to say we've identified the toxin...it's the same one that caused our teachers to be hospitalized. We'll keep you posted as we learn more. But because the perpetrators might still be on campus, we must all remain vigilant. And Nujran, please don't share this information with anyone outside this room."

Nujran nodded. "Yes, of course, Detective." He put his thumb and forefinger together and drew them across his mouth. "My lips are sealed."

"Sarnoff, what do you make of the drone?" Amsibh inquired, changing the subject.

"We've sent it to our forensic laboratory for analysis," Sarnoff replied. "It will take a few days for their report."

"Any preliminary thoughts?" The question came from Leongatti.

"I sent a picture of the markings on the hull to my cousin, Pholtorimes," Sarnoff responded. "He confirmed what Amsibh suspected. The insignia is the same one that Hoanan's rebels used during his failed coup attempt in Loh'dis."

It's great that Sarnoff is reaching out to Pholtorimes for assistance, Nujran thought. *My father would have approved.* Aloud, he asked, "So, Hoanan's now sending in drones to monitor the campus?"

"Well, let's not jump to that conclusion just yet," Sarnoff cautioned. "Remember he's just escaped from prison with Yarozin. I would have thought it would take him some time to marshal resources and put any type of operation together. More likely it's some of the rebels acting independently. The news of the prison break has leaked out now, so perhaps they're gathering information, anticipating that their leaders may need it."

"What type of information?" Nujran posed the question, realizing what the likely answer was even as the words emerged from his mouth. He did not feel fearful, just resigned to the obvious inference that he was a target once again. At this point, it was just another day in the life of a prince.

Amsibh looked kindly at him, his eyes searching the prince's face. "I think it's fairly obvious, Nujran. You've probably guessed this by now…they're interested in you. You're not new to that, though. But rest assured…we're all here, and it's our job to protect you and keep you safe."

Chapter Fifteen

PERIL ON CAMPUS

Nujran exited Leongatti's office in a somewhat tense frame of mind. Knowing that he was once again a target of some nefarious plan dreamed up in the minds of Yarozin and Hoanan had brought back old fears. During the period of Hoanan's aggression against Rababi, there had been efforts to take the young prince captive, including a successful attempt that Amsibh had quickly aborted. It had been an uneasy period in Nujran's life. While he had grown from those experiences, the apprehension now seemed to be returning. Somewhere in a corner of his brain, a small dark cloud had formed and was threatening to grow. *But I'm a different person now... more mature*, he reasoned, trying to reassure himself. *And Amsibh is around; that counts for a lot. There's no point in being fearful...that doesn't really help at all.*

He closed his eyes and tried to deliberately re-focus his thoughts, a technique that had worked for him before. *Imagine a happy place*, he told himself. His thoughts drifted to the golden sands on a beach in Narcaya, rays of Yarus bouncing off azure waters. It was an idyllic location on a picture-perfect day. Managing to bury his fears deep within his psyche, he suddenly felt a gnawing feeling in his stomach and realized that he was famished. He had headed over to the dean's office directly from the gym, not having had any time to eat after his exercise. Worry had suppressed his appetite, and as he deliberately controlled his angst, the hunger had resurfaced. Subconsciously, he had already been walking in the direction of the cafeteria, so he quickened his steps and entered the hall.

There were a few students scattered around at various tables. His eyes searched the room for a familiar face, and he was pleased to spot Miriana. She was seated by herself in a corner, reading a book, sipping a hot beverage. *She kissed me twice last night, and it's the first time today I'm reflecting on it,* he thought. *What's wrong with me? I really should be celebrating...or, at least, in a far more upbeat frame of mind.*

Approaching the table where Miriana was seated, he planted himself next to her. He hesitated for a moment, then kissed her firmly and noisily on her cheek. "Hi, Miriana, my day's not been that great so far. But seeing you has made it a whole lot better!"

That sounded pretty banal, he thought, just as he said it. Miriana didn't seem to mind, though. She smiled, turned to him, and gave him a warm embrace. "Nujran, you poor thing. I can only imagine how worried you must be. Anything more we know about where the drone came from? Was it dispatched here by the enemies of Typgar? That's what the rumor mill around campus is saying today. Does Amsibh have any further thoughts about it?"

Nujran was in two minds. On one hand, he was feeling a tad vulnerable, so Miriana's sympathetic disposition and kind words were certainly comforting. On the other hand, he wanted to come across in control of the situation and not appear weak in front of his girlfriend.

"It's with Sarnoff's team now, Miriana. They will examine it carefully. We'll hear from them soon, I hope."

"But Amsibh obviously believed it was after you, did he not? Why would he have pushed you down to the ground, otherwise?"

Nujran hesitated, wondering how much he should share. He owed Miriana some information, yet he did not want to worry her too much.

"The markings on the drone were the same ones used by Hoanan's rebel forces. But Sarnoff's not sure where exactly it came from, so I guess it's best to wait for more data. No point in being unduly worried at this stage, don't you agree?"

"That's a great attitude, Nujran. I admire your courage."

"Fear of the unknown brings no gain, Miriana."

"That sounds like something Amsibh would say, Nujran."

The prince smiled. "You're right, Miriana. I've heard him use the expression. It's a good one, isn't it?"

Miriana nodded. "Nujran, I know you probably want to chat, but I've got a few things I have to finish in my room before class."

"Which lectures are you attending?"

"I'm going to 'Introduction to Languages.' I heard that the monk who will teach the class is an expert."

"Yes, that would be Glyoptula," Nujran noted. "She knows my mother and has actually spent time at my home, the palace in Loh'dis. She's a brilliant linguist, fluent in many tongues."

"That's great, I look forward to it. Any classes you're going to today?"

"Andron is doing one: 'Religious practices and beliefs, past and present.' I'm not religious myself but have always been a bit curious about the topic."

"Sounds interesting, Nujran. Enjoy the lecture. Perhaps we could catch up later in the day."

"I'd really like that, Miriana. Dinner tonight?"

"Sure, I'll see you in the evening, then." Miriana stood up, gave Nujran a quick kiss on the lips, and then strolled out of the cafeteria.

Nujran helped himself to a bowl of fruit from one of the counters in the cafeteria. Still somewhat hungry after consuming it, he grabbed a packet of nuts on his way out. Munching them, he emerged from the cafeteria and spotted Tyora and Miko, taking a stroll.

"Hi Tyora, hi Miko," he called out.

They came over to where he was standing, at the door of the cafeteria. Miko smiled and gave him a wave.

"How's your morning going, Nujran?" Tyora inquired.

"Pretty good, so far," he replied, a smile on his face.

"Ah, Miriana kissed you again. No wonder you are happy."

"Are you reading my mind, Tyora?"

"I'll stop if you don't want me to, Nujran."

"No, I don't mind…I guess. It's an amazing skill. How did you learn to do it?"

"It's hard to explain, Nujran. It started a couple of years ago, just after Zhinso's death. I realized that I could listen to people's thoughts. Andron really helped me to focus my energy and fine-tune the skill. I've gotten quite good at it."

"But don't people object, Tyora? After all, you're reading thoughts they consider private."

"Yes, I have to be really careful about how I use it," Tyora admitted.

"I suppose it's a lot like Amsibh's cephavid," the prince pointed out. "I remember being uncomfortable when he first used it on me. And we debated its use on prisoners, without their consent. Your talent is remarkable…you can do what he does without a machine."

"Mommy…hungry," Miko interjected, pointing her index finger at her mouth.

"Do you mind if I grab her something to eat, Nujran?" asked Tyora. Not waiting for an answer, she walked into the cafeteria, Miko following closely behind. Nujran ambled back in after them. He waited till Tyora had served Miko a bowl of porridge and then sat down beside them.

"So, how much have you told Miko about Zhinso?" the prince inquired softly.

"Well, I've shown her pictures of him. I've explained to her that he is her father, and he is not with us. I think it's all quite abstract for her now, but I'm sure she will ask me more questions about him as she grows up."

Nujran fell silent for a while, reflecting on memories of Zhinso. They were warm and pleasant recollections, as the monk had been a wonderful friend to him. *If only Zhinso had stayed on the ship, and not boarded the aircraft above, he would still be alive,* Nujran thought. Then recollecting Amsibh's advice about not tying himself in knots contemplating what might have been, he dragged himself back to the present.

"I used to wonder about the very same thing, Nujran." Tyora was reading his thoughts again. "But it just got me depressed, so I try not to go down that path much these days."

There was another brief silence, and then Tyora spoke again. "Can you look after Miko for a couple of hours this afternoon, Nujran? After your classes finish, of course. I have a few things I need to attend to."

"I'd be happy to," the prince responded. "She's such a sweet child." He looked at his watch. "Sorry, Tyora, I have to leave now; it's time for Andron's class. I'll see you both later today."

He walked briskly over to Rababi Hall, where Andron's lecture was just about to commence. The auditorium was only half full, but students were still arriving. Andron had taken his place at the podium. Yin'hua was beside him, adjusting the microphone which suddenly came to life, generating a screeching sound that caused several in the audience to cover their ears with their hands. Fortunately, it only lasted seconds, to the relief of everyone in the room. Andron coughed a couple of times and then started to speak.

"My lecture today is on religious practices. My apologies, I will not be using any visual aids. And unfortunately, unlike my friend Amsibh, I don't own a cephavid, so I will not be projecting my thoughts."

There was scattered laughter through the hall. Nujran smiled and thought, *He's got everyone relaxed now.*

"We live on a planet with numerous religions and beliefs," he began. "And what's more...these beliefs have changed and evolved over time. Our ancestors were largely nature worshippers. They revered our son Yarus, our three moons, the wind, the rain, our oceans and rivers, the mountains and valleys, and so on. That's understandable when you think about it a bit more...they were at the mercy of the elements, you see. So, it's hardly surprising that they felt the need to propitiate the natural forces controlling their lives."

As Andron spoke, the prince marveled at how he had instantly captured the attention of the class. *Logical thought, clear diction, and simple arguments...that's what it takes. Yet, many teachers just don't have it.*

"At various points in history, individuals with vision and insight emerged as spiritual leaders," Andron continued. "People flocked to them, and their popularity grew. Sometimes the flock dissipated with the leader's death, and that was the end of the story. But every so often, a spiritual teacher would emerge whose philosophy and concepts would gain such widespread attention that they would outlive the individual. Over time, the teachings would be consolidated into a religion, with temples and priests, and an entire infrastructure would emerge that was autonomous and self-perpetuating."

"Side by side, as these religions developed around spiritual teachers, nature worship gradually started to decline. Scientific curiosity stimulated a better understanding of natural phenomena. So, while people still feared calamitous acts of nature, these were now de-mystified. As a result, the ancient traditions of reverence and awe for the elements were slowly replaced by other belief systems."

Wow, he explains it so beautifully, Nujran thought. *A crystal-clear description, so easy for anyone in the class to follow!*

The lecture continued for another forty minutes or so. Andron spent some time discussing two major religions, namely Hariscatiny and Didubism. Nujran had met both Hariscatins and Didubists in Typgar but realized he understood very little about either religion. He listened carefully to the maestro's descriptions, taking notes on his Zogo. Hariscatiny was based on the teachings of a prophet who lived in Baariya several centuries earlier and had been murdered for his beliefs. It was the predominant religion in both Typgar and Foalinaarc. Didubism was an ancient faith that had originated in Nadii, then spread to Inchea, and now had followers across the planet.

At the end of the lecture, Andron opened the floor to questions. Yin'hua went up to the podium to assist him by calling out students in the audience. Several hands in the hall were already raised. A girl in the first row, whom Nujran thought was familiar but did not recognize by name, asked the first question.

"Maestro, several of the Monks of Meirar, I understand, have special powers. Do you have followers, as a group or as individuals?"

"If you're asking if we started a religion, the answer is a firm no," Andron responded, a smile across his face. "And we don't have special powers…rather, we prefer to think of them as inherent talents that we have developed and honed over time, with lots of practice."

"Are you a religious order of monks?" asked a young man with a thick mop of curly brown hair, seated in the third row. Nujran identified him as Trimiod, someone whom he had observed hanging out with Tazloe from time to time.

"No, we are not," came Andron's reply. "We adhere to certain philosophical principles. We practice meditation and introspection on a daily basis and are detached from the usual responsibilities that most on Syzegis have. But we welcome all religious beliefs, or none… it's really up to the individual."

A hand went up in the same row where Nujran was seated. He recognized Lincus and was pleased when Yin'hua invited him to ask his question.

"My understanding is that there are lots of folks now who don't follow any religion at all," Lincus remarked. "My family and I are in this category. What are your thoughts on how this has come into being?"

Andron reflected for a moment. "We call that agnosticism. In fact, it's estimated that over half the planet is agnostic to any religion. Nothing wrong with that; it's a choice people make for themselves. It may surprise some of you that I am an agnostic as well. I believe that as long as people are good and behave in a righteous manner, they're on the right track. Religion and belief in a supernatural power aren't a mandatory requirement to achieve that goal."

Nujran felt relieved. He was not a follower of any particular faith and could not recall any phase in his life thus far when he was. That was probably because neither Rababi nor Roone were adherents to a religion, although the queen did occasionally indulge in the practice of certain Hariscatin rituals, especially those native to Yarwone, her country of origin. And he had once overheard Rababi say that if he were to practice a religion, it would likely be Didubism.

The prince was about to ask a follow-up question when Andron announced, "I think we should conclude now. We can continue our discussion when we next meet."

Nujran headed back to the cafeteria to pick up Miko as he had earlier promised. Tyora was waiting outside the door, but Miko wasn't with her.

"She's running around inside," Tyora informed him. "She's just very excited to have so much space. Except for the short sojourns we've had on land when Flomo has dropped anchor, she's spent most of her life on the ship."

Tyora stuck her head into the cafeteria. "Miko," she called out, "Nujran is here."

"Perhaps I'll show her around campus then," the prince suggested. "We'll take a walk through the corridors, maybe visit the gym, and then she can play in Reinhart's Green, the field at the center of campus, next to the library."

"I think she'll really enjoy that." Tyora sounded grateful. "I truly appreciate your help, Nujran. I've got a few domestic chores to do, and then I need to run an errand for Andron."

"No problem. By the way, Tyora, why don't you teach a class on mind-reading? I think there would be a lot of interest."

"I'm not sure, Nujran. I admit I'm starting to be reasonably good at it, but teaching a class? I don't think I'm ready. Maybe I'll give you a few tips…one on one, I mean. Sorry, I've got to run now."

Miko had just emerged from the cafeteria, an ice cream cone in one hand and a smile on her face. Tyora bent down and gave her a hug. "Chef Eramsen has been spoiling you again, hasn't he," she remarked.

"Ice…cream…" said Miko, pointing to the cone with her other hand and licking it happily.

"I'll see you both later." Tyora turned around and walked away.

Nujran waited for Miko to finish her ice cream cone, then took her hand. They wandered through a couple of corridors and strolled across a quadrangle. Miko pointed to a row of shrubs and then to her hair. The prince wasn't sure what she wanted. Miko repeated the gesture, and this time Nujran understood. Striding over to the plants, he plucked a large maroon flower with white stripes on its petals. He beckoned to Miko, who ran over to him. He then placed the flower in her hair, securing it with her hair clip.

A cherubic smile lit up her face. "Nice flower," she said, patting it down on her head.

They continued their walk around campus. Students greeted them as they passed by. Miko seemed to be enjoying herself. Nujran marveled at how well behaved she was, and how easy she was to manage. Shortly after, they arrived at Reinhart's Green at the center of campus. They were on the side across from the library, standing on a path. A row of trees stood behind them, like sentries guarding the edge of the field. It was largely empty, except for a couple of youths who were kicking a ball around, not too far from the library entrance. As Nujran wondered what he should do next with Miko, he heard a rumbling sound in the distance. It was faint at first but steadily grew louder. Miko appeared to have heard it too; she was pointing toward the sky.

Looking up, Nujran noticed a funnel-shaped cloud extending down toward the ground. Wobbling from side to side across the landscape, it reminded him of an inebriated sailor of gargantuan proportions. As they watched, it seemed to be advancing in their direction quite rapidly. There was something at the top of the cloud, an indistinct dark object, but the prince could not make out what it was. Through the corner of his eyes, he noticed that the youths had stopped kicking the ball and were staring upwards too. The cloud reached the middle of the field and stopped, hovering above for a few seconds.

Nujran was unsure what he should do. He felt a sudden sense of unease welling up inside him. Miko had stopped pointing, her eyes now fixated on the cloud. And then without warning, the tail of the funnel snaked across the field in their direction. They heard a loud whooshing noise that rapidly increased to a crescendo. The prince felt himself being sucked upwards, unable to resist. Fearing for Miko, he grasped her hand even more tightly. He sensed that he was being lifted into the air and then spun around in a wide circle. Miko was holding on to him, her tresses flying above her head, the flower in her hair no longer there. Nujran thought he heard her scream. The spinning became faster and more forceful. Feeling quite dizzy now, he closed his eyes. He thought he heard a loud bang, and then… everything went dark.

Chapter Sixteen

KIDNAPPED BY A TORNADO

When Nujran's eyes opened, he was not sure how long he had been unconscious. He felt quite dizzy, the back of his head hurt, and his vision was blurry. He closed his eyes again for a few seconds, before opening them to take another look. His surroundings gradually came into focus. He appeared to be in a window-less room with gray walls. The ceiling was white, the room dimly lit with a single yellow light bulb dangling on a short length of wire. Attempting to sit up, he found that he could do so with minimal difficulty. But when he tried to stand, he realized that his left wrist was chained to the floor. He strained on the chain, and although it rattled noisily, it did not yield. He heard a soft sob from the corner of the room. As his eyes adjusted to the dim light, a child's silhouette gradually took shape. A shocking realization came over him, and an uncomfortable sensation welled up in the pit of his stomach.

"Miko, is that you? Are you alright?"

The sobbing stopped. Miko stood up and rushed toward him. Nujran was relieved that their captors had not chained her. *Thank goodness*, he thought. *Through no fault of hers, she's become my fellow prisoner. But at least she's free to move around the room. Perhaps whoever kidnapped us isn't that cruel after all.* Miko fell into his arms, and he gave her a hug, the chain attached to his left wrist rattling as he did.

"Don't worry, Miko. I'll take care of you. We'll make sure that we get out of here safe."

Miko wiped the tears off her cheeks with the back of her hands. She gave Nujran a smile.

"Did you get some sleep?" Nujran asked.

Miko shook her head from side to side. She used her thumbs and forefingers to prise open her eyelids, signaling that she had stayed awake. Nujran hoped that she had at least managed a brief nap.

"Are you scared?" *That's a silly question*, he thought, immediately after he posed it. *Of course, she must be scared. She's just a little girl.*

To his surprise, though, she shook her head again. She gave him another smile.

"You're so brave," he said reassuringly. He patted her on the head, admiring her poise in the situation they found themselves in.

Suddenly, the soft silence which blanketed the room was perturbed. Nujran felt his heart skip a beat…there were footsteps at the door. Miko heard them too, and the prince thought he felt her tremble beside him. He looked at her; she was gazing nervously ahead. Nujran's palms were drenched with sweat; he felt a shiver down his spine. His legs quivered and he tugged on his chain, but his arms seemed to have turned into lead. Then for some inexplicable reason, the aroma of one of the special palace dishes of his childhood, a Typgarian meat platter, entered his consciousness, followed quickly by a lashing of bile rushing up his throat. Nausea…he closed his mouth tightly…he didn't want to stain his shirt.

He heard a bolt scrape against its metal housing, rending the air like a rusted blade. The door swung slowly inward, and from its seemingly gaping maw, a guard clad in billowing black emerged, as if the shadows were sending an emissary. He stretched his hands out, and Nujran shielded Miko, bracing for the worst.

"Eat," the guard barked tersely. In his roughshod hands were a plate of food and a glass of discolored water. Unpleasant, but not deadly. "The boss wants you both to eat." He placed the plate and the glass on the ground directly in front of Nujran.

The prince did not respond. The guard squatted, his eyes now level with Nujran's, searching his face. They stared at each other briefly, neither uttering a word. Their silent confrontation lasted a few moments. The guard then stood up, looked over briefly at Miko, turned around, and left the room. The door banged shut behind him, and they heard the sound of the bolt grinding back. They were locked in again.

"Looks like a splendid meal," Nujran remarked, trying to be jocular and lighten the mood for Miko's sake. The plate had a few blackened pieces of meat, a greenish blob that appeared to be a scoop of mashed vegetables, and a dry slice of white bread. There were a couple of spoons on the plate. The prince picked up one of them, using its side to cut the pieces of meat into small chunks. It was not easy since it was quite tough, and the edge of the spoon was blunt. Nevertheless, he managed to chop it up into bits that were small enough for Miko to chew. Offering her the other spoon, he invited her to eat.

"We need to keep up our strength, Miko," he explained. "The food may not be the best, but it's all we have at the moment."

Picking up the spoon from Nujran's hand, Miko looked at the plate. She then turned to the prince, waiting for her cue to start eating. Nujran dished out a little food, placed it in his mouth, and encouraged Miko to do the same. She began eating, and the room fell silent except for the sounds of spoons clanging on the plate. Very soon, the food was finished. They shared some water, and then Miko collapsed beside Nujran, using his chest as a pillow. She quickly fell into a deep slumber, her breathing slowing down noticeably, her eyelids slightly parted, her eyes moving rapidly from side to side. *She must not have slept much after we were kidnapped and brought here,* he thought. *I wonder how long it has been.* And then another thought occurred to him. *Surely, by now, someone must have noticed our absence from campus. Hopefully, they're starting to be concerned.* As he pondered the questions, sleep began to overtake him, and shortly after, his anxieties notwithstanding, he entered the land of dreams.

Back at the university, several hours had passed since the first appearance of the tornado-like phenomenon. Many students had observed it from different angles on the grounds, or through their windows. But no one had made the connection yet between the funnel-shaped cloud and Nujran's and Miko's disappearance. In fact, it was not until later that evening that anyone noticed they had vanished. Tyora had not discussed picking up Miko at any particular time; all she had said to them before departing was, "I'll see you both later." In her mind, Miko was with Nujran, they were wandering around campus, and all was well. However, just before sunset, when Yarus was starting to approach the horizon, she began to get worried. Having finished her chores and run an errand for Andron, she had searched the campus for Nujran and Miko without success, finally arriving at the entrance to the cafeteria. There were several students in there, but no sign of either her daughter or the prince. She asked a few students if they had seen Nujran or a little girl, but everyone she spoke to politely shook their heads. She decided she would wait for them, then took a seat at a table close to the door, from where she could look out. Shortly after, Amsibh walked in. His eyes scanned the room, and seeing Tyora, he walked over to her.

"Have you seen Nujran?" he inquired.

"No, I left Miko with him earlier today. I'm waiting for them to come back from wherever they went."

"He was supposed to meet with me and Leon about an hour ago. But he was a no show. That's not like him at all."

There was now obvious concern on Tyora's face. "He was going to take Miko for a walk and show her around the school. The plan was for them to end up in the field at the center of campus. I've searched everywhere, but there does not seem to be any sign of them. I'll be honest, maestro...I'm starting to worry."

Amsibh did not respond. Furrows had appeared on his brow. He stared into the distance, stroking his long beard.

One of the students in the cafeteria had noticed the maestro and strolled over. He was a stocky bespectacled lad with light brown hair and a face covered with freckles. "Maestro, can you tell us anything about the tornado that touched down here today?" he asked. "There was hardly a reference to it on the local news."

"Your dean, Leongatti, mentioned it to me earlier. It's highly unusual in these parts, apparently. Where exactly did it make contact with the ground?"

"I saw it from a distance. The tip of the funnel briefly touched down on Reinhart's Green."

"Where's that?" Amsibh asked.

"It's the official name of the field at the center of campus, next to the library."

Tyora was now looking at Amsibh, extreme concern writ across her face. A lot of thoughts were running through her mind, none of them particularly cheerful.

"Come with me...we have to leave, now." Amsibh's tone was one of urgency. They strode out of the cafeteria. As they did, the maestro extracted a small Zogo-like device from one of his pockets and typed a few words on it.

"Where are we going, maestro?" Tyora inquired, regaining her composure.

"We need to go immediately to Leon's office," Amsibh answered. "I just sent him a message, informing him that we're coming over. Hopefully, he would have contacted Sarnoff by the time we get there."

"Yes, I know, maestro. But I'm reading something else. You seem worried..." She closed her eyes tightly. "You're confirming my worst fears...you believe Miko and Nujran might have been kidnapped." Tyora's voice trembled a little; she could barely conceal her trepidation now. She opened her eyes; there was fear in them.

Amsibh stopped in his tracks. "Andron told me you can read minds. I was trying hard to conceal my concerns from you, yet you managed to get in. Alright, that's exactly what I suspect. You have a right to know since Miko is involved."

They headed over to the dean's office. As they approached the garden in front of the old red brick building, the sky was now darkening, the last rays of Yarus just visible. Handac and Iandic had both made their appearance, a few scattered clouds partially dimming their light. Entering the building, they observed Sarnoff waiting for the doors of the glass elevator to open. Seeing them through his rear-facing eyes, he swung around and greeted them.

Amsibh introduced Sarnoff and Tyora to each other. The elevator arrived, and they ascended together, exiting into the dean's office. Leongatti was standing over his desk, staring at images playing on its surface. He looked up when they entered.

"Come and have a look at this," he called out. "A tornado-like structure designed specifically to abduct people...a technique originating from Inchea. Hasn't been used in a while, apparently." It was then that he noticed Tyora following Sarnoff and Amsibh into the room. He quickly changed his tone. "We don't really know if that's the case here, though," he pointed out, trying to sound reassuring.

"Whatever it is, Dean Leongatti, I need to know." Tyora sounded calm, effectively concealing the unease that had taken residence in her mind. "If Miko and Nujran were kidnapped, then we need to understand what happened and figure out how to bring them back."

They looked at the images playing on the dean's desk. It had transformed into a screen, and as he touched it in various parts, it responded by throwing up new information. Sarnoff seemed particularly fascinated, his front-facing eyes darting around as he studied it closely.

Amsibh looked up at the circular clock on the wall above the sofa. He was stroking his beard, a pensive look on his face. "Leon, can we use your time machine? Let's go back to earlier today and see what really happened."

"Time machine?" Sarnoff and Tyora blurted out in unison, a look of surprise on their faces.

The dean nodded. "Yes, that odd-looking clock up there…it's a tempusmachina…it can take us back in time. It's an invention of mine." There was a tinge of pride in his voice.

Tyora appeared to be very interested in this suggestion.

"Such machines really exist?" Sarnoff sounded quite skeptical. "How is that possible? I don't think I've ever seen one."

As they walked over to the time machine, it seemed to look back at them with its customary lopsided grin. "I'll turn the clock back with this hand," Amsibh proposed, raising one of his arms. "You grab this other arm, Sarnoff, while Leon and Tyora can hold on to the remaining two. That way, with each of you holding on to me, we can travel back together."

"Ah, I see you have done this before, Amsibh," Leon remarked, a knowing smile on his face.

Amsibh did not respond. One of his hands moved up toward the clock, his others extending in various directions to his three companions. He deftly turned the short hand backward, retreating several hours in time, to the early afternoon. The room began to spin, and everything became blurry, similar to when he had done this before. Once things settled into focus, Amsibh walked back quickly into the elevator, pulling his companions along with him. They descended, holding tightly on to his arms, as he had asked them to. Walking out into the garden, they noticed that the scene in front of them had come into focus. They cut across a quadrangle and strode quickly through a couple of corridors. A few students passed them by but appeared to see right through them. A few moments later, they found themselves in front of the library.

They looked across Reinhart's Green and saw Nujran and Miko standing on the opposite side. Tyora instinctively wanted to run across to Miko, but Amsibh's hand was now holding hers firmly. She tried to say something, but no words emerged. They stood watching, helpless spectators transported back from a time later that day. As they continued to observe, they saw a funnel-shaped cloud approach the ground. Something mechanical was evidently spinning at the top, creating the tornado from above. And then, before their eyes, the bottom of the funnel snaked across the field and lifted Nujran and Miko into its furious embrace. Tyora's hand broke free from Amsibh, and she tried to run forward, but was hardly able to take a single step. She collapsed to the ground, apparently forced back by gusty winds emanating from the tornado as it ascended into the sky. Sobbing, she watched helplessly as it wound its way away from them, its two captives firmly in its clutches, finally disappearing into the distance.

Chapter Seventeen

SURVIVING CAPTIVITY

Nujran was suddenly awoken by footsteps outside the door of his cell. He realized he must have dozed off. Miko was lying curled up next to him, hands tightly closed, her back arched, knees almost touching her chin, fast asleep in this fetal position. Cut off from sunlight, and with the absence of any devices showing him the time, he did not know how many hours had passed since they had last eaten. He reflected on his conversation with Miko prior to falling asleep. To his credit, he had tried really hard to keep her spirits up, attempting all the while to stay hopeful himself. He had reassured her that he would protect and take care of her as best as he could. She had listened quietly, her demeanor surprisingly tranquil. The prince wondered if her young mind was able to comprehend the enormity of what had happened to them. She would undoubtedly have realized that something was seriously amiss. *Being carried away by the tornado and separated from Tyora were bad enough,* Nujran thought. *Ending up in a window-less chamber and seeing me chained to the floor must have been really stressful.* She had obviously been crying when Nujran had first come to, but to all appearances had remained resolutely serene after that. He could not help but feel some admiration, that someone so young could deal so calmly with a situation fraught with so much uncertainty.

His thoughts were interrupted by the grinding sound of the bolt being dragged across to open the door of his cell. It swung open suddenly, and a guard dressed in black appeared. It was not the same man who had brought them food earlier, but his attire was identical. His face bore several curvilinear scars on his forehead and cheeks, and his left eyelid was drooping, leaving it half shut. *Are these the wounds of past battles?* Nujran wondered. *Or perhaps the result of a rough upbringing in the streets?*

"The boss is going to pay you a visit soon," the man announced, in a dry, rasping voice.

Nujran did not reply. He thought briefly about waking Miko up. But she looked so peaceful in repose that he decided he would not disturb her. *Who is the boss the guards refer to?* he wondered. *Could it be Hoanan or Yarozin? They had recently escaped from prison and were on the run. Given their track record, and their propensity for mischief, they were likely hatching some nefarious plot once again. But could they have really organized themselves well enough, in so short a time, to engineer such an abduction?* It didn't seem very likely.

Fortunately, he did not have long to wait. A few minutes later, the door swung open once again, and someone appeared. In the dim light of the room, Nujran could make out a tall slender individual dressed in black, with a red armband just above the left elbow.

"I trust your stay so far has been uneventful, and the guards have treated you well." It was then that the prince realized, with some degree of surprise, that 'the boss' was a woman. For a brief instant, as she stood silently in front of him, he reflected on his unconscious bias. *Am I a sexist for assuming that the boss was a man?*

Aloud, he inquired politely, "And who are you?"

"Be quiet!" barked the guard with the scarred face, from his position behind her. "You don't get to ask the questions."

"No, that's alright," the woman said, gesturing to the sentry to remain silent. "He's entitled to know why he's here. We cannot keep him in the dark forever, as others have probably done his entire life."

She stepped forward directly under the light, and Nujran looked up at her curiously. She was tall and statuesque, with dark hair and high cheekbones. He could not help thinking that she looked very familiar…a blurred memory of sorts from his past…but he could not place her.

"I'm Vilania. I believe you knew my brother."

"Your brother?" Nujran seemed a tad confused. Miko stirred on the floor next to him, and shifted her posture gently, but did not awaken.

"He was killed by your father's head of security," Vilania continued.

It was like she was giving him clues and he had to solve a puzzle. He shook his head, then looked up at her again. She was staring down at him, an impassive look on her face. And then, in that instant, he saw the resemblance and realized who she was.

"You're Manolos' sister!" he exclaimed.

"We have a bright young man here," Vilania remarked, a smirk on her face. The guard standing behind her snickered noisily, causing Miko to stir again.

"But you can't fault Dannigan for killing him," Nujran protested. "It was seconds after Manolos assassinated my father, the King of Typgar."

Vilania shrugged her shoulders. "Well, that's the official story. And I don't blame you for repeating it."

"It's exactly what happened!" Nujran's tone was emphatic. "I was there." There was movement on the floor next to him. Miko was now awake. She sat up, rubbed her eyes, and stared at Vilania.

"I'm not here to argue the details surrounding the death of my brother," Vilania stated blandly. "We have to decide what to do with you both."

"Are you going to kill me?" Nujran asked. Almost immediately he wished he hadn't. *Why on earth would I pose a query like that?*

"I don't know yet," came Vilania's reply to his question. "To be honest, you may well be more useful to us alive."

Nujran changed the subject promptly. "This young girl next to me…her name is Miko…she shouldn't be involved in any of this. She just happened to be with me when I was…uh…kidnapped. She's an innocent bystander. Why not return her to her mother, back on the university campus? I'm sure she must be going crazy with worry."

"It was never our intent to bring her here," Vilania pointed out. "It was supposed to be just you. But the vortex picked you both up."

"You mean the tornado?"

"Yes, that's what it looks like, doesn't it? It's actually a mechanical vortex created by a machine. We bought it from a military distributor in Inchea."

Nujran wondered why she was telling him all this. She did not seem unfriendly, and her manner was very similar to that of Manolos. He remembered how his bodyguard had betrayed him and his family, unexpectedly turning traitor in the end. And now the prince was his sister's captive. His head was spinning a bit; he could not fully comprehend what was going on. He was also extremely hungry, a fact which compounded his sense of discomfort. Realizing that Miko was also probably just as famished as he was, he looked up at Vilania.

"Do you think we could have some food? Neither of us has eaten for a fair while. Please?"

Vilania thought for a moment, then looked at her watch. "Yes, we will give you something to eat."

"Thank you. Manolos was always kind to me. We got along well."

"And yet, your people killed him." There was now a harsh edge to Vilania's tone. "He was paid for his kindness with death."

She seems convinced of a different version of why Manolos was killed, thought Nujran. But he decided this was not the best time to press

Vilania for her version of the story. As though reading his thoughts, Vilania spoke, this time in a softer voice.

"Your father could have been killed by anyone in the crowd. Knowing my brother, and his sense of loyalty, he would have never betrayed your family. He was probably protecting you and your father, from his position on the turret."

Nujran was perplexed by what he was hearing. Vilania's narrative did not correspond to what he had experienced on that fateful day, when a gunman had fired down into the crowd. His father had been fatally shot, in attempting to shield the prince from the bullets that rained down on them from the turret above. Agent Dannigan, the head of his father's elite forces, had felled the assassin with a single bullet and discovered, to everyone's amazement, that it was Manolos, Vilania's brother. At no stage had any doubt been expressed that the killer was anyone other than Manolos.

Vilania then beckoned to the guard to come closer and mumbled something to him. Nujran could not make out what she said and wondered if it was a different language. Abruptly, she pivoted around on her heel and marched out through the door. The guard lingered a few moments, scratching his head. Nujran noticed that Miko was staring intently at the open door and wondered if she was going to make a run for it. *I can't really move; I'm still chained firmly down to the floor. I would need to break free before I even contemplate any escape attempt.* It was a discouraging feeling, and he decided he needed to re-focus his thoughts.

The guard, who had said very little up to this point, spoke again in his dry, rasping voice. "I'll be back shortly. The boss has asked me to feed you both." His face contorted briefly into a scowl as he turned around and left the room, bolting it shut from the outside.

Nujran dragged himself on the ground as close as possible to the center of the room, where the light appeared to be brightest. Arching his back and bending his neck as far as he could, he examined his left wrist. The chain was attached to a clasp, which was locked shut around the wrist. Observing his actions, Miko walked over to where he was, picked up his hand, and stared closely at it. She seemed to be studying the clasp carefully, with an intensity unusual in a child just over two years of age. Staring at it for a few minutes, she passed her fingers over it, as though gaining a thorough understanding of its material and shape. And then, closing her eyes, she started to hum quietly.

Clicking sounds emerged from within the metal clasp, and then to the prince's astonishment, it slowly started to open and disengage from his wrist. He was not entirely sure what was happening, whether Miko was doing this, and if so, how. Her eyes were still closed, and she appeared deeply contemplative. Moments later, Nujran was able to slip his hand out, and the clasp fell away to the floor, making a clattering noise. Miko opened her eyes and clapped her hands together softly, conscious of not making much of a sound.

"Open," she said, a broad smile on her face.

The prince was amazed. Until this very moment, he had not realized that she had any special abilities. *Has she just freed me, using her mind to undo the clasp that restrained me? What an amazing skill! But then again, she's the daughter of Zhinso and Tyora, two incredibly talented monks. Perhaps I shouldn't be surprised at all!*

The sound of someone approaching the door on the outside interrupted his thoughts.

"Quick, get behind me," he whispered to Miko, a sense of urgency in his voice. He placed his wrist back on the now open flanges of the clasp and swiftly pushed it behind him, hiding it from view.

There was the grinding sound of the bolt opening again, and the door swung inward once more. It was the same guard who had left a few minutes earlier. He was back bearing a large bowl and a bottle of water. On entering the room, he stopped for a moment and looked around, as though determining where exactly to put them down. After a few moments, he decided to place them in front of Nujran.

The bowl contained a thin gruel, with some meat and vegetables floating around. Unappetizing in appearance, but an inviting aroma nevertheless...doubly so to the two hungry occupants of the cell.

"Thank you, sir," said Nujran, genuine gratitude in his voice. Truth be told, he was now positively ravenous, and thus appreciative of any nourishment that was on offer.

The guard stared at him for a moment, then grunted. He looked at Miko, his face softening almost imperceptibly. "Make sure you give her some too."

"Of course," came Nujran's reply. *I hope he doesn't come around and see the open clasp*, he thought. *He can't know that Miko has set me free.* The prince leaned back a bit further, rocking back onto his haunches, tucking his left hand firmly and tightly against his lower back.

Fortunately, the guard was lacking in either curiosity or powers of observation, for he showed little interest in the prince's peculiar posture. Shortly thereafter, he turned around, strode rapidly toward the door, and exited the room, bolting the door shut behind him. Nujran waited until his footsteps had receded into the distance.

Taking a deep breath, the prince turned to Miko. "What you did was remarkable!" He brought his left hand forward from behind his back, grasping the clasp. Pointing to it with the other, he asked, "How did you do that?"

Miko smiled, deliberately raised the index finger of her right hand, and placed it gently on her temple. "Mind...power," she stated, slowly and simply.

"Incredible!" exclaimed the prince, shaking his head. "I had no idea you had that ability. Tyora never mentioned anything about it." He thought for a moment, then continued. "And now that I'm free, we must plan our escape. But first, let's eat."

Chapter Eighteen

COMMOTION ON CAMPUS

By this time, the news of Nujran's kidnapping had spread like wildfire on campus. Although he did not flaunt it, he was unquestionably a celebrity...the Prince of Typgar. Other princes from numerous kingdoms across the planet had studied at the school. But Nujran stood out as one whose story was of much interest to ordinary folks. His parents were famous and widely loved, the news of his father's tragic assassination had been broadcast to all corners of Syzegis, and the fact that Rababi had died protecting his son in a final embrace made the recounting of the story particularly poignant. And so, while it was standard practice at the university that all pupils were treated alike, most students on campus knew who Nujran was. The legends that surrounded him as he had grown up had, in fact, already entered the realms of popular folklore.

When the prince had first enrolled at the school, Leongatti had attempted to explain the institution's philosophy regarding celebrity students to Roone. "Our campus attracts the sons and daughters of famous people. But here, on our school premises, they are just students like any other, and we try to help them blend in. We believe that this gives them the best chance of a normal education, free from the trappings and distraction of fame."

"Am I to understand that none of the students has bodyguards?" Roone had inquired.

"No, we discourage that," the dean had replied.

But now, with a strange tornado having descended on to the university grounds and taken Nujran away with it, that very question was being actively revisited in the student community.

"It seemed all too easy...why wasn't he being protected?" Tazloe was making his opinion known in the cafeteria. "He's a prince, his family has enemies, they should have known this was going to happen."

"I guess no one is allowed bodyguards on campus." It was Lincus, recalling something Leongatti had mentioned during student orientation. "Supposedly, we're all equals here."

"Yes, I know that," Tazloe continued. "But Nujran's case is clearly different. He's survived a kidnap attempt previously. Two criminal politicians who were imprisoned for threatening his kingdom recently escaped from custody and are fugitives at large. It doesn't take a genius to conclude that he requires extra protection."

"Isn't that why Amsibh was sent here?"

"Precisely, Lincus. But, as you well know, Amsibh is an old man. Highly intelligent, no doubt, but still an old man. That's certainly not equivalent to having a bodyguard beside him."

"Amsibh has protected him before, though, has he not?" The question came from the table behind them. Tazloe and Lincus turned around. It was Miriana who had posed the query. Her brow was furrowed, and she looked stressed.

"Oh, hello Miriana, didn't realize you were behind us." Tazloe's tone was mildly apologetic.

"I know that the prince was with the maestro in Narcaya when the palace was under siege by Hoanan's rebels," said Lincus. "But I don't know the details."

Miriana took a sip from a glass on the table in front of her. "Nujran told me that Amsibh saved him twice, once on the ship and again when they were taken captive by some of Hoanan's rebels."

"The maestro is skilled in the martial arts, apparently." There was admiration in Lincus' tone of voice.

"But that didn't help Nujran this time," Tazloe pointed out.

"I don't think that's fair," Miriana protested. "Amsibh wasn't even around when the tornado arrived. Nujran had taken Miko for a walk."

A few more students had gathered around, interested in the conversation. "Are you saying Nujran was actually kidnapped by a tornado?" one of them asked.

"It would appear so," Tazloe responded.

"I've never heard of that happening before," another student remarked.

"Apparently, Leongatti was telling some of the seniors that a tornado-like phenomenon was used to abduct people by some outlaw groups in Inchea," said Lincus.

As if on cue, the cafeteria door, which someone had closed shut, swung open and Dean Leongatti entered. Seeing the group that had congregated around Miriana, he walked over to them.

"Dean Leongatti, we were just discussing Nujran's abduction," Lincus volunteered.

Leongatti looked at Miriana, then came around and sat down beside her. "Don't worry, Miriana, we have alerted the authorities. There's a massive effort currently underway to track the path of that tornado and determine where it may have touched down, depositing Nujran and Miko."

"How are you so certain that it was an abduction?" Miriana asked, her voice slightly strained. "Couldn't it have been a natural phenomenon? Perhaps Nujran and Miko were just unlucky enough to have been picked up."

Leongatti reflected on Miriana's question for a moment. He didn't really want to go into details of how they had traveled back in time and observed the spinning device at the top of the tornado. Clearly, someone's hand was behind it, controlling it remotely. Aloud, he said, "We have evidence that it was created by a mechanical device. Sarnoff and his team are looking into it and have alerted security forces both here in Foalinaarc as well as in Typgar."

"Do they think Hoanan and Yarozin might be behind it?" Lincus inquired. "It's curious that this has happened so soon after their prison break. Surely there must be a connection?"

"Hard to say," came the dean's reply. "I'm sure they're considering all possibilities."

"How's Tyora?" Miriana asked. "She must be beside herself, given Miko's disappearance."

"Yes, she's quite distraught, as you can imagine. Perhaps you could spend some time with her, Miriana, and comfort her. Right now, she would benefit from the company of a friend."

Miriana looked doubtful. "I'm not sure what I could say to comfort her."

"It's not so much about the content of what you say. In her circumstance, it's just nice to know there are others who care. In addition, she is aware that you and Nujran are close friends. She would understand you share some of her anxiety."

Miriana nodded. "Alright, I'll go and see her. Where is she now?"

"Just outside the library, with some of the other monks," answered the dean.

Miriana walked out of the cafeteria and slowly made her way to the library. Her heart was heavy, and her mind filled with angst. *Why did Nujran have to be kidnapped in such a fashion, just as our relationship was starting to solidify? I do hope he's alright, wherever he is.* Her thoughts then turned to Miko. *And why would they take a two-year-old? What kind of sick people snatch away a child so young?*

Arriving at the steps in front of the library building, she looked up. There was a bench near the entrance, in the shade cast by the edifice. Seated on the bench was Tyora, flanked on either side by Yin'hua and Ronanya. Tyora was resting her head on Ronanya's shoulder, and as Miriana approached, she looked up and wiped away her tears. Miriana bent forward and gave her a hug, then nodded at Yin'hua and Ronanya.

"I've been speaking with Dean Leongatti," she began. "He was telling us that a major effort is underway to track the path of the tornado and find out where it touched down. I'm sure they'll find Miko and Nujran and bring them both home soon." Miriana stopped and looked up, aware that Ronanya was staring at her, her piercing eyes scrutinizing her face, studying her with apparent interest. Although she found Ronanya's gaze quite disconcerting, Miriana refrained from saying anything. She remembered Nujran once describing Ronanya as an odd individual, so this wasn't particularly surprising.

"So, you are Nujran's new interest, I believe," Ronanya commented, her eyes continuing to be fixed on Miriana. "What a lovely young lady you are! It's not difficult to see why the prince likes you."

"Thank you, Ronanya, that's very kind," Miriana responded, trying to sound unflustered.

"Are you from Ersipia?" Ronanya continued. "You look Ersipian to me."

"No, I'm from Zilbaros, in Aaltin."

"Ah yes, beautiful people, the Zilbarians. I've known many over the years. And such an upbeat culture."

Miriana was trying hard not to be irritated. She had come over to comfort Tyora and offer whatever solace she could, not to discuss her heritage. *Was Ronanya not concerned about Tyora's state of mind?*

"What does Amsibh think?" Miriana asked, directing her question at Tyora and trying to change the subject. "Any leads on where they might have ended up?"

Tyora stayed silent, but Yin'hua responded. "Sarnoff's taken over Leongatti's office...he's monitoring the search from there. He's in touch with law enforcement in several different countries. An overlord of surveillance across the lands, it would appear...and he seems quite gifted at it. I'm not sure what the latest updates are. I haven't heard anything in that regard."

Miriana thought for a moment. "Yin'hua, you have the ability to pinpoint people anywhere on the planet, right? Can you locate where they are now?"

"It doesn't quite work like that," Yin'hua explained. "I first need the coordinates. Once I have those, I can visit the location in my mind's eye and describe the scene in as much detail as needed."

"I see." Miriana thought for a moment. "Perhaps we should take you to Sarnoff. Surely, they must be close to locating where on Syzegis the tornado touched down. I'm sure you can be helpful to him, if a rescue is being planned."

Yin'hua looked doubtful. "I'm not sure. Neither Amsibh nor Andron has sought my assistance. Perhaps we should wait."

"Well, how's that going to help?" Miriana sounded annoyed.

"I guess it couldn't hurt to try, Yin'hua." It was Tyora. "Anything that would help bring Miko and Nujran back to us." Her voice sounded weak. She was obviously tired, and her anxiety was apparent.

Miriana looked at Yin'hua. "I'm heading over to Sarnoff's office now. Would you be willing to come with me? We could at least find out if the investigation has made any progress."

"Please help if you can," said Tyora. She had a forlorn expression on her face, and once again her eyes were brimming with tears.

Yin'hua thought for a moment and nodded. He then stood up and followed Miriana, who had started walking briskly ahead. It was late afternoon, and the shadows were lengthening all around. Yarus was hiding behind clouds, and the air felt cool. Neither Miriana nor Yin'hua spoke. As they approached the old red edifice that was the dean's office, Miriana broke the silence.

"I'm sorry, Yin'hua, I was a little rude to you earlier. I'm worried about Nujran; I'm not quite myself."

"No need to apologize, Miriana. I know it's a taxing time. I'll provide any assistance I can, if it will bring Miko and Nujran back."

They entered the building, and a robotic voice greeted them. "State your business." There was no one around.

"We're here to see Detective Sarnoff," Miriana announced. She looked around for a video camera, but wherever it might have been, it was well concealed. A moment later, the glass doors of the elevator opened, and they entered. As they went up, Miriana realized this was the first time she was visiting the dean's office. It was a privilege that few students on campus experienced during their years at the school. Meanwhile, Yin'hua's face remained impassive, his arms folded across his chest. Miriana couldn't help being impressed by how serene he appeared. *It must be the years of meditative reflection*, she thought. *I wish I could stay so calm*.

Entering the dean's office, they were somewhat surprised by what they saw. There was a cacophony of electronic voices arising from all corners of the room. Several devices and screens were scattered around. Amsibh was seated behind the dean's desk, staring at various images moving across it. Sarnoff was standing near Leongatti's whiteboard, his back to the door. He spotted Miriana and Yin'hua through his rear-facing eyes and turned around to greet them.

"Hello Miriana, what brings you here? Is this one of Andron's monks?"

"Hello Yin'hua," Amsibh said, looking up.

"Yin'hua…ah yes." Sarnoff scratched his head, then smiled. "Pholtorimes has told me about you. You were very helpful to him during Typgar's troubled times. You're very talented, from what I have heard. A geographical seer, right? I've never met anyone with that ability."

Yin'hua bowed, acknowledging the compliment. "I merely did what Andron and Amsibh asked of me. It was nothing. But I'm glad I was able to help."

"What you did was extraordinary," Amsibh remarked. "You gave Pholtorimes and Dannigan extremely useful information when it was most needed."

"And that's why I brought him to you," Miriana chimed in. "I thought he could help you with the investigation."

Sarnoff nodded approvingly. "Your timing is perfect. Our satellite technology has just pinpointed the location where the tornado touched down. It wasn't easy, you see...whoever was controlling it was using some sort of masking know-how. In the end, someone from the Central Meteorology Laboratory in Loh'dis was able to override the electronic barriers and give us the information we were seeking."

"So, where did it touch down?" Miriana inquired, trying hard not to sound impatient.

"At the old barracks not far from Cherstwine Castle. I may be stating the obvious...it's as we suspected...this has Hoanan's and Yarozin's hands all over it."

Chapter Nineteen

PLANNING AN ESCAPE

Back at the prison, Nujran and Miko had finished the paltry meal offered to them. Thoughts of escape were paramount in the prince's mind. *I have to get Miko back to Tyora.* He could only imagine how concerned Tyora must be about her little girl's disappearance. *She had placed her confidence in me, entrusting Miko to my care. And now she must be beside herself with worry.* He was no longer anchored to the ground by the chain, Miko having freed him. But there remained the challenge of a locked door, bolted firmly from the outside. He had been considering his options a while, until an idea finally struck him.

"Miko," he began, speaking slowly and softly, "Did you see the bolt on the outside of the door when the guard opened it?" He made a sign with his hand that indicated lifting a bolt handle and sliding it horizontally across to open a door.

To his surprise, Miko nodded. *For a two-year-old, she's astonishingly bright. She's probably a child prodigy.* For a brief moment, his mind wandered to thoughts of his friend Zhinso, who had been killed in a skirmish when intruders had boarded the Floating Monastery. *It was so unfortunate that Zhinso had never known Miko. Or did he? He would have to seek Ronanya's input on this question.*

"Do you think you could open it…with your mind power?" He placed his index finger on his temple, as she had done before.

Once again, Miko nodded. Nujran smiled warmly at her and gave her a quick hug. "You're amazing, Miko. Let's do this. But first of all, let me check if there's anyone on the outside."

Walking over to the door, he placed his ear to it, straining to detect any sounds on the outside. He heard nothing but continued to listen for a short while, just to be sure. Convinced there was no one out there, he beckoned to Miko to come over.

"Do your thing, Miko. But move the bolt across nice and slow, so it doesn't make a sound." He placed a finger vertically over the center of his lips, indicating the need to work as quietly as possible.

Miko toddled over to the door and stared hard at it. Then she put her index finger on her right temple, her facial muscles starting to tense up. At first, nothing happened. Suddenly, Nujran heard a soft grinding sound on the outside, causing the door to vibrate a tad. *I hope no one heard that*, he thought. *The last thing we need is to draw attention to ourselves, even before we've had a chance to exit.* His heart was beating faster, and beads of sweat were forming on his brow. Miko meanwhile had her eyes shut tightly, her face now taking on a reddish hue, her breath fast and shallow. Abruptly, the grinding stopped, and the door opened just a crack. Nujran approached it tentatively, then pulled it open a bit more. He stuck his head out, craning his neck, his eyes darting from side to side in order to survey the scene outside. The corridor was dimly lit and appeared empty. He motioned to Miko to follow him, and they both stepped outside the cell. He pulled the door behind him and deliberately bolted it shut again, taking pains to minimize any sounds that might alert the guards. Now the first decision had to be made. *In which direction should we go?*

The corridor on the left seemed shorter, so he headed that way, holding Miko's hand tightly. Reaching the end, he had to make a choice again. This time he thought he saw light from the right, so he took that course. Sure enough, in a few steps, they came to the edge of a small open courtyard, rectangular in shape. Two of its sides were flanked by a red brick wall, the remaining two by corridors looking out onto the courtyard. Directly across from where they stood, embedded in the brick wall, was a wooden door. *We'll have to make our way over to it,* he thought. *I'm not sure what's on the other side, but it's worth a shot. That door hopefully opens out to our escape path.*

Nujran stepped out tentatively into the courtyard, holding Miko's hand. Looking up and behind him, he noticed a second level above the corridor they had just traversed. He cast his eyes across it, and it appeared empty, so he decided it was safe to walk across the quadrangle. Heading toward the door, they reached it in a few quick steps. But when the prince tried to open the rusty metal bolt by which it was secured shut, it refused to open. Long years of corrosion had sealed it tightly closed, and opening it seemed physically impossible. *Miko just opened the cell door with her mind, would she be able to open this one too*? he wondered. *That would be an unreasonable amount of effort*, he decided. *There must be another way.*

Suddenly, they heard voices from the upper floor. The prince looked around him, quickly surveying the scene. He noticed that the rays of Yarus did not reach the corner of the courtyard closest to them, at the confluence of the two arms of the brick wall. Protected by a lofty turret, there was a zone of shade on the ground. Grabbing Miko's hand, he sped over toward it. Pressing themselves back into the corner, they stayed quite still, hoping that the guards patrolling the upper level would not look out in their direction. Luck was on their side. The guards seemed too busy conversing with each other to notice them. But they lingered a while, and time seemed to drag on forever. Nujran's heart began to race again, and he felt a bead of sweat trickle down his forehead, onto his nose. *What are they doing?* he thought. *I wish they would just move on*. Almost on cue, they did, completely disappearing from view. Emerging from the shadows, the prince took a long hard look at the wall, considering his options. He noticed a section not far from the door where aging had crumbled the brick structure, causing its upper part to disintegrate. *We should be able to climb over that*, he thought. *It's a lot lower there.*

His first task was to get Miko over to the other side. Approaching the wall, he cupped his fingers together and then bent down so that Miko could use them as a step. She understood immediately what he was trying to do. She placed her left foot in his hands, then reached for his shoulders and climbed up. Her eyes searched for a place on the wall she could use as a second step, and she found a small recess among the bricks where she could place her right foot. Then, finding another one up higher, followed by yet another, she clambered up, and very soon, she was at the top of the wall. Crossing over, she disappeared from the prince's view.

It was Nujran's turn. He decided he would take a different approach. He walked back into the courtyard, then sprinted forward a few steps, and jumped as high as he could. His right hand sought the top of the wall but did not find it. He slid down against the bricks, tearing the skin on his right thigh and knee as he fell to the ground. Fortunately, the soft grass cushioned his fall. He winced as the pain from the bruised skin on his leg burrowed its way into his consciousness. Trying to ignore it, he quickly picked himself up, dusted off adherent bits of grass, and repeated the motions. This time his right hand found its target, and he was able to secure his grip on the top of the wall, approximately at the same location where Miko had gone over. He then swung his left arm up and over, pulling his body up, his feet searching for support on the wall below wherever they could find it. A few seconds later, he had cleared the wall and vaulted over to the other side. The landing wasn't as soft as it had been in the courtyard, as the terrain was rocky and uneven. Picking himself up again, and ignoring the additional bruises he had just sustained, he looked around for Miko. He spied her at the bottom of the hill, seated patiently on a rock, waiting for him to approach.

"Are you alright, Miko? Did it hurt when you jumped down from the wall?"

"Didn't jump, climbed down," she explained simply.

What an amazing child, Nujran thought. *Zhinso would have been so proud of her.* He took a deep breath as his mind coped with conflicting emotions. He was relieved that they had been able to escape, astonishingly with no resistance whatsoever. But as he glanced around, the realization dawned on him that he had absolutely no idea where they were. The landscape was hilly, and it made sense to walk downward, away from where they had been held. Carefully making their way between rocks and boulders, they approached a clump of trees. Yarus was in partial descent toward the horizon and it would be nightfall in a few hours. *Should we enter the woods*? Nujran pondered. *Or perhaps skirt its perimeter? Staying in the open means risking discovery; the better option would be to take cover.* He extended a hand to Miko and guided her into the woodlands ahead.

They wandered among the trees for a while and soon heard the pleasant sound of running water. Heading in its direction, they reached a meandering brook, lined by steep banks. They worked their way through tall grass, almost Miko's height, and gently slid down the embankment to the water's edge. It suddenly dawned on the prince how thirsty he was, and he figured that Miko must be feeling the same way. Their liquid intake in the cell had been very restricted, so not surprisingly they were both moderately dehydrated. They went down on their hands and knees, eager to imbibe. Bending down low over the water, they cupped their hands and drank to their heart's content. Miko let out a satisfied burp, then placed a hand over her mouth, looking mildly embarrassed.

"It's alright, Miko…no worries," said Nujran. "Are you hungry?"

Miko shook her head.

"I guess we can wait then. Let's try and figure out what we should do. We can look for food a bit later."

They climbed back up the embankment and followed the brook for a short distance downstream. Abruptly, they came upon a parting in the trees and immediately saw something that made the prince suck in his breath.

"Wow! What have we here?"

A short distance beyond the trees, perched halfway down a hill, rose an impressive castle. They had a good view over the ramparts of numerous bartizans, and an edifice at the center from which arose a towering steeple. The grounds appeared unkempt, and at first glance, the place looked completely empty. There was something vaguely familiar about it, and then an uncomfortable feeling came over Nujran as he realized what he was looking at.

"That's Cherstwine Castle!" he exclaimed. "It's where Dannigan arrested Hoanan and Yarozin, at the end of the conflict in Typgar."

Miko looked at him uncomprehendingly.

"Sorry, Miko, of course those names mean nothing to you." He paused for a moment. "Bad men..." he continued, "Bad men used to live there. But I'm not sure if there's anybody on the premises now."

No sooner had he said that than two men emerged through the front doors of the castle. They were a long distance away, and it was unlikely that the prince and Miko would be spotted. Still, as an abundance of precaution, Nujran decided to retreat into the trees. *Best to stay hidden for a while,* he thought. *Would our absence from our cell have been discovered by now? I hope not...our captors only came to check on us infrequently, so that should work in our favor.*

They walked back toward the brook, and Nujran decided that their best course of action was to stay close to the water. They made their way toward the edge of the embankment and started walking alongside the brook, in a direction away from their site of captivity.

Every now and again, they had glimpses of the castle to their right, between the trees. By following the brook's meandering path across the landscape, they gradually put some distance between themselves and the castle. Yarus appeared intermittently, just above the horizon, and from its position the prince was able to confirm that he was heading south. That was roughly the direction they needed to proceed to get back to the university campus, although they would probably have to deviate a little to the west as well.

"You must be hungry now," he said to Miko. She had marched beside him for quite a while, quiet and uncomplaining. She shook her head.

"Anyway, let's keep an eye open for nuts, berries, anything that we can eat," Nujran suggested.

Miko nodded and continued walking. The brook had now broadened into a stream, and a little further down, the waters parted around a small island. There was a tree on the island, replete with luscious yellow ognam fruit dangling from branches that almost touched the ground.

"There's our dinner," Nujran remarked.

But getting to the ognams would not be as easy as it appeared. At this point in the stream, the current appeared extremely strong; trying to swim across would be quite dangerous. Furthermore, there were large rocks further downstream that they could easily be smashed against if they lost their foothold.

He looked at Miko. "I'm not sure what we should do. It's not safe to cross. Perhaps we should try to find a fallen branch that we can place across the water. It would have to be strong enough to hold our weight, though…"

He looked around, contemplating his next steps. He remembered Amsibh's advice to plan properly before launching into action. As he did, he noticed Miko approach the water's edge through the corner of his eye. Before he could ask her to stop, she had placed her foot over the water. And then something astounding happened. In front of his disbelieving eyes, she began to levitate, floating across the rapid currents on a cushion of air. She reached the island in a few seconds, upon which her feet descended, landing gracefully on the ground. Turning back, she smiled and waved at Nujran. She pointed happily at the ognams, then placed her face close to the low-hanging boughs, allowing their scent to waft into her nostrils.

Nujran threw his head back and laughed. "Miko, you never cease to astonish me. First your mind power, and now this. I should have guessed. After all, you're the daughter of two amazing monks, Zhinso and Tyora."

Chapter Twenty

FINDING NUJRAN

Back in Dean Leongatti's office, the task of rescuing Nujran and Miko had begun in earnest. At Sarnoff's request, Yin'hua was preparing to locate Nujran, using the coordinates the detective had provided him. The monk was seated on the sofa, beneath the clock. The room was silent and dark; Sarnoff had dimmed the lights to help Yin'hua concentrate. Amsibh had poured him a glass of fruit juice, remembering from prior experience that the effort would likely sap his energy to a significant degree. This was Miriana's first experience of seeing the monk perform this feat. She looked on quietly, unsure of what to expect next.

Yin'hua closed his eyes and breathed in deeply, his back upright and head slightly bowed. His body began to sway from side to side, and then suddenly, he started to speak. "I'm in a courtyard...it's empty. I see brick walls to my right. The building to my left looks like some sort of old military quarters. I see a corridor; it's empty as well." He fell silent for a short while, his breathing beginning to quicken. "I'm now walking along the corridor. I see a couple of guards just ahead of me…I'm following right behind. One of them is carrying a tray…looks like there's a bowl on it, with perhaps some food. They're turning left and proceeding down another corridor. Wait...they're stopping now at a door. One of them is opening it, sliding a bolt across. They're entering the door...let me follow them. Oh, the man carrying the tray has just dropped it on the ground...he looks surprised. The other guard appears to be shouting, not quite sure what he's saying...I'm going around to try and see what they're looking at. Hmmm...there's no one else here in the room...just some chains on the ground."

Sarnoff and Amsibh were looking at each other.

"Are you thinking what I'm thinking, Amsibh?" Sarnoff whispered.

"I'd hope this means Nujran and Miko have escaped," Amsibh responded quietly.

Yin'hua's breathing was now significantly labored, but he continued, "The alarm seems to have been raised, several more guards are here. And now someone...I think it's the officer in charge... has arrived. It's a woman...she seems quite angry...she's barking out orders, and some of the guards have rushed out. I'm back in the corridor now... there are men running in all directions. I'm going to have a look around; there are a few more corridors to explore." There was silence for a few moments, the monk's body continuing to rock gently from side to side. A short while later, he announced, "I've looked everywhere...there's no sign of Nujran or Miko." At this point, his body shuddered a little, the swaying stopped, and his eyes opened as he emerged from his trance.

"How did I do?" he inquired.

"We've got an interesting situation on our hands," Sarnoff replied. "Judging from the surprise the guards showed, and the brouhaha that followed, they were unable to find Nujran and Miko. That's assuming, of course, that those were the two occupants of the cell the guards just entered. Our best guess from what you just described, Yin'hua, is that they have escaped."

Yin'hua seemed exhausted from the activity. He took a sip from the glass of juice that Amsibh had poured him earlier, then stretched out on the sofa. Miriana approached him, looking concerned.

"Are you alright, Yin'hua?" she inquired kindly.

"Give him a few minutes," Amsibh suggested softly. "This exercise always drains him; it's quite an enormous effort for him. Fortunately, he usually recovers pretty quickly."

"So, where do you think they might be?" Miriana asked, addressing her question to Sarnoff.

"It's hard to be sure," the detective answered. "But if they managed to get away, my best guess is that they are in the hills near Cherstwine Castle. I've already been in touch with the palace at Typgar, and Queen Iolena has arranged for a rescue mission. Finding Nujran and bringing him back to this campus is now her highest priority. Agent Dannigan, who heads Typgar's special forces, is working with a team from Foalinaarc as we speak. I need to update him on what we have just learned from Yin'hua."

Miriana nodded. "Nujran has mentioned Dannigan before. He described him in glowing terms. So, what's the plan?"

"Well, we have to locate them first. Then we can plan a rescue mission. Currently, it's like looking for a polar bear in a snowstorm."

Miriana looked perplexed. "What do you mean? Don't we have a pretty good idea where they are?"

"Yes, but they could be anywhere over a fairly broad expanse. The area around the barracks is hilly and wooded. They probably took cover under the trees, so it would not be easy to spot them from the air."

"Dannigan's team will likely employ infrared sensors from aerial positions," Amsibh chimed in. "They can detect heat signatures from the air, an approach we've used in military combat for many years. If they're out there in the woods, it's just a matter of time before we locate them."

"That's if we find them before their captors do," Sarnoff pointed out. "Judging from the pandemonium in the barracks that Yin'hua described, I'd guess the kidnappers are none too pleased. I would assume they are looking for them right now. Dannigan's troops need to move quickly."

Sarnoff's bluntness made Miriana feel a little uncomfortable. Nevertheless, she realized that as a detective, it was his duty to consider all angles. And he did not have the same emotional involvement in the situation as she did. *I hope Nujran is alright*, she thought. *I really care for him a great deal; he's such a wonderful person. And I know he will look after Miko, doing everything he can to keep her safe.*

"What do you know about Eramsen?" Sarnoff inquired, interrupting her thoughts.

"Eramsen? Our head chef in the cafeteria? Why do you ask?"

"This may come as a surprise to you…he is now the main suspect in Shamirah's murder. And we also think he may have had a hand in the poisoning of the teachers."

"Really? I am shocked!" Miriana responded. "I find that hard to believe. He's always been so nice to us all."

"Our investigations show that he has links to Hoanan," Sarnoff explained. "He used to work for Lumisio and Alamira."

"Who are they?"

"Hoanan's parents." It was Amsibh who responded.

"But I thought Hoanan was estranged from them," said Miriana.

"True, but we don't know where Eramsen's loyalties lie," said Sarnoff. "The evidence suggests that the mysterious illness which affected the teachers originated in food. And as we had discussed with Nujran earlier, Shamirah's death may have been a test run. I had asked him not to speak about this with anyone, so I assume this is the first time you're hearing about this."

Miriana nodded. "He hasn't shared that with me. Or anyone else, as far as I know. But this is a complete surprise. I would have never suspected Eramsen. We've generally thought of him as a very agreeable chef, willing to go the extra mile for a student. We have scholars from all corners of Syzegis, some with unusual or stringent dietary requests. I've always known him to be quite accommodating, at least in that respect."

"We're not sure, of course," Sarnoff cautioned. "But as you can see, we have to explore all possibilities."

"Has Dannigan set out yet?" Amsibh asked, returning to the matter at hand.

"Not yet," Sarnoff replied. "But I'm sure he will leave Typgar pretty soon. I understand that he's heading to Cherstwine Castle on Alcon, accompanied by his team."

"What's Alcon?" Miriana asked.

"It's a specialized type of stealth aircraft that Dannigan's elite forces use," Amsibh explained. "It's his favorite vehicle for rescue missions because it's also a command center."

"Let's wish him success." Sarnoff was voicing the collective hopes of the group. There was a sound from the sofa. Yin'hua was pulling himself up from a reclining to a seated position.

"Glad to see you're alright," said Miriana.

Yin'hua didn't answer but just nodded his head weakly. "I could go back in there, and try to find out more," he volunteered.

"You've done enough for now," Amsibh noted firmly. "Dannigan and his team will use all resources at their disposal to find Nujran and Miko."

Miriana leaned over to Yin'hua. "Maybe we should leave. Let's go back and join the others."

"We may ask you to come back in if we need your expertise," Sarnoff called out after them as they exited the room into the elevator.

Amsibh turned to Sarnoff. "I think I might join Dannigan and his men. I could be of help to them if they encounter resistance."

"How will you get there?" the detective inquired.

"In my personal drone," came Amsibh's reply. "I had rented one to come to campus."

"Alright then, I'll continue monitoring things from here." Sarnoff delved into his pocket and fished out a small disk-shaped object. "Keep this on your person, I can monitor your movements," he added. "It's a tracking device."

Amsibh took the device, looked at it for a moment, then placed it in his cloth bag. "Thanks, I'll make a move now." He left via the elevator, as Miriana and Yin'hua had done moments earlier.

Sarnoff turned back to Leongatti's desk, which had now lit up with a view of Alcon at the aerospace terminal in distant Loh'dis. Touching the desktop, he swiped his finger to the left, and the screen changed, bringing up an image of Dannigan.

"Everything ready there?" Sarnoff asked.

"Yes, the countdown has started," came the reply. "About 30 minutes to takeoff."

"So, what's your plan?"

"In essence, we are going to target the areas around Cherstwine Castle and the barracks," Dannigan began. "Assuming they have escaped, they must be hiding where they could take cover. We know that it's a hilly region…there's a lot of vegetation in the vicinity, shrouding the landscape and potentially impeding our search. But there's another possibility…they've escaped from their cell and are now hiding somewhere else within the barracks, out of sight of their captors."

"Are you planning to use infrared technology?" Sarnoff remembered what Amsibh had told them.

"Yes, indeed," Dannigan responded. "We can look for heat signals from up above...a young adult with a small child...shouldn't be too difficult to pick up if they're in the woods."

"And if they're still hiding in the barracks?"

"That's going to be much more challenging. Usually, walls and ceilings are pretty opaque to infrared, but we could scan the courtyard, any terraces, and so on. We're assuming that there are a lot of people in the barracks, so that might confound our search as well."

"Any news of Hoanan and Yarozin?" Sarnoff asked.

"My counterparts in Foalinaarc have reported increased activity in and around Cherstwine Castle," Dannigan replied. "But as fugitives, Hoanan and Yarozin would be somewhat foolish if they returned directly to the most obvious place we would be looking for them. My guess is that they are hiding elsewhere, and someone on their staff is commanding operations at the moment."

"Any idea who that might be?"

"Well, we've been speaking with Arondello, who used to be their head of operations. Do you know that name?

"No, I don't," Sarnoff admitted.

"He turned out to be the father of Nujran's girlfriend at the time, a young lady named Zaarica. Toward the end of Hoanan's siege of Loh'dis, Arondello crossed over to our side. Amsibh played a big role in convincing him to switch his loyalty. He ended up receiving a pretty light sentence and now works in our counter-terrorism unit. He's been a tremendous resource. He has mentioned a few names of people who might be leading Hoanan's team, but we are not really sure." Dannigan looked at his watch, which was now beeping. "I've got to go now, almost time for takeoff." He waved at Sarnoff and disappeared off the screen.

Chapter Twenty-one

HOMEWARD BOUND?

Nujran and Miko had eaten their fill. The ognam fruits hanging from the tree, on the small island in the stream, had proven delicious beyond imagination. Miko had delivered them to Nujran two at a time, plucking them off the low-hanging branches and then gliding back gracefully across the water back to the prince. Watching her with a tinge of envy, Nujran considered attempting to levitate across to the island himself. It was something he had done once or twice before in Narcaya, floating across the water to board Flomo. However, on this occasion, he was dissuaded by the strong currents in the stream, concerned that he might be swept away if he stumbled and fell. In the end, Miko had gone back and forth multiple times, with speed and agility, transferring more than a dozen fruits over to his side. They consumed them one by one with great gusto, savoring every bite as they sunk their teeth into the soft delicious flesh. Tossing the bare seeds into the water, they watched them being carried away by the rapid flow and then disappear into the currents downstream. When finally satiated, they picked themselves up and walked a little further. Soon it was nightfall. The last light of Yarus had receded, and two of the three moons now illuminated the night sky.

"I think it's time for us to stop and rest," the prince suggested. Miko nodded in agreement. They were both clearly exhausted and ready to sleep.

They found a tree close to the bank, below which the ground was relatively flat. Stretching out, they closed their eyes. Almost immediately, a pleasant somnolence overtook them, induced by the exertions of the day, as well as by the postprandial impact of a full stomach and the sugar in their bloodstream. Before long, a deep sleep had engulfed them both.

"Wake up!" It was a soft whisper, but the tone was urgent.

Nujran opened his eyes. He was unsure how many hours had passed since they had fallen asleep. Darkness had set in, and it took a short while for his eyes to adapt. It was Miko, her face close to his, who had awoken him.

"What's the matter, Miko?"

She pointed upwards to the night sky. Through a gap in the trees, in the light of the three moons, Nujran was able to see what she was indicating above. There was a giant triangular object in the sky. It was advancing slowly in the direction of the barracks. Despite its enormous size, no sound emerged: it moved in silence like a colossal bird heading toward its nest.

"That's Alcon!" Nujran exclaimed. "They must be looking for us. We need to attract their attention."

He stood up quickly and started to wave his arms around, weaving his way along the ground to try and keep the aircraft in sight. This was not easy, since the trees had created a dense canopy, almost completely obscuring the sky from view. Suddenly, he felt Miko tug at his leg from behind. He turned around to look at her. She had her finger placed vertically across her lips.

"Shush," she said. She then cocked her head to her left and cupped her ear.

"You hear something?"

Miko nodded. She pointed in the direction of the barracks, from where they had escaped. "Men coming," she said simply.

It could be our captors seeking us out, Nujran thought. *Or it might be soldiers who had parachuted down from Alcon, fanning out to look for us.*

Aloud, he said, "We need to be sure they are friends, not foes. So, let's hide someplace we can observe them from."

Miko pointed up a tree.

"Good idea," said Nujran appreciatively.

They ran over to the base of the tree trunk. Nujran lifted Miko up to the lowest hanging bough. Grasping it, she pulled her body up and over, until she was seated on it. Moving into a crawling position, she dragged herself higher and then nestled herself comfortably astride a Y-shaped fork in the trunk. Backing up a bit, Nujran ran forward a few steps and then jumped, reaching for a higher branch. He missed and fell heavily to the ground, his knees buckling under his weight. He lay down where he had fallen for a moment, caught his breath, then rolled over and pulled himself up to his feet. He checked himself quickly for injuries, but the landing had been soft, so there were none. Repeating his attempt from earlier, he took another running jump, and this time he was able to clutch on to the branch that he was aiming for. He repositioned his hands to get a better grip, then hauled himself upwards, making his way up the tree to just above where Miko was seated. Positioning himself where he could see the ground below, unobstructed by the leaves of the tree, he waited and watched intently.

A few minutes later, Miko prodded his leg to get his attention. Nujran looked at her, and she was pointing in the direction of the castle. The prince's eyes searched the darkness. Initially, he couldn't see a thing, but slowly he started to make out silhouettes in the distance, close to the ground. And then flashlights came on, moving up and down, and from side to side, searching the landscape. The lights got closer, and now they could make out the shapes of several men dressed in dark attire. One of them flashed his light upwards into the tree, causing them to sway out of its path in order to stay hidden.

Suddenly, there was a sound from above. A distant rumble, gaining in intensity, unusual and yet familiar. Nujran looked up and saw a small low flying aircraft in the sky. The men on the ground collectively turned their flashlights upwards, causing a myriad of reflections from the aircraft's shiny base. As it approached, a rectangular box on the underside of the aircraft came into view. Nujran instantly realized what it was.

"That's Amsibh's drone," he whispered to Miko. "First Alcon, now Amsibh! Clearly, a rescue effort is underway."

However, the immediate problem was still the men on the ground. As if sensing the situation, Amsibh's drone hovered over them a while.

The maestro is probably determining what he should do next, Nujran thought.

Abruptly, the drone plunged into a descent, rapidly approaching the clearing below, where the men were standing. Nujran heard shots…the men appeared to be firing at the aircraft. Luckily, the bullets just bounced off the bottom of the chamber where Amsibh was seated, so he did not seem to be in any danger. From their vantage point in the tree, they had a good view of the drone during its descent, and at one point, Nujran thought he could discern Amsibh's form seated within.

If only we could somehow get the maestro to see us, he thought. *But how do we do that? The drone is under attack from the men on the ground. Any attempt to attract Amsibh's attention could draw fire in our direction.*

As if responding to the prince's wish, the drone started to move sideways, in their direction. As they watched, it approached them in the tree, drawing really close. It then came to a halt in mid-air, its sides brushing up against the leaves, pushing a few boughs out of the way.

The door of the drone sprang open, and Amsibh looked out directly at Nujran and Miko.

"Get in!"There was urgency in his voice.

Nujran reached for Miko's hand and helped her into the drone, then quickly stepping inside himself. There was a renewed salvo of firing from below. *The last thing we need is for a stray bullet to hit one of us*, the prince thought. He seated himself quickly, Miko in his lap, and fastened the restraint across them both. Amsibh pulled a lever to one side, causing the aircraft to move away from the tree. He pushed a button, and the drone rose rapidly, then swung around and started to move in a direction away from the castle.

Nujran tapped Amsibh on the shoulder. "Maestro, how did you know that Miko and I were seated on that particular tree?"

"It was Miko," Amsibh responded.

"Miko? What did she do?"

"She communicated with me…telepathically."

"Really? Wow!" Nujran's face showed surprise. "First mind power, then levitation, and now telepathy. You are so talented, Miko!"

Miko just smiled but said nothing.

The ride home was absolutely spectacular. Although Yarus had not appeared yet, its early light spilling over the horizon created some amazing views of the landscape. The hills below were covered by evergreen trees, amongst which the stream meandered its way across the terrain. As the prince took in the view, he was reminded of a journey a few years previously, traveling in a bubble from Loh'dis to Narcaya. *Amsibh was with me on that journey as well. And Manolos and Linaea, my two bodyguards at the time. We were headed to Narcaya…it was only then that I realized that Manolos and Linaea were lovers. Such a pity that Manolos turned out to be a traitor in the end. But wait…could Vilania be right? Was there another assassin, and could Manolos have actually been innocent of the crime? No, that can't possibly be…I was there…I saw it. Or did I?*

His thoughts were suddenly interrupted by what sounded like gunfire.

"There's an aircraft pursuing us," Amsibh called out. "Stay down."

Nujran pushed Miko down to the floor. Instinctively, he took a quick look behind him and spied a small airplane just above and to their left. *I hope the glass from which this drone was made is bulletproof,* he thought. *If it isn't, we're in big trouble.* He remembered bullets bouncing off the bottom of the drone as Amsibh had hovered above them, just before he had approached them in the tree.

Suddenly, he felt a searing pain in his upper chest, near his left shoulder. He looked down and noticed blood spurting out, a fountain of red drenching his garment.

"Amsibh, I think I've been shot!" he cried out.

Amsibh turned and looked over at him, quickly assessing the situation. "Press your right hand as hard as you can on the wound," he instructed. He then pushed a couple of buttons on the aircraft control panel. The drone went into full throttle, then soared up skyward. Expertly, Amsibh maneuvered the aircraft through the sky, weaving in and out of the clouds. He then pulled a lever, causing the drone to dive toward the ground and stay low, just above the trees. They were being propelled forward extremely fast and felt themselves hurtling from side to side, propelled helplessly by the physical forces of the aircraft motion. Abruptly, it settled into a steady forward pace.

There was a loud click as Amsibh released his seatbelt. "I used the drone's high-speed setting…I think we've shaken them off our tail." He reached for a yellow box under his seat and opened it quickly. Grabbing a couple of pieces of gauze, a pair of scissors, and some tape, he jumped up and turned his attention to Nujran. He cut through the upper half of Nujran's now bloody shirt and applied a large wad of gauze directly to the wound. Taping the gauze down firmly, he declared, "That should hold back the bleeding for a short while. Keep your hand pressed down on it, Nujran. We should be back on campus very soon."

The maestro helped Nujran back into his seat. Miko was by his side, holding his hand reassuringly. She must have realized that Nujran had been hurt, but the prince was unsure if she fully comprehended what had just happened. A short while later, the drone started to descend. Reinhart's Green, at the center of the university campus, came into view. *That's where the tornado picked Miko and me up*, Nujran thought as he looked out. The ground came rapidly upwards, getting closer by the second. The prince now started to feel light-headed and a little queasy in his stomach. And just as the drone touched down on the grass, he felt the blood drain from his face. A few seconds later, his head fell forward, his chin hit his chest, and he passed out in his seat.

Chapter Twenty-two

GUNSHOT WOUND

When Nujran opened his eyes, he found himself on a bed in a large rectangular room. Sunlight was streaming in through open windows. The sky was a cerulean shade of blue, and there were a few scattered white clouds that looked like giant balls of cotton, drifting slowly across. Wondering where he was, his eyes wandered around the room. As objects came into focus, he realized he was in the campus infirmary. To his right, there was a pole next to his bed, to which he was connected via several feet of plastic tubing. He tried to get up but felt a sharp stabbing pain on the left side of his chest, below his collar bone. He winced, cursed softly under his breath, and collapsed back into the bed.

"I wouldn't do that for now. You've just had surgery; you need to rest." Nujran looked up, recognizing Sheena, the head nurse.

"Surgery? What for?" Nujran's voice showed surprise.

"A gunshot wound. You don't remember? You were shot, just after Amsibh rescued you and Miko. The bullet was successfully removed. Since the recovery room at the hospital still has teachers convalescing from the mystery illness that afflicted them, your surgeon thought it better to transfer you to our infirmary."

"How long have I been here?"

"Just a few hours. We'll likely keep you a day or two at the most."

"I still feel a great deal of pain. Is that normal?"

"Yes, the bullet penetrated quite deep into your chest. I believe it nicked one of your ribs. You also lost quite a bit of blood, so they gave you a transfusion. Overall, you're pretty lucky, you know. A slightly lower trajectory would have hit your heart."

"So, I could have died?"

"Yes, indeed."

A pregnant silence followed as the prince contemplated Nurse Sheena's pronouncement. It wasn't his choice to live perilously, yet danger seemed to appear frequently, and when least expected. He had not anticipated being kidnapped by a tornado and certainly could not have predicted being shot on the night of his rescue. On the bright side, the bullet had missed his heart, and he was alive. He closed his eyes and took a deep breath, wincing again as the discomfort from his injury surfaced once more.

"Can you give me something for the pain?" he asked Sheena. *My voice sounds weak,* he thought. *I wonder how much blood I lost.*

"There's medication in the intravenous infusion that you're receiving," Sheena replied. "Oh, it looks like it's run out. I'll replace the bag. You'll have some relief in a few minutes."

Nujran closed his eyes, trying to think of something serene and peaceful. His mind drifted to the palace gardens, back at his home in Loh'dis. Sheena exchanged the empty bag hanging on the pole with a fresh fluid-filled one. Shortly after, the prince had dozed off again.

Where am I now? It looks like an orchard in Narcaya. Zaarica is with me…what's that fragrance? Must be some herbs that Amsibh recently planted; he's always doing that. He leaned over to kiss Zaarica. *Oh, you're not Zaarica, you're Miriana! How did that happen?*

"Hope you were able to get some rest. You sleep like a Foalinaarcian bear in hibernation!" A booming voice roused him from his slumber, extracting him from the reverie. Even with eyes shut, Nujran recognized the unmistakably resonant tones of his teacher, who had just entered the room.

"Hello, maestro." His eyes remained closed.

"Hello, Nujran. Sheena tells me you're showing signs of recovery."

"Getting better slowly, I think. I still had some pain, but it's decreased now. Nurse Sheena topped up the medication." *Is this still part of the dream, or am I awake now?* The prince opened his eyes and recognized the infirmary. Amsibh was standing next to his bed, smiling down at him. *I'm definitely awake…unless my mind is playing tricks on me. I feel a bit weird…what exactly did Sheena put in that bag?*

"Thanks for saving me again, maestro. I would not be here, alive, were it not for you."

Amsibh smiled and one of his hands landed gently on Nujran's right shoulder. "You saved my life when our helicopter crashed during the battle to retake Loh'dis from Hoanan. And earlier today, I was able to rescue you in return. So, I guess we are now in each other's debt. But the main thing is…you're on the road to recovery."

"I am certainly grateful, maestro." The prince's mind wandered back to the woods, and he thought about how Amsibh had rescued them from their refuge in the tree. Amazingly, he had been guided there by telepathic messages from Miko. Aloud, he asked, "How is Miko doing, maestro? Is she alright?"

"She's back with Tyora…it was a joyful reunion. Tyora will be stopping by a little later to chat with you, and to thank you for looking after her."

"It was the reverse, maestro. She looked after me…she is an amazing kid. And so talented…she levitates, uses mind power to move objects, and communicates by telepathy. And she was able to use each of these skills to extricate us from difficult situations."

"Yes, indeed. And she's really strong…she did not panic when you were shot. She stayed calmly by your side until we landed the drone."

"Does my mother know what happened to me?" Nujran asked Amsibh. "If she knew I had been kidnapped, she would be beside herself with worry."

"I've been in communication with the palace in Loh'dis, right through your ordeal. Yes, Roone was aware you had been taken by a tornado…and yes, she was extremely concerned for your safety. But we've now informed her that we were able to rescue you and bring you back to campus. Needless to say, she's relieved you're safe."

"And do we know who kidnapped Miko and me? Or what exactly it was all about?"

"Dannigan's forces stormed Cherstwine Castle and the barracks where you were held. They arrested a lot of rebel soldiers and have taken their leader into custody. It turned out to be a woman; her name is Vilania."

"Yes, she's Manolos' sister. She seemed to have a very different version of Manolos' death and my father's assassination. She said it wasn't Manolos who killed my father. According to her, he was an innocent bystander."

"People believe what they want to believe," Amsibh remarked. "Manolos' treachery was in full view of hundreds of people, so that is not in doubt. Perhaps she was brainwashed into accepting a different version as true."

"Who is she working for?" Nujran inquired.

"Most likely Hoanan and Yarozin. But we're not completely sure. Dannigan and his team will interrogate her to find out more."

"So, what happens now, maestro?"

"Well, it looks like the immediate threat has passed. Dannigan's working hypothesis is that a group of rebels masterminded your kidnapping, using Cherstwine Castle as their base. The technology they used to generate the vortex to abduct you and Miko is expensive and sophisticated, so they must have had help from somewhere."

"And what about the fugitives, Hoanan and Yarozin?"

"Dannigan's team is working with Foalinaarc's special forces to try and track them down. As long as they remain at large, the threat of some new attack persists."

"Is there anything I can do to help?" Nujran inquired.

"Sarnoff would like to chat with you and get a detailed description of everything you went through. He will pass it on to Dannigan and his counterpart in the Special Forces in Foalinaarc. It's important that every detail is documented so that the case investigators have all the facts before them."

The prince nodded. "I'd be happy to speak with Sarnoff. When can I meet with him?"

"Not so fast, you still need to rest a bit, Nujran." It was Nurse Sheena, who apparently had overheard the last part of the conversation.

"Yes, I completely understand," the maestro said. "But at the same time, we don't want to wait too long, lest his memories of the event begin to fade."

Nurse Sheena pondered for a moment. "Perhaps later today or early tomorrow morning?"

"That makes sense. I'll see you later, Nujran."

No sooner had Amsibh left than Nujran fell asleep once again. The sedative effect of the post-operative medications was quite potent. Several hours later, he was awoken by a voice at his ear.

"You have a visitor, Nujran." It was Nurse Sheena, who was attempting to rouse him from his slumber.

Nujran opened his eyes. Miriana was sitting on a chair beside his bed. She was holding his right hand, and her face looked tense.

"Oh, hello Miriana. It's nice of you to come and visit me."

"How are you feeling, Nujran?"

The prince chuckled and squeezed Mariana's hand. "Overall, not too bad, considering I was shot. Just a bit of pain beneath my left shoulder, that's all."

Miriana forced a smile. "Glad to see you're in good spirits. I understand you were pretty lucky. The bullet wasn't very far from your heart."

"Yes, indeed! It could have been a lot worse." He was going to add, "I could have died," but thought better of it. Instead, he said, "And it was fortunate that Amsibh was with me. He knew exactly what to do to stop the bleeding."

"You've had quite an adventure, Nujran. First, the tornado that kidnapped you, then a captive in the barracks, and then a gunshot wound while being rescued. I was so worried about you. But I'm really glad you're alright." She leaned over and gave him a soft kiss on the lips. "Welcome back! We'll have to celebrate your homecoming when you're feeling better."

Nurse Sheena had returned to the bedside. "Sorry, Miriana, I have orders from the surgeon to let him rest. Perhaps you could come by again later in the evening."

Mariana got up, preparing to leave. She gave him another kiss, this time on the cheek. "I'll see you later, sweetheart."

Nujran felt really good about Miriana's visit. Her concern and warmth were reassuring. From the signals she was sending, he was now sure that she was interested in him. *Is she my girlfriend now?* he asked himself. *She just addressed me as her sweetheart. I'd say she is.* A pleasant feeling suffused his body, and he fell once again into a deep sleep.

When he awoke, the rays of Yarus had lengthened, and a few clouds had gathered in the twilight sky. Looking out of the window, he noticed that Handac had made its appearance.

"Ah, you're awake. Good timing." Nurse Sheena's voice invaded his consciousness. "Sarnoff will be here shortly...he wants to get your story."

A few moments later, almost on cue, the detective walked in, accompanied by Amsibh.

"Are you feeling better?" Amsibh asked.

The prince replied, "Yes I am. Thank you maestro. I had a very long and refreshing sleep. Happy to answer any questions now."

"Did you see the tornado coming, or were you caught by surprise?" Sarnoff began.

"I saw it through the corner of my eye," replied Nujran. "But it all happened so fast. We were airborne in an instant."

"Did you remain conscious? Or did you pass out?"

"I was briefly aware of what was happening, long enough to grab Miko's hand. I remember being really concerned about her safety. After all, she's so little…I feared she would just be blown away."

"So, you didn't stay conscious very long?" Sarnoff asked.

"No, probably just a few seconds. And then it all went dark pretty quickly."

"What happened next?"

Nujran then explained how he came to in the prison cell and found Miko there with him. He described the interaction with the guards, Vilania's appearance, Miko's role in their escape from the cell, and their seemingly unchallenged exit from the barracks.

"Wait a minute," Sarnoff interrupted. "Let me understand what you just described. The cell was bolted from the outside, yet Miko was able to open it? That's incredible!"

"It certainly was amazing," agreed Nujran. "I've never seen anything like it before. She told me she was using her mind power."

"And what happened after you got out of the barracks?"

"I really didn't know what to do," Nujran continued. "We made for the woods and then stumbled on a stream. I thought it wise to just follow it, in a direction away from the barracks. We saw Cherstwine Castle not too far away, which is when I realized where we were."

"How did you survive?" Sarnoff asked. "I mean…you were out there for a while…what did you eat?"

"Well, Miko was once again a star. We came across an island in the stream. She levitated across the water to retrieve fruit from a tree on it. Once again, I was astonished at what she was capable of. After all, she's just two years old!"

"She is the daughter of two accomplished monks," Amsibh explained to Sarnoff. "Her father was sadly killed when intruders boarded Flomo, during those difficult days of the siege of Loh'dis. Levitation came naturally to both her parents, so it's not surprising that she can too."

"How is it that Amsibh found you both on a tree?" Sarnoff inquired.

"We were awoken in the middle of the night by Alcon…and then we heard sounds of men prowling around the woods," Nujran responded. "We thought it wise to hide. Miraculously, Amsibh found us…apparently, Miko contacted him telepathically."

Sarnoff's jaw dropped. "Extraordinary!" he muttered softly, stroking his chin, then turning toward the maestro.

"I suddenly heard a voice talking to me inside my head," Amsibh said. "I recognized it as Miko's. She guided me toward where she and Nujran were hiding."

"She's probably the most talented two-year-old on the planet!" Sarnoff exclaimed. "It's just remarkable, what she seems capable of doing."

All of a sudden, Nujran clutched his chest. "Maestro, my chest hurts. I…can't…breathe." He looked quite uncomfortable. His respiration had quickened, and he appeared to be in a lot of pain. Abruptly, his arm fell away from his chest, and his head rolled to one side as he fell back into his bed.

At first, there was blackness, and then suddenly there was light again. Nujran's consciousness returned, but he felt a strange sense of floating in the air. He looked down and saw Amsibh and Sarnoff standing beside his bed. As the scene below gradually came in to focus, he saw someone lying on his bed. It took him a few seconds to realize what was happening. His consciousness was now outside his body, and he was staring down at himself.

"Nurse Sheena, I need a needle," he heard Amsibh call out. He observed the maestro bend forward and loosen the dressing on Nujran's chest wound. A moment later, he saw Nurse Sheena appear with a large needle, which Amsibh picked up and plunged into the Nujran's chest, just below his left collar bone. There was an audible whooshing sound as air rushed out of his chest. Almost immediately, the aerial projection of Nujran's consciousness reacted; the prince felt himself being sucked downward into his unconscious frame. There was a momentary blacking out again as the prince's breathing started to return to normal. A few seconds later, he awoke, back in his own body. He now seemed to be in a lot less pain.

"What just happened?" Sarnoff asked. He had observed Nujran's distress and Amsibh's intervention in silence, stepping back and staying out of the way.

"Nujran had what medical professionals refer to as a tension pneumothorax," Amsibh explained. "It's directly related to his gunshot wound. The bullet probably nicked his lung, and there was a delayed leak of air into his chest cavity. It's quite serious, requiring immediate attention but, as you just saw, resolves with the right treatment."

"How did you know what to do?" Sarnoff inquired.

"I've been around a long time," the maestro responded with a smile. "And I've encountered the condition on battlefields. If not treated immediately, the subject can die."

"Thanks, maestro," said Nujran. "In fact, I think I was briefly dead… whatever you just did…it brought me back to life."

Chapter Twenty-three

AN OUT OF BODY EXPERIENCE

Nurse Sheena had placed a tube in Nujran's chest wall that continued to drain the air from his chest. There was a jar below his bed with liquid in it that bubbled in response to his breathing.

Nujran related his out of body experience to Amsibh and Sarnoff. "I was watching you both from up there." He pointed to the ceiling. "It was really weird. I had this sense of floating in the air."

"But you were clearly unconscious, my young friend," Sarnoff noted, some skepticism in his voice. "Are you sure you were observing the situation from above?"

"Let's test him," Amsibh suggested, a smile on his face. "Tell us exactly what you saw."

"I first saw you both," Nujran began. "I was looking down on you. And then, I realized that my body was on the bed. I was looking at myself from outside my body. It was incredible."

"Hmmm…ok, what happened next?" Sarnoff continued to sound doubtful.

"The maestro called for a needle…Nurse Sheena emerged, carrying one. I saw the maestro plunge it into my chest. I heard air rushing out…and then I was sucked back into my body. The intense pain I had felt was all gone."

"Well, it looks like he watched it all, despite being unconscious," Amsibh remarked, smiling at Sarnoff. "And he even got the sequence of events right."

Sarnoff did not respond immediately. There was a pensive expression on his face.

"This is not the first time I'm encountering this," the maestro continued. "Lots of subjects who have experienced sudden death, and then been revived, have reported something similar to what Nujran appears to have experienced. When you think about it from a strictly scientific perspective, it's hard to be sure of what actually happens. Can consciousness actually exist outside the body, or is it just some trick of the brain? Honestly, I don't really know."

"This is the first time I'm observing it," Sarnoff confessed. "I'm not sure I believe it. But I have to admit that Nujran just gave us a perfect description of what happened.

"Even though he was unconscious at the time," the maestro reminded him.

"Well, for me there's no doubt that something strange happened," Nujran chimed in. "I was watching you both from up above. I'm sure of what I saw. It was all a little blurry at first, and then things became crystal clear. I've never experienced anything like it before. It chills me to the core of my spine, thinking back about it now."

"Yes, but you have a really good story to tell," Amsibh pointed out, smiling again. "Not a lot of people can claim to have died and then been revived, enjoying an out of body experience in the process. It's something only those privileged few survivors, and perhaps certain monks, can speak to, but princes…now that's another story entirely."

Shortly thereafter, Amsibh and Sarnoff left the infirmary. Time was starting to weigh on Nujran's mind. He was now wide awake and did not have much to keep himself occupied.

"When are you going to let me leave?" Nujran called out to Nurse Sheena.

"We can determine that just as soon as your surgeon gets here," came Sheena's reply. "I need to show him your chest tube, and we have to confirm that your lung is fully expanded."

"Could you let him know that I'm keen on getting out? I have nothing to do here. I'm beginning to get really bored."

Sheena laughed. "Alright, I will. Obviously, you can't leave until the chest tube is pulled out. But you need to be patient. And how can you be bored? You've had a constant stream of visitors."

"Two more are here now," said someone from behind Sheena.

Nujran recognized the voice instantly. "Hi Tyora, it's so great to see you." He looked down beside her. "Hi Miko, all well with you?"

"She's fine, Nujran," Tyora responded. Miko nodded in agreement.

"How are you feeling?" Tyora inquired. "Are you in pain?"

"Not really, just a bit of discomfort from this tube that's been inserted in the side of my chest," the prince replied. "Nurse Sheena has taken excellent care of me. But I just had a near-death experience. A tension pneumo something...Amsibh saved me."

"It's called a tension pneumothorax," Nurse Sheena explained. "It's caused by leakage of air into the chest cavity. In Nujran's case, it was probably a late effect of his gunshot wound."

Tyora leaned down and gave the prince's hand a squeeze. "Well, I'm glad you're alright now." Nujran winced slightly as he felt the tube move in his chest wall.

"My apologies," said Tyora, noting his discomfort. She pulled herself upright again. Spreading her palm on her forehead, she placed a thumb and forefinger on each temple and closed her eyes. A few moments later, she opened them and looked at the prince. "Wow, so you died and came back to life?"

"You were reading my thoughts again, weren't you?" Nujran asked.

Tyora nodded. "Sorry, I should have obtained your consent. But I assumed you would be alright with it. What happened, exactly?"

"I had an out of body experience as Amsibh was reviving me. It was pretty amazing."

"That's incredible!" exclaimed Tyora. "I've heard a few people speak about it, but they were always a lot older than you. That's such a unique experience. You're always going to remember it…you'll probably be talking about it when you're as old as Amsibh."

The prince had a vision of himself with long white hair and a flowing beard. A smile played on his lips.

"You died?" It was Miko, who had returned to the bedside after a stroll around the ward.

"Yes, how did you guess?"

"She listens to everything, Nujran. I can just read minds, but she can communicate telepathically as well."

"I know," said Nujran. He proceeded to describe to Tyora how Miko had helped them escape, brought food from the island in the river by levitating, and finally mentally communicated with Amsibh where they were hiding in the tree. "She is so talented, Tyora. You should be proud of her. Zhinso would be too."

At the mention of Zhinso's name, Tyora's face became pensive. She looked into the distance, as though recalling times past. A teardrop started forming in her left eye; it welled up and slowly ran down her cheek. Miko looked up, noticed the tear, and gave her a hug.

"He would be delighted with Tyora, wherever he is," the prince commented. "She really is an extraordinary little girl."

Tyora wiped her eyes. "Thank you, Nujran. That's very kind of you to say."

"What news of Dannigan's prisoners?" Nujran asked, adroitly changing the subject.

"Funny you should ask," Tyora responded. "Leongatti said that Dannigan was bringing Vilania and a couple of the guards here to this campus. Apparently, he wants our assistance in interrogating them because, at the moment, they aren't saying very much."

"So, I guess he wants Amsibh to use his cephavid, right?"

"Exactly. And Leongatti asked if I would use my mind-reading ability, but I'm undecided."

"Ah yes, a moral dilemma," the prince noted. "Amsibh and I have discussed this at length. He believes that it's permissible to interrogate prisoners against their will in times of war. But I've always been concerned about the ethical implications."

Tyora nodded in agreement. "Nothing is easy. A lot of life's questions are complex. We have to use our best judgment."

"When are the prisoners arriving?" the prince asked.

"Later today," came Tyora's reply. "The interrogations will take place in Leongatti's office."

"It would be so interesting to observe them. I'd like to be a fly on the wall."

"I'm sure Sarnoff will be fine with that."

Later that day, Nujran's surgeon Sarjenkel stopped by to remove the prince's chest tube. He was a kind man, with an excellent bedside manner.

"So, you're a prince from Typgar?" he asked. "I was trained by a wonderful surgeon there, a man by the name of Setrosko. He was at the main health center in Loh'dis."

"Yes, I remember meeting him," the prince responded. "He was looking after the victims of the terrorist bombings on the trains, orchestrated by Hoanan and his rebels. He has a great reputation all over Typgar."

"Yes, indeed," Sarjenkel agreed.

"Can I go now?" Nujran inquired. "I've missed classes, and there are a few other things I need to do."

"If you're feeling alright, I don't see why not. The chest tube is out. You may have twinges of pain where it was placed, and at the site of the bullet wound. Nurse Sheena will give you some painkillers on your way out, so you can use those if you need them. Don't take more than three of them daily, and let's aim to get you off them in about a week."

Nujran returned to his room. His body felt stiff, and he walked slowly. The hour was almost twilight, and lengthy shadows spilled into the corridors he traversed. Only once, as he turned a corner, did he feel a twinge of pain. When he got back, Tazloe wasn't in; all was quiet. Seated on the sofa, he felt sluggish and heavy-eyed. He wondered if his somnolence was caused by one of the painkillers he had consumed on his way out of the infirmary. He dozed off for a while but was awoken by a knock on the door.

It was Amsibh. "Sheena told me you were back in your room. Dannigan has arrived with Vilania and a palace guard. I'm going to interrogate her in Leongatti's office. I thought you might be interested in coming along. That's only if you feel well enough to do so. If you just want to rest, that's fine too."

The groggy feeling in Nujran's head appeared to have lifted. For the moment, he did not have any pain either. "I'll come along, maestro. I'm curious to watch."

When they entered the dean's office a few minutes later, Sarnoff was already there. The prince recognized Amsibh's colorful sack on the dean's desk. The maestro walked over to it and extracted the cephavid with its accompanying helmet, in preparation for his interrogations. A few moments later, the elevator doors opened and Dannigan strode into the office. Behind him was Vilania, in handcuffs, walking with a firm upright gait, looking straight ahead. And right behind Vilania was a guard, massive and muscular in frame, with a shaven head and tattoos on his arms. Nujran instantly recognized him as Nyawandus, a member of his father's Royal Guard from Typgar.

"Greetings, Agent Dannigan," said Sarnoff.

Dannigan nodded at Sarnoff, then at Amsibh and Nujran.

"Nyawandus, it's great to see you again. It's been a long while." The prince ambled over to the guard and gave him a warm hug. He felt a twinge of pain in the left side of his chest as he did so and winced imperceptibly. He wondered if he should have taken another one of the painkillers Sarjenkel had prescribed, before leaving his room.

"It's really nice to catch up again, Prince Nujran," Nyawandus responded. "I hope college life has been treating you well."

Amsibh asked Vilania to sit down on one of the armchairs next to the dean's desk. She did not protest, doing as the maestro requested.

"Do we really need these handcuffs?" Amsibh asked Dannigan. "I'd prefer if they were removed."

Dannigan nodded and tossed a key to Sarnoff, who proceeded to open the handcuffs. Amsibh placed the helmet on Vilania's head. He turned on a switch, and several tubes emerged from the helmet, projecting images in different directions.

"I'm going to ask you a few questions," he began. "Here's the first one. Where did you and Manolos grow up?"

Nujran saw one of the tubes project an image of a house, and a boy and a girl were running around in it. Even though the prince had watched Amsibh use the cephavid before, it always amazed him to see it work. There were images of a man and a woman, who he assumed were their parents. The maestro asked additional questions about Vilania's life growing up and then, without warning, posed the most crucial one: "Where are Hoanan and Yarozin hiding?"

Vilania's eyes closed tightly. Most of the images went blurry, and a couple of projections turned completely blank.

Amsibh leaned over to Sarnoff. Nujran overheard him whisper, "She's deliberately blocking her thoughts to prevent us from seeing them."

That's quite impressive, the prince thought. *It can't be easy to do. Someone must have trained her in countering this interrogation technique.*

The maestro tried several times again but to no avail. Each time he called out Hoanan's or Yarozin's name, the images would become nebulous, sometimes disappearing altogether. After an hour of trying, he walked over to Vilania and flicked off the switch on her helmet. The images faded away, and the tubes withdrew back into the helmet.

The maestro approached Dannigan, who was standing near the exit. He lowered his voice. "I'm going to try something else," he said. "Let's arrange for Vilania to spend some time with Tyora."

"How is that going to help?" Dannigan asked softly.

"Tyora can read minds," Amsibh whispered in reply. "Vilania does not know that. They can engage in casual conversation, and by dropping appropriate clues or questions, I'm sure Tyora can uncover the information that we seek. I think she might be more successful than my cephavid."

Amsibh left the room through the elevators and returned a short while later with Tyora. Sarnoff placed the handcuffs back on Vilania. Nujran stifled a yawn and realized he was starting to feel tired. He would have to return to his room fairly soon and get some rest.

Amsibh addressed Vilania directly. "This is Tyora, one of the Monks of Meirar. She will accompany you to our cafeteria so that you can have some food and refreshments. We don't want to leave you with the impression that we mistreat our prisoners."

Tyora led Vilania out of the dean's office. Nyawandus waved to the prince and followed them into the elevator.

"Let's give them some time," Amsibh said to Sarnoff.

"What's she going to do?" Sarnoff asked.

"As I just explained to Dannigan, she reads minds," the maestro replied. "I have instructed her on the nature of the information we need on Hoanan and Yarozin. She was reluctant at first, but when I reminded her that they were most likely the people behind Miko's kidnapping, she agreed to help us."

Chapter Twenty-four

A CAMPUS RETURNS TO NORMAL

By this time, most of the teachers had been discharged from the health center. Many had returned to campus, eager to resume their teaching activities. Some of them had started giving lectures again, others were in the process of preparing to do so. Only a handful remained under observation at the health center, specifically those who had been admitted in a particularly serious state and needed a few extra days to recover fully.

"Any update on Chef Eramsen and his role in all this?" Nujran asked Amsibh when they met the next morning.

"Apparently, he confessed to being responsible for poisoning the food," came the maestro's reply. "Hoanan's people threatened to kill his children and granddaughter if he didn't, so he maintains that he did not have a choice. He also admitted to accidentally overdosing Shamirah in a trial run. He says he had no intention of killing her; he was just testing the dose required to incapacitate someone. He picked her because she mostly sat alone in the cafeteria and didn't seem to have friends."

"What was the motive? Why did Hoanan plan this?"

"That's not entirely clear. Actually, I think it was most likely Yarozin's idea; he's the more devious one in the duo. I guess he wanted to cause major disruption on campus. Fortunately, no teacher died...

that could have easily happened, given Shamirah's fate. And it's very likely that mass murder was on Yarozin's mind."

"What do you mean?" Nujran asked.

"When Eramsen confessed, he said that the message he received from Hoanan's people was to wipe out the entire faculty. But after Shamirah's death, our chef felt so distraught that he backed off on the dose. He says he defied his instructions and tried to mitigate the effects of the poison, making sure the teachers only got sick."

"So, what happens to him now?"

"Sarnoff has him in custody, and interrogations continue in the hope that he may have information on Hoanan's and Yarozin's whereabouts," Amsibh replied. "At some stage, he will be charged and will stand trial for his crimes."

Meanwhile, on campus, excitement was brewing, as there were going to be several final classes taught by the Monks of Meirar that week. Andron, Glyoptula, and Ronanya were all scheduled to deliver lectures. Nujran also spotted Amsibh's name on the schedule; Leongatti had requested him to deliver a farewell oration on a subject of his choice.

The first lecture that Nujran attended that day was by Ronanya. Miriana and Tazloe accompanied him. At one point during the walk to the lecture theater, Nujran felt a sharp stab of pain on the left side of his chest.

Miriana looked alarmed. "Are you alright, Nujran?"

"Yes, just felt a twinge at the site of the chest tube. I had similar pains earlier today, and they passed quickly."

Miriana looked very concerned. "Why don't you just sit down a minute?" she suggested.

They found a bench near the perimeter of one of the quadrangles they were walking through, and the prince parked himself on it.

"Should I run and get you some pain medication from Nurse Sheena," Tazloe inquired sympathetically.

"Actually, I have some in my pocket. Thanks, Taz. All I need is some water."

"I always carry some," Miriana responded, obligingly producing a bottle from the backpack she was carrying.

"I'm feeling a lot better now," Nujran remarked, a few minutes later. "Let's go hear what Ronanya has to say."

Ronanya's lecture turned out to be fascinating. It was on her subject of expertise, namely death and the afterlife. Nujran was a little disappointed that only a couple of dozen students showed up; he had expected many more.

"It's understandable, Nujran," Miriana whispered to the prince. "Let's face it, not a lot of folks of our age are thinking about the afterlife."

"Of all the topics we wrestle with, death is probably the most mysterious," Ronanya began, her soft voice coming through quite clearly on the loudspeakers around the room. "So many people think it is final, but I assure you it is not! It's merely a transition, a middle ground of sorts, but hardly the termination of our travels. I have communicated with many on the other side; it's just a matter of being able to pick up the signals." She gave a little cough, then continued, "It's interesting that most cultures on Syzegis mourn the departed, but there are a few places I've visited where it's actually a time to rejoice. It is understood, in those places, that death heralds another stage of existence. The thinking there is that the individual has moved on to a better place, so it's appropriate to celebrate his or her life and be happy for them."

A hand went up in the audience. It was a bespectacled youth seated in the front row. Nujran did not know his name.

"How do you make contact with those who have passed on?" he inquired.

"I was coming to that a bit later," Ronanya responded. "But since you have asked the question, let me explain. I just place my mind in a receptive state, and then I feel their presence. It's definitely not in the same way that I am communicating with you. It's more that I'm aware they're nearby." Ronanya paused, then stared vacantly at the ceiling. She didn't speak for a few minutes, and as time passed, there was some murmuring in the audience.

Miriana looked at Nujran. "Should we say something? She seems to have gone into a trance."

Just as Nujran was about to respond, Ronanya began to speak again. "Sorry about that, I was feeling a presence in the room as I spoke. I have just communicated with her. She's one of your fellow students, who recently crossed over to the other side. She said her name was Shamirah."

For a brief moment, there was a stunned silence in the audience. Then the murmurs started again, students whispering to each other. The bespectacled youth in the front row raised his hand again.

"I'm a bit skeptical," he began cautiously. "How do we know if we can really believe you? Someone might have told you about Shamirah after you arrived here."

"Well, I'm not really here to convince you," came Ronanya's reply. "Each of you can and should believe exactly what you want to believe. But if one of you knew Shamirah really well, please come up to the podium, and I will tell that individual what she just communicated to me."

Nujran nudged Miriana. "You knew her well, didn't you?"

"Not really…but I did speak with her a few times, and I'm curious to see what Ronanya has learned."

Miriana sauntered up to the podium. Ronanya moved the microphone away from her face, then whispered something in Miriana's ear. A look of surprise came over Miriana's face.

A moment later, Miriana leaned over to the microphone. "Ronanya has just told me something that very few people know about Shamirah. I'm not at liberty to share the information, but trust me, it's quite impressive that Ronanya was able to learn this from her."

"Well, you've got to tell us," the bespectacled youth in the front row piped up. "Otherwise, how can we believe you?"

"Well, I really can't…it's confidential information that almost no one on campus knew about Shamirah," Miriana replied. "It's not appropriate for me to share it."

Another hand went up in the audience. This time, it was a brunette with a freckled face, seated in the third row. "Did Shamirah reveal who her killer was?" she asked.

"Her killer?" Ronanya seemed confused.

"The rumor on campus is that she was murdered," the brunette explained.

Ronanya shook her head. "No, she did not say anything about how she died." She paused and stared into the distance again.

By this time, Miriana had walked back to her seat. Ronanya cleared her throat, then continued her lecture.

"She told you Shamirah was transgender, right?" Nujran asked Miriana.

"Yes, indeed…and also that she always wanted to be a girl, even from a very young age."

Ronanya's lecture went on for another half an hour or so. The prince felt that although it was somewhat rambling and unstructured, it was still fascinating. Most students seemed engaged; some were taking notes. When she finished, several hands shot up in the audience.

The bespectacled youth in the front row asked the first question again. "My mother passed away when I was very young, and I did not really know her. Do you have the ability to put me in contact with her?"

Ronanya stared at the questioner for a few seconds and then began, "It is rare that I reach out deliberately to the other side. Let me explain…it is usually souls from the other side who reach out to me. I place myself in a state of receptivity and am thus able to pick up their signals more easily. In terms of your question…can I place you in touch with your mother? I think that would be quite difficult since she passed a long time ago. Usually, the souls who reach out are those who departed Syzegis fairly recently."

"I'm not convinced at all that there is life after death. So, I find everything you have just said fairly hard to believe." The statements came from a female student in the third row. She was a brunette with blond streaks in her hair and a nose ring. The prince was sure that he had seen her around campus a few times and on one occasion with Tazloe.

"Well, I'm not really here to persuade you one way or the other," came Ronanya's reply. "As I said, each of you is free to have his or her own beliefs. I can only tell you what I have experienced. And based on the experience of being contacted by so many who have died, I am sure that there is some type of connectivity between us and the other side. It's a matter of keeping an open mind."

Ronanya took a few more questions, and the class concluded.

"Let's head over to the cafeteria and get something to eat," Nujran suggested to Miriana. As they walked over, Miriana asked the prince, "Do you think there is life after death, Nujran?"

"I'm really not sure," Nujran answered. "After Tyora's partner, Zhinso, was killed, I was convinced that he was communicating with me. I even had a vision of him floating past me during the funeral.

But I can't be certain if it actually happened, or whether it was just a combination of wishful thinking and an active imagination."

"I'm pretty sure it's all over when we die," said Miriana. "A depressing notion perhaps, but one I'm totally comfortable with."

The prince did not reply, but his face appeared pensive. His thoughts were about his father, Rababi, who had frequently appeared in his dreams shortly after his assassination.

"When the dead show up in our dreams, are they projecting themselves into our brains, or are we simply thinking about them as we sleep?" he asked out loud.

"I think you know the answer to that one," Miriana replied.

Nujran was just about to respond, when they bumped into Amsibh and Tyora coming out of the cafeteria.

The maestro addressed Nujran. "Can we speak to you for a moment?"

"Go ahead and grab some food, Miriana," Nujran said. I'll join you in a few minutes." Miriana nodded and entered the cafeteria.

"So, what's up?" Nujran inquired.

Tyora began to speak. "I've spent some time with Vilania, reading her thoughts. It took a while, but finally, her mind wandered to where Amsibh and Sarnoff wanted it to go."

"You know where Hoanan and Yarozin are?"

"Yes, they have traveled east, far east actually. Apparently, they are hiding out in Nadii."

Chapter Twenty-five

THE SEARCH FOR THE FUGITIVES

Amsibh and Nujran met for an early morning walk. Yarus had not yet made its appearance, but its light had begun to spill over the edge of the horizon. As the pair walked in silence, the chirping of an avian orchestra was distinctly audible.

"Is there an effort to go after Hoanan and Yarozin?" Nujran inquired.

"Yes, Dannigan and his men will be on their way to Nadii shortly," Amsibh replied. "Leon has once again offered his office so that Sarnoff and I can watch the proceedings. I'm not sure how helpful we can be, but it's nice that Dannigan is allowing us to do so."

Dannigan had asked Queen Iolena for permission to use Alcon in order to travel to Nadii. He had contacted Nadii's Chief of Security, a man named Izvan, to coordinate the efforts to find Hoanan and Yarozin.

"It will not be an easy task," Dannigan had explained to Amsibh earlier that day. "As you know, Nadii is a vast country, and seeking out two fugitives in that expanse is like looking for a pair of needles in a haystack."

"So, what will your strategy be?" Amsibh asked.

"We shall seek the assistance of folks on the ground. Hoanan and Yarozin must have help from someone there. We will need to offer rewards, encourage informers to come out, interrogate any eyewitnesses, and use all means necessary to find them."

In the early afternoon, Amsibh and Nujran went over to the dean's office. Sarnoff was already there, looking at something on the screen, his back to the door. Leongatti was hovering over his desk.

Sarnoff spotted them enter through his rear-facing eyes and turned around to address Amsibh. "Dannigan's already on the ground in Nadii."

"That was quick," the maestro responded.

"Yes, usually a sixteen-hour flight but cut in half by the speed at which Alcon can fly," Leongatti observed. "An amazing aircraft, that's for sure. Hopefully, some version of it will be used in commercial aviation one day."

A few moments later, the screen flickered, and Dannigan's face appeared. His brow was moist with perspiration, and he looked a little tired. He glanced over his shoulder at someone who was out of the camera's range and asked, "Where is this being transmitted to?"

"The palace in Loh'dis and Leongatti's office at the university," came the reply.

Dannigan turned back to face the camera. "Hello, everyone," he began. "I'm in Bammubi, Nadii's most densely populated city. Our intelligence sources here told us that this is our fugitives' most likely destination."

"But really, they could be anywhere in the country, right?" Nujran recognized the voice as Queen Iolena's, from the palace.

"That's true," Dannigan admitted. "Nonetheless, Nadii's head of security received a tip that two men resembling our fugitives had disembarked several days ago at the port of Bammubi. So, we thought we would start our search here. Using the few details we have, we can perhaps start tracing the course of their escapades. Put your detective hat on, my friends, we are going hunting!"

"What's the temperature there?" Nujran inquired.

"As you can see from my sweaty face, it's pretty hot here," Dannigan responded. "High-nineties, high humidity, not very comfortable outside."

"What's the plan?" Sarnoff asked.

"My local counterpart on the ground here is a very experienced intelligence officer named Rihana. She's been great to work with. She has informants in every nook and cranny of Bammubi, and we'll start by interviewing those who have any leads."

"Well, thanks for reporting in," Iolena chimed in from the palace. "Let's not hold you up. I'm sure you have a lot to do."

The screen in the dean's office went blank.

Back in Bammubi, Dannigan removed the earpiece he had been using for the transmission and stepped away from the camera. A tall woman wearing white attire and a peaked cap approached him.

"We're ready for you, Agent Dannigan."

"Thank you, Officer Rihana. Let's get started."

Dannigan followed Rihana into an old building that looked like it needed a fresh coat of paint. Once they entered, though, it was surprisingly modern inside. There were screens on the walls and holographic images in various parts of the room.

One of the holograms approached them: it was the replica of a man of imposing stature. "Welcome to our facility, Agent Dannigan!" he said. "I am Izvan, head of Nadii's Internal Security. We had spoken earlier when you were in Typgar. Rihana will look after you and help you with your search." The hologram then waved at them both, began to disintegrate in front of their eyes, and finally disappeared altogether from view.

They walked up a flight of stairs and then along a corridor. Halfway down, Rihana opened one of the doors, and Dannigan followed her in. There was a young man with unkempt hair and a beard seated at a table, arms folded across his chest.

"This is one of the eyewitnesses who saw two men meeting the description of Hoanan and Yarozin," Rihana whispered into Dannigan's ear. "You can ask the questions; I'll translate for you."

Dannigan pulled up a chair and sat down at the table, across from the man. "How do you know that the men you saw are the ones we are interested in?"

Rihana translated the question.

"I was shown photographs," the man replied. "Those were the same men."

"Are you certain?" Dannigan persisted.

"Yes, I am sure. Definitely the same men."

"What were they doing when you saw them?"

"They had just walked off a ship. They sat down on a bench for a while, talking to each other. Then a group of men arrived, and they walked away with them."

"A group of men?"

"Yes, probably half a dozen. A few of them were dressed in black, and a couple were wearing black hats."

Dannigan posed a few more questions, then asked Rihana to accompany him outside the room.

"Quite convincing," he remarked. "The man does not seem to be in any doubt at all. Now we need to interview the others and try and connect the dots."

"I've already done that, and the trail leads to Central Bammubi," Rihana responded.

"That's helpful," said Dannigan. "Can we search that part of the city…street by street, door to door?"

"It's not that easy. There is a huge slum in the city center, a lot of the areas are not fully mapped, and the landscape is constantly changing. The people there mistrust law enforcement, so it's quite difficult to get anything out of them."

"That does sound like a huge problem," Dannigan agreed. "What about your informants there?"

"I've put the word out and am waiting to hear back," Rihana replied. "There are a number of young adults on our payroll, our eyes and ears in that community. With any luck, some of them would have seen the fugitives."

"I remain hopeful. Let's wait and see what turns up."

Dannigan returned to his hotel to get some sleep. It had been a long flight on Alcon, and he was starting to be very tired. He dozed off as soon as his head hit the pillow. He was awoken several hours later by the buzzing of his hand-held Zogo, which he had placed beside him on the bedside table.

"We have a lead." It was Rihana.

"I'm listening."

"We just received a report that two men meeting the description of our fugitives entered the home of a drug lord. The home is on the outer edge of Central Bammubi. It's heavily fortified, but we are planning a raid in a couple of hours. You're welcome to join us."

"Yes, I'd like to be there."

"I'll send a vehicle to pick you up. Be ready in ten minutes." Rihana hung up.

The car that pulled up to the front door of the hotel looked old and rickety but was surprisingly comfortable on the inside. The driver was a middle-aged man, with a gap-toothed grin that seemed fixed on his face.

"We need to go at once, sir. Madam Rihana asked me to bring you as soon as possible."

Dannigan wondered how such a rickety vehicle could move quickly. But no sooner had the car started than he realized that despite its deceptively decrepit appearance, its engine and controls were in excellent shape. The driver expertly maneuvered it at high speed through the streets of Bammubi, deftly avoiding obstacles along the way. In a few minutes, he pulled up outside a dimly lit building. A door opened, and Rihana emerged with two more uniformed officers; all three jumped into the car. Dannigan noticed a garage next to the building, the door of which was starting to open. Suddenly, a fleet of small black cars emerged, one behind the other, through the door. He counted about six of them; they took off ahead at high speed, the driver of Dannigan's vehicle following the convoy directly behind. They found themselves zigzagging rapidly through the narrow streets of Central Bammubi.

"The drug lord's den is on the other side of the city," Rihana explained to Dannigan. "It will take us a few minutes to get there."

"Will we have air cover?" Dannigan inquired.

"Not until we request it. Once our men are in the compound, and approaching the building, I'll call for it. If the helicopters arrive earlier, our quarry may hear them coming and vanish into the night."

A short while later, the cars pulled up on a narrow empty street, alongside a high brick wall.

"This is the outer perimeter of the property," Rihana pointed out. "We'll have to jam the cameras first, before our troops climb over the fence."

A guard emerged from one of the cars, holding a rectangular device with an antenna. He twiddled a few knobs on the device, then gave a 'thumbs up' sign to the others. The remaining guards, all wearing dark green helmets, got out of the vehicles ahead. Finding footholds on the wall, they climbed up and over it with speed and alacrity. In a few seconds, they had all but disappeared from view.

Rihana was holding a rectangular tablet in her hand. She pressed a button, and its screen came alight. As the image shimmered into focus, the troops came into view.

"Our guards are wearing cameras on their helmets," she explained. "So, we can easily watch the action from here."

She then spoke into her hand-held device, a locally manufactured version called a Xivo. "This is Officer Rihana, requesting helicopter backup. You have the coordinates." She turned to Dannigan. "They should be here in less than five minutes."

They watched on the screen as the guards approached the building inside. One of them kicked a door open, and the team entered behind him. It was dimly lit, but they could see men within, awakening in surprise at the nocturnal raid. Bursts of light penetrated the darkness as guns were fired. The guards spread out through the building, and a few of them ran down a flight of stairs. Rihana moved her finger across the screen, switching cameras so that the basement of the building came into view. The guard whose helmet camera was transmitting the image stopped briefly, and a large room came into focus. Two men were visible on the far side of the room.

"Can you zoom in?" asked Dannigan, seated in the car next to Rihana.

Rihana spread her thumb and forefinger on the screen to enlarge the image, and two faces came into view.

"That's them!" exclaimed Dannigan. "Hoanan and Yarozin! We need to capture them, alive if possible."

Rihana barked a few words into her hand-held device, and the guards advanced rapidly, but withholding their gunfire. The situation was intensifying with each breath, each heartbeat, each buzz of the Xivo. A door suddenly opened at the back end of the room, and the two men stepped through it, pulling it shut behind them. The guards rushed toward the door. It took them no time to get there. They kicked it open and found themselves in another chamber. They shone their lights around the room, up and down the walls, and even scanning the ceiling. Several of them were shaking their heads. It was all becoming irrefutably clear.

"There's no one here," one of them finally remarked, breaking the uncomfortable silence. "The targets seem to have literally vanished!"

Chapter Twenty-six

AFTER THE RAID

Back on campus, the news of Yarozin and Hoanan's narrow escape was the topic of conversation on everyone's lips. Nujran and Amsibh were having breakfast together in the university cafeteria.

"Such a pity they got away," Amsibh remarked.

"Apparently, they just disappeared into thin air," said Nujran. "What do you think happened?"

"There must have been a trap door in the floor or some hidden exit through one of the walls. Dannigan told us that they had a quick look and found nothing, but a more detailed search will take place in daylight."

"Nadii is a big country," the prince pointed out. "They could be anywhere now."

"Exactly. But Dannigan will continue working with the local security services. His hope is that since they were able to locate them the first time, they could likely find them again."

"But they might have escaped to another country. What if they are now somewhere in Inchea? That's another huge geography to cover." The comments came from Miriana, who had just arrived and seated herself across the table from the prince and the maestro.

"That might happen, but not so quickly," Amsibh responded. "Bammubi is a long way from the border between Nadii and Inchea. There is also a fairly high mountain range, the Limhays, between the two countries, where the terrain is not easy to negotiate."

"So, where do you think they are?" Nujran asked.

"They've probably taken refuge somewhere else in the city," Amsibh answered. "The drug lord who sheltered them has numerous connections, so it's most likely they're hiding out in one of his other warehouses. Or they could have escaped out to sea. Bammubi is a port on a bay, and there's plenty of little inlets they could have accessed to escape on a boat."

At this point, Nujran's hand-held Zogo started to vibrate. He extracted it from his pocket and looked at it. "It's my mother. I should take this."

He stepped out of the cafeteria to speak with her.

"I guess you have heard the news, Nujran," Queen Roone began.

"Yes, the maestro was just updating me on what he heard from Dannigan," replied the prince. "It's unfortunate that they got away."

"Don't worry, we will track them down. It's only a matter of time." Roone's voice sounded reassuring, but Nujran realized that she was concealing her concerns.

"Will the maestro now return to Narcaya?" Nujran inquired. "He's pretty well-liked on campus, and there are many students who want him to stay."

"Well, I'd prefer that he remains there. But it's really up to him and Iolena. I'm not sure if they have discussed it yet. And we don't want to impose; we're probably keeping him from things he'd like to be doing back at his home. On another note, son, how is school going?"

"As best as can be expected, Mother."

"What do you mean, son?" Roone now sounded slightly alarmed.

"It's just that we've had lots of interruptions, Mother, as you know. You remember I told you about the mystery illness that a lot of the teachers came down with? Luckily, the Monks of Meirar were anchored close by on Flomo, so they were able to assist on campus. We had some excellent lectures, and the maestro helped as well. The regular curriculum ended up being disrupted, but I don't think we missed much."

"That's good to hear, Nujran. Yes, you did mention the illness that affected your teachers. Are they all back now?"

"Most of them are, I believe. Perhaps one or two remain at the health center."

"Anything else happening on campus?" Roone asked.

Nujran debated briefly in his mind if he should tell her about Miriana. The queen knew that he had broken up with Zaarica when he left for college, but they had not discussed it in detail.

"Mother, I'm going out with someone; her name is Miriana. She's a year ahead of me; she's from Zilbaros."

There was a short pause. "I'm delighted for you, Nujran. I hope you are both happy. I'd like to meet her at some stage."

The conversation ended a few moments later. Nujran walked back into the cafeteria. Amsibh had just finished his breakfast. Miriana was still seated across from him, sipping a hot brew. The prince walked over, bent down, and kissed her cheek.

The maestro smiled. "That's my cue to leave," he said, getting up from the table. "I have a meeting with Leon."

Nujran and Miriana wandered out shortly after. They did not seem to be in any rush, since neither had a class till early afternoon.

"I just told my mother about you," the prince remarked.

"That's nice, Nujran. I'd certainly like to meet her sometime."

Nujran smiled. "That's exactly what she said. I'm sure I can arrange that."

Nujran reached for Miriana's hand and grasped it gently. Miriana reciprocated with a squeeze—a reminder to the prince that despite all the problems of the world, the warmth of another could be so reassuring. They continued to walk down a corridor, holding hands. A sharp gust of wind blew in from the courtyard to their right, dying down almost instantly. Yarus had now lit up the campus, but there were no other students in sight.

"Are you worried that the fugitives are still at large?" Miriana asked.

"Not really," the prince replied. "They're a long distance away. And Dannigan is still on their tail, so hopefully, they will be located soon."

They emerged from the shade of the corridors, entering a quadrangle. It was the same one where Shamirah's body had been found. There were now no security tapes; everything had returned to normal. A faint scent of sycamund bushes wafted pleasantly across their path. The only sound audible was the distant chirping of birds. They continued their walk, in no particular direction, just enjoying each other's company. Nujran felt a sense of comfort, conscious that he was with someone he really liked, perhaps even loved. The sky was now a bright cobalt blue; it was a good day, he was happy.

THE END

Made in the USA
Monee, IL
17 September 2020